Critics rave about THE DARKENING DREAM by Andy Gavin:

"Gorgeously creepy, strangely humorous, and sincerely terrifying"

— Publishers Weekly (starred review)

"Wonderfully twisted sense of humor" and "A vampire novel with actual bite"

— Kirkus Reviews

"Inventive, unexpected, and more than a little bit creepy — this book has something for everyone!"

— R.J. Cavender, editor of the Bram Stoker nominated Horror Library anthology series

"This is a story that is rich in visual and verbal treasures. The Darkening Dream is an unbelievable first novel."

— Vampire Librarian

"This book will satisfy any fan of the vampire genre and then some!"

— Must Read Faster

"In a similar vein to George R.R. Martin's writing style, Gavin often dangles his characters in the maws of danger and doesn't shy away from ... their blood being spilled."

— Andrew Reiner, executive editor of Game Informer magazine

"Now this is a vampire novel! It flows so perfectly between character point of views, it's a great blend of historical fiction, mythology and paranormal."

— Little Miss Drama Queen

"Action-packed and suspenseful, and there were twists all over the place."

— Les Livres

"Andy Gavin has taken a bevy of supernatural elements, compelling characters, and an intricate and superbly developed storyline, and expertly weaved them together to create an original and enthralling book."

— Word Spelunking

"Like going into a used bookstore and finding a rare and hidden gem... highly entertaining, fast-paced, innovative, original horror read..."

— Darkeva's Dark Delights

"I am in awe of this author's writing style."

— The View from Fairview

"I love the ending. It makes me want a lot more, now."

— Caught Between the Pages

"Perfectly written to the dot"

— Subtle Chronicler

"No words that I can use to adequately describe just how gloriously insane this book is."

— Word Vagabond

Untimed

Andy Gavin

Illustrations by Dave Phillips

Mascherato
Publishing

UNTIMED
by Andy Gavin

Illustrations by Dave Phillips

This book is a work of fiction. Names, characters, places, and incidents are either products of the author's imagination or used fictitiously. Any resemblance to actual persons living or dead, events, or locales is entirely coincidental.

MASCHERATO PUBLISHING
PO Box 1550
Pacific Palisades, Ca, 90272
publishing@mascherato.com
http://andy-gavin-author.com

MS version: 3.20a LV version: 1.5a
75,300 words, September 25, 2012, 12:47:21 PM PDT

Cover Photo-Illustration copyright © Cliff Nielsen 2012
Interior Illustrations copyright © Dave Phillips 2012
Book Design by Christopher Fisher

E-book ISBN 978-1-937945-05-3
Hardcover ISBN 978-1-937945-03-9
Trade Paperback ISBN 978-1-937945-04-6

Contents

Chapters

Illustrations

Chapter One:
Ignored

Philadelphia, Autumn, 2010 and Winter, 2011

My mother loves me and all, it's just that she can't remember my name.

"Call him Charlie," is written on yellow Post-its all over our house.

"Just a family joke," Mom tells the rare friend who drops by and bothers to inquire.

But it isn't funny. And those house guests are more likely to notice the neon paper squares than they are me.

"He's getting so tall. What was his name again?"

I always remind them. Not that it helps.

Only Dad remembers, and Aunt Sophie, but they're gone more often than not — months at a stretch.

This time, when my dad returns he brings a ginormous stack of history books.

"Read these." The muted bulbs in the living room sharpen the shadows on his pale face, making him stand out like a cartoon in a live-action film. "You have to keep your facts straight."

I peruse the titles: Gibbon's *Decline and Fall of the Roman Empire*, Asprey's *The Rise of Napoleon Bonaparte*, Ben Franklin's *Autobiography*. Just three among many.

"Listen to him, Charlie," Aunt Sophie says. "You'll be glad you did." She brushes out her shining tresses. Dad's sister always has a glow about her.

"Where'd you go this time?" I say.

Dad's supposed to be this hotshot political historian. He reads and writes a lot, but I've never seen his name in print.

"The Middle East." Aunt Sophie's more specific than usual.

Dad frowns. "We dropped in on someone important."

When he says *dropped in*, I imagine Sophie dressed like Lara Croft, parachuting into Baghdad.

"Is that where you got the new scar?" A pink welt snakes from the bridge of her nose to the corner of her mouth. She looks older than I remember — they both do.

"An argument with a rival… researcher." My aunt winds the old mantel clock, the one that belonged to her mom, my grandmother. Then tosses the key to my dad, who fumbles and drops it.

"You need to tell him soon," she says.

Tell me what? I hate this.

Dad looks away. "We'll come back for his birthday."

While Dad and Sophie unpack, Mom helps me carry the dusty books to my room.

"Time isn't right for either of you yet," she says. Whatever that means.

I snag the thinnest volume and hop onto my bed to read. Not much else to do since I don't have friends and school makes me feel even more the ghost.

Mrs. Pinkle, my ninth-grade homeroom teacher, pauses on my name during roll call. Like she does every morning.

"Charlie Horologe," she says, squinting at the laminated chart, then at me, as if seeing both for the first time.

"Here."

On the bright side, I always get B's no matter what I write on the paper.

In Earth Science, the teacher describes a primitive battery built from a glass of salt water covered in tin foil. She calls it a Leyden jar. I already know about them from Ben Franklin's autobiography — he used one to kill and cook a turkey, which I doubt would fly with the school board.

The teacher beats the topic to death, so I practice note-taking in the cipher Dad taught me over the weekend. He shows me all sorts of cool things — when he's around. The system's simple, just twenty-six made-up letters to replace the regular ones. Nobody else knows them. I write in high-lighter and outline in red, which makes the page look like some punk wizard's spell book. My science notes devolve into a story about how the blonde in the front row invites me to help her with her homework. At her house. In her bedroom. With her parents out of town.

Good thing it's in cipher.

After school is practice, and that's better. With my slight build and long legs, I'm good at track and field — not that the rest of the team notices. A more observant coach might call me a well-rounded athlete.

The pole vault is my favorite, and only one other kid can even do it right. Last month at the Pennsylvania state regionals, I cleared 16' 4", which for my age is like world class. Davy — that's the other guy — managed just 14' 8".

And won. As if I never ran that track, planted the pole in the box, and threw myself over the bar. The judges were looking somewhere else? Or maybe their score sheets blew away in the wind.

I'm used to it.

Dad is nothing if not scheduled. He and Sophie visit twice a year, two weeks in October, and two weeks in January for my birthday. But after my aunt's little aside, I don't know if I can wait three months for the big reveal, whatever it is. So I catch them in his study.

"Dad, why don't you just tell me?"

He looks up from his cheesesteak and the book he's reading — small, with only a few shiny metallic pages. I haven't seen it before, which is strange, since I comb through all his worldly possessions whenever he's away.

"I'm old enough to handle it." I sound brave, but even Mom never looks him in the eye. And he's never home — it's not like I have practice at this. My stomach twists. I might not like what he has to say.

"Man is not God."

One of his favorite expressions, but what the hell is it supposed to mean?

"Fink." For some reason Aunt Sophie always calls him that. "Show him the pages."

He sighs and gathers up the weird metallic book.

"This is between the three of us. No need to stress your mother."

What about stressing me? He stares at some imaginary point on the ceiling, like he always does when he lectures.

"Our family has—"

The front doorbell rings. His gaze snaps down, his mouth snaps shut. Out in the hall, I hear my mom answer, then men's voices.

"Charlie," Dad says, "go see who it is."

"But—"

"Close the door behind you."

I stomp down the hall. Mom is talking to the police. Two cops and a guy in a suit.

"Ma'am," Uniform with Mustache says, "is your husband home?"

"May I help you?" she asks.

"We have a warrant." He fumbles in his jacket and hands her an official-looking paper.

"This is for John Doe," she tells him.

The cop turns to the man in the suit, deep blue, with a matching bowler hat like some guy on PBS. The dude even carries a cane — not the old-lady-with-a-limp type, more stroll-in-the-park. Blue Suit — a detective? — tilts forward to whisper in the cop's ear. I can't hear anything but I notice his outfit is crisp. Every seam stands out bright and clear. Everything else about him too.

"We need to speak to your husband," the uniformed cop says.

I mentally kick myself for not ambushing Dad an hour earlier.

Eventually, the police tire of the runaround and shove past me as if I don't exist. I tag along to watch them search the house. When they reach the study, Dad and Sophie are gone. The window's closed and bolted from the inside.

All the other rooms are empty too, but this doesn't stop them from slitting every sofa cushion and uncovering my box of secret DVDs.

Mom and I don't talk about Dad's hasty departure, but I do hear her call the police and ask about the warrant.

They have no idea who she's talking about.

Yesterday, I thought Dad was about to deliver the *Your mother and I have grown apart* speech. Now I'm thinking more along the lines of *secret agent* or *international kingpin*.

But the months crawl by, business as usual, until my birthday comes and goes without any answers — or the promised visit from Dad. I try not to let on that it bothers me. He's never missed my birthday, but then, the cops never came before, either.

Mom and I celebrate with cupcakes. Mine is jammed with sixteen candles, one extra for good luck.

I pry up the wrapping paper from the corner of her present.

"It's customary to blow out the candles first," Mom says.

"More a guideline than a rule," I say. "Call it *advanced reconnaissance*." That's a phrase I picked up from Sophie.

Mom does a dorky eye roll, but I get the present open and find she did well by me, the latest iPhone — even if she skimped on the gigabytes. I use it to take two photos of her and then, holding it out, one of us together.

She smiles and pats my hand.

"This way, when you're out on a date you can check in."

I'm thinking more about surfing the web during class.

"Mom, girls never notice me."

"How about Michelle next door? She's cute."

Mom's right about the cute. We live in a duplex, an old house her family bought like a hundred years ago. Our tenants, the Montags, rent the other half, and we've celebrated every Fourth of July together as long as I can remember.

"Girls don't pay attention to me." Sometimes paraphrasing helps Mom understand.

"All teenage boys say that — your father certainly did."

My throat tightens. "There's a father-son track event this week." A month ago, I went into orbit when I discovered it fell during Dad's visit, but now it's just a major bummer — and a pending embarrassment.

She kisses me on the forehead.

"He'll be here if he can, honey. And if not, I'll race. You don't get your speed from his side of the family."

True enough. She was a college tennis champ and he's a flat-foot who likes foie gras. But still.

6

Our history class takes a field trip to Independence Park, where the teacher prattles on in front of the Liberty Bell. I've probably read more about it than she has.

Michelle is standing nearby with a girlfriend. The other day I tapped out a script on my phone — using our family cipher — complete with her possible responses to my asking her out. Maybe Mom's right.

I slide over.

"Hey, Michelle, I'm really looking forward to next Fourth of July."

"It's January." She has a lot of eyeliner on, which would look pretty sexy if she wasn't glaring at me. "Do I know you from somewhere?"

That wasn't in my script. I drift away. Being forgettable has advantages.

I tighten the laces on my trainers then flop a leg up on the fence to stretch. Soon as I'm loose enough, I sprint up the park toward the red brick hulk of Independence Hall. The teachers will notice the headcount is one short but of course they'll have trouble figuring out who's missing. And while a bunch of cops are lounging about — national historic land-mark and all — even if one stops me, he won't remember my name long enough to write up a ticket.

The sky gleams with that cloudless blue that sometimes graces Philly. The air is crisp and smells of wood smoke. I consider lapping the building.

Then I notice the man exiting the hall.

He glides out the white-painted door behind someone else and seesaws down the steps to the slate courtyard. He wears a deep blue suit and a matching bowler hat. His stride is rapid and he taps his walking stick against the pavement like clockwork.

The police detective.

I shift into a jog and follow him down the block toward the

river. I don't think he sees me, but he has this peculiar way of looking around, pivoting his head side to side as he goes.

It's hard to explain what makes him different. His motions are stiff but he cuts through space without apparent effort. Despite the dull navy outfit, he looks sharper than the rest of the world, more in focus.

Like Dad and Sophie.

The man turns left at Chestnut and Third, and I follow him into Franklin Court.

He stops inside the skeleton of Ben Franklin's missing house. Some idiots tore it down two hundred years ago, but for the bicentennial the city erected a steel 'ghost house' to replace it.

I tuck myself behind one of the big white girders and watch.

The man unbuttons his suit and winds himself.

Yes, that's right. He winds himself. Like a clock. There's no shirt under his jacket — just clockwork guts, spinning gears, and whirling cogs. There's even a rocking pendulum. He takes a T-shaped key from his pocket, sticks it in his torso, and cranks.

Hardly police standard procedure.

Clueless tourists pass him without so much as a sideways glance. And I always assumed the going unnoticed thing was just me.

He stops winding and scans the courtyard, calibrating his head on first one point then another while his finger spins brass dials on his chest.

I watch, almost afraid to breathe.

CHIME. The man rings, a deep brassy sound — not unlike Grandmom's old mantel clock.

I must have gasped, because he looks at me, his head ratcheting around 270 degrees until our eyes lock.

Glass eyes. Glass eyes set in a face of carved ivory. His mouth opens and the ivory mask that is his face parts along his jaw line to reveal more cogs.

Charlie confronts the clockwork man
at Franklin Park

CHIME. The sound reverberates through the empty bones of Franklin Court.

He takes his cane from under his arm and draws a blade from it as a stage-magician might a handkerchief.

CHIME. He raises the thin line of steel and glides in my direction.

CHIME. Heart beating like a rabbit's, I scuttle across the cobblestones and fling myself over a low brick wall.

CHIME. His walking-stick-cum-sword strikes against the brick and throws sparks. He's so close I hear his clockwork innards ticking, a tiny metallic tinkle.

CHIME. I roll away from the wall and spring to my feet. He bounds over in pursuit.

CHIME. I backpedal. I could run faster if I turned around, but a stab in the back isn't high on my wishlist.

CHIME. He strides toward me, one hand on his hip, the other slices the air with his rapier. An older couple shuffles by and glances his way, but apparently they don't see what I see.

CHIME. I stumble over a rock, snatch it up, and hurl it at him. Thanks to shot put practice, it strikes him full in the face, stopping him cold.

CHIME. He tilts his head from side to side. I see a thin crack in his ivory mask, but otherwise he seems unharmed.

CHIME. I dance to the side, eying the pavement, find another rock and grab it.

CHIME. We stand our ground, he with his sword and me with my stone.

"Your move, Timex!" I hope I sound braver than I feel.

CHIME. Beneath the clockwork man, a hole opens.

The manhole-sized circle in the cobblestones seethes and boils, spilling pale light up into the world. He stands above it, legs spread, toes on the pavement, heels dipping into nothingness.

CHAPTER ONE: IGNORED

The sun dims in the sky. Like an eclipse — still visible, just not as bright. My heart threatens to break through my ribs, but I inch closer.

The mechanical man brings his legs together and drops into the hole. The seething boiling hole.

I step forward and look down....

Into a whirlpool that could eat the *Titanic* for breakfast. But there's no water, only a swirling tube made of a million pulverized galaxies. Not that my eyes can really latch onto anything inside, except for the man. His crisp dark form shrinks into faraway brightness.

Is this where Dad goes when he *drops in* on someone? Is the clockwork dude his *rival researcher?*

The sun brightens, and as it does, the hole starts to contract. Sharp edges of pavement eat into it, closing fast. I can't let him get away. Somehow we're all connected. Me, the mechanical man, Sophie, and Dad.

I take a step forward and let myself fall.

Chapter Two:
Yvaine

Unknown Locale

I fall hard onto wet cobblestones.

A pair of horses bears down on me fast. I roll into the gutter to avoid being trampled.

It's seriously raining, a genuine Noah's Ark deluge. Between the downpour and the low clouds, you'd hardly know it's daytime.

The horses pass, drawing a covered coach behind them. Coach?

The driver huddles in his cloak, a triangular hat pulled low against the downpour. Two flickering lamps hang from the vehicle's rear.

Tourists ride coaches in Independence Park, and the drivers wear Revolutionary War outfits like this guy — but who takes a scenic ride during a rainstorm?

Then again, I just followed a clockwork man through a Hanna-Barbera hole.

I'd been halfway hoping the hole would lead to my father, but I look around and realize I'm the only one on the street — even the clockwork guy is long gone. Way to make my dad proud. *Act after analysis*, he'd say. Instead, I jumped into a wormhole to wherever.

And where is *wherever*? It's a city street, a little like old Philly but there's no sidewalk. Just a nasty strip of mud and refuse between the road and the building fronts. I take a few steps — and look down at my shoes, which are pinching my feet. Instead of sneakers I see old-fashioned black leather shoes crudely sewn and covered in mud, but they go with my waterlogged stockings, tattered knee-length pants, and ratty wool coat.

Like the coach driver or a mock pilgrim in the Thanksgiving Day Parade.

What the hell?

I limp down the empty street. The air seems different. January in Philly is always cold and dry, unless it's snowing. Nothing like this slashing rain that makes me wish the Goretex jacket I put on this morning wasn't lost in translation.

I hear my mother's voice in my head: *Get inside or you'll catch cold.*

While I don't think you can catch the temperature, I better call her. Maybe even check the GPS and see where I am. I grope my strange pants and find the bulges made by my wallet and mobile. Rain and my new iPhone are not something I want to mix, but the nearby townhouses have covered porches like the ones on Society Hill.

I hop up a trio of marble steps to get out of the downpour, lean against a wooden column, and reach into my pocket for the phone.

But that's not what I find. My fingers extract a small notebook covered in brown leather. I open it carefully, trying not to drip.

On the first page are some names written in blotchy ink. In my handwriting!

My name, my mom's, our doctor's, Dad's, Aunt Sophie's. The phone numbers and addresses underneath. On the next page is the embarrassing script that ought to be entitled *The Tragedy of Charlie and Michelle* — still enciphered. Whew!

Chapter Two: Yvaine

I flip another page to find a charcoal sketch of my mother and me, posed exactly like that photo I took with my phone.

My life has always been pretty weird — like me. The ticking clock dude and the hole in the world were extremely weird.

But this is beyond weird. My mobile phone has mutated into a notebook!

I put it away and take out my wallet — um, leather pouch, full of silver and copper change. I don't see any Washingtons or Jeffersons, only pirate coins.

I'm not dreaming. My wet clothes chafe against my skin, and when I run a finger down my jacket sleeve, I feel every bump in the rough wool. I study the street, easier on the porch without water pouring down my face.

Another carriage passes, this one with four horses and two drivers. A couple of people scurry along near the edges of the buildings trying their best to stay dry. A man helps a lady pick her way through the mud. She wears huge skirts and a bonnet. He's sporting knickers, a long jacket, and a tri-corner hat atop his big white wig.

A spontaneous historic celebration? Magic mushrooms slipped into my Frappuccino? No, I'm me, and I'm not in Philadelphia. And I better find my dad or at least a way back, so I step out into the rain wishing I wasn't the only one without a hat.

I make it about ten feet before the mud literally sucks one of my crappy shoes right off my foot. I kneel to pull it from the earth's thieving grasp and someone collides with me from behind, knocking me face down into the muck.

"Pardon me, so sorry." The accent is funny, but the voice is lilting.

I roll over to find a soaked rat of a girl backing away. Her dress is ragged and the yellow-brown hair escaping her bonnet is plastered against her filthy face. Even so, she stands out brightly against the drab cityscape.

"Where are we?" I ask.

Her eyes, too large for her face to begin with, seem to grow even larger.

Then she bolts down the street.

I try to knock the mud out of my shoe but the stuff is as thick as... mud.

And I notice my pants feel light — both my wallet-turned-purse and the phone-become-notebook are gone.

The girl is making good headway — she's halfway down the block, running — and I notice her footprints have toes.

She's barefoot *and* she picked my damn pocket!

I remember I'm only wearing one shoe, pull it off, and sprint after her in stocking feet.

In summer, at our shore house in Ventnor, I run barefoot on the beach every morning. This is like that, only colder, stickier, and way weirder.

"Give me back my stuff!" I yell after the girl.

She glances over her shoulder, lifts her skirts, then puts the pedal-to-the-metal — whip-to-the-nag? — and pulls even farther ahead. But that feeling comes over me, the one you get after a couple minutes of running when the pain goes away and you're in the Zone and you think you can go on forever.

In no time, she's only a few feet in front. The rain is letting up, but moisture hangs thick in the air, lending everything a dull blurry look. Except her. Bright legs stand out under caked mud. They pump furiously but she's beginning to flag. She probably doesn't run track. Not that they have track here.

Wherever — or whenever — *here* is.

She hooks a hand on an iron lamppost, whips herself around a corner, then we're on another street, this one crowded with people and carts.

Everyone's in costume. Yep. I've either dropped back two hundred years or gotten stuck in a rerun of *Sliders*.

I follow the girl's bobbing head as she weaves through the crowd, often losing sight of her but finding her easily again thanks to her white bonnet and dirty-blond hair. She dodges to the side and ducks behind a cart piled with raw fish.

I pull up short. I noticed before, but now, breathing hard, I *really* notice.

This place stinks. Like horse shit, like cat piss, like dead fish. I can only imagine what it smells like on a day that isn't cold and rainy.

I try to stay out of her sight but keep after her. I want the picture of Mom, and I'll probably need the money. Which I'd still have if I'd remembered Dad's oft-repeated advice: *When you're alone in a strange place, guard your things.*

Even on his rare visits, he's never been the take-your-kid-to-the-zoo type father. He and Sophie drove me to strange neighborhoods and made me find my way home without money or a phone. This charming family tradition started when I was, what? Five? No older than six, anyway.

I dodge past a well-dressed gentleman in a purple tailcoat and slide around the fish wagon.

No blond girl. "Damn!"

The vendor lady — a fishmonger? — glares at me.

Despite the setback, I feel giddy. I'm betting Dad's aborted final lecture wasn't about divorcing Mom or being an international super spy. No, he was going to tell me that in our family we run from clockwork cops and jump through holes in time.

Which would be extremely cool if the past didn't smell like rotten fish and flies weren't biting my ears.

The rain lightens to a drizzle. Beyond the fish wagon, scrappy retailers hawk cloth. I wander down the street, and it isn't long before I catch the sound of the girl's lilting voice. The few words I heard before made an impression, and she's not speaking softly.

I find her in a courtyard, near a red and white brick church half covered in scaffolding.

This time I stay out of sight, peering around the edge of the gatepost. She's talking to a man.

"Ben, you needs help me."

He's older, maybe twenty, and wearing the now-familiar knee-length pants and high socks. No jacket, just a loose white shirt and a leather apron. His long hair is tied back in a ponytail and he's holding a silvery mug with black-stained hands.

"How do I even know it's mine?"

"*He's* yours," the girl says, holding her arms rigid, her fists clenched.

This Ben guy shrugs.

Now that I'm not running headlong, I notice she *really* stands out. Not her street thief clothes, but her. Even the bare foot she's stomping is crisper, more focused than the mud it splashes around.

"Who else would you have me turn to?" she says.

"Tipple of ale?"

The guy in the apron hands her the mug, which, surprisingly she drinks down as if it were water.

"Be reasonable," he says. "I don't even remember your name."

My heart skips a beat.

She hurls the mug at his feet. "Yvaine!" she yells.

I can't help but sympathize.

"Come again?" Ben says.

Her lips are frozen in frustration.

**Arguing with Ben Franklin
at the St. Barts printhouse**

I might be sympathetic, but I still want my money back. Aunt Sophie had one thing to say about bullies: *take the fight to them*. I dash into the courtyard and grab the girl by the arm.

"Give me my stuff!"

She tries to twist away, but I hold firm.

"Ouch! Let go!"

The Ben guy's hairline is beating an early retreat from his oval face. His generous forehead — more a fivehead — wrinkles in amusement.

"Who's this? Another contender?"

"Charlie," I say. "Charlie Horologe."

Ben gives me the usual confused stare. He's tall, a tad overweight but muscular.

"Doesn't matter." He turns from me to the girl. "You'll have me believe I'm the only one, when this fellow comes looking after you."

"She just picked my pocket on the street," I say.

Ben smirks. "Watch out, boy, she knows more than one way to pinch a man's purse."

Yvaine is so red I think she might explode any second.

"But—"

Another young guy in an apron pokes his head out the church door.

"Mr. Franklin, the type's ready for your approval."

My eyes track Ben as he bows and heads inside. Ben Franklin? No way—

Yvaine slaps my face hard, scattering the gathering cloud of my thoughts. Bright specks wriggle across my vision and I nearly let go of her arm.

"You've ruined me proper!" She kicks at me with a filthy foot.

Close up she looks a little older than me, maybe sixteen, but much smaller, under a hundred pounds for sure. Her eyes are huge and really green, which almost makes her limp hair look that color too. Her chapped, makeup-free lips stretch thin.

"Hey," I say. "You're the one who stole my money!"

CHIME. The all-too-familiar sound echoes across the brick-boxed churchyard.

I feel Yvaine's arm stiffen.

CHIME. The noise is slightly above us, to the left.

CHIME. I turn to see the clockwork man sitting on the wall of the courtyard. His suit is still blue, but his hat now has three corners. He's holding something in his hand, like a book made of shiny brass, and his gaze flicks from it to us and back again.

CHIME. He puts the book away then unfolds upward to stand on the wall.

CHIME. He hops down into the yard. My insides knot. I found him. Or he found me.

CHIME. Yvaine screams. She tugs out of my grip and bolts toward the gate.

CHIME. I turn to see the clockwork man draw his sword. The mask of his face betrays nothing. Dad and Sophie probably had good reason to duck out when he knocked at the door.

CHIME. I sprint after Yvaine and pull the little gate shut as I pass. It isn't locked or anything, but a few extra seconds can't hurt.

CHIME. Glancing over my shoulder, I see the man standing behind the iron bars. His head pivots to follow me but he makes no move to open the gate.

We sprint through the cloth seller's street. My nose stings: chemical fumes. With the rain dying down, more vendors have emerged, making our race more a slalom than a dash.

Yvaine is still moving, but I can see she's running out of gas. She staggers into a cart and knocks a bundle of yellow cloth in the mud.

The owner hollers but she keeps going — and going — into an alley where she collapses onto a pile of garbage, gasping for air.

I'm breathing hard but doing fine — yay, four-hundred meter dash! — so I pounce and start patting her clothing.

"Watch the... hands!" She's almost panting too hard to speak.

She looks pathetic, and I do feel bad — but not bad enough to stop groping her. I find her stash bound around her thigh and take back my purse and notebook.

But I return the three purses that aren't mine.

She's sobbing now and I feel even worse.

"I be cursed," she says. "Men!" She kicks at me again. "You'll ruin a girl, take her money. An' a goddamned Tick-Tock?"

"Hey! I'm the victim here!"

The once-over she gives me is like my mother picking a watermelon.

"So when are you from, Charlie?"

Chapter Three:

Bar Talk

London, Spring, 1725

"Huh?" The oddity of hearing my own name addles my wits.

"You think me daft, do you?" the girl in the refuse pile says. "You're from the future."

Living the last hour in a high-budget documentary has made me a time travel believer, so I'll take her word for it.

"How do you know?"

"Boys always be from the future. What's me name?"

"Yvaine?" I say.

Her smile is so genuine it startles me.

"There you go. I haven't never heared that since I was a wee bit."

I know how she feels even if I only *mostly* understand what she says.

"Help a lady up, Charlie."

I take the hand she extends, pull her upright, then kick my feet into the dirty pair of shoes I took off when I ran after her. Her scruffy outline stands out with unnatural clarity.

This cinches it. I know how to spot the historically homeless!

Dad's history books, all his lessons, swirl in my head. He totally knew! If us extra-in-focus-no-names are time travelers, and he and Sophie have been off visiting the Crusades or whenever, why'd they wait till right before the clockwork cop showed up before trying to tell me?

"Are you from the future too?" I ask.

"You know nothin', dinna you?" Yvaine cuffs me on the arm. "Boys are from the future, girls are from the past."

"Where? I mean when? And when is now?"

"Let's cosy someplace warm." She tugs me toward the alley entrance. "We'll be lucky not t'catch cold."

"That's what my mother would say."

"I'm not your mother."

Yvaine leads me down grimy steps into an even grimier cellar. Inside is a pub, candle-lit and smoky but not crowded.

She takes a seat on a rickety stool before a tiny table.

I join her. "I don't even know what time of day it is, where I am, when."

"Late afternoon, March 15, 1725. London."

Good God. Two-hundred and seventy years before I was born! Not to mention five-thousand miles away. I thought we were in Philadelphia at least.

She puts her palms up in front of her face. "The Ides of March are come!"

"Is that important?" I say.

"Make of it what you will. How far uptime you from?"

"Uptime?"

"The future."

"2011."

"You be lying! You ain't old enough to travel that far."

Her gaze is intent, and it's focused on me. All on me. I'm not used to it. Not even Mom ever paid me that much attention.

"I'm fifteen, and I woke up this morning in Philadelphia, January 2011."

Chapter Three: Bar Talk

"You sayin' you traveled all that way in but one hop?" She takes my hand across the table — not much of a reach, the top being the size of a medium pizza.

I nod.

"Well, if you ain't lying most awful rotten, you're not goin' nowhere soon. There always be some recovery time — "

"What's your pleasure?" a serving wench asks.

I don't normally think of women as wenches, but this woman looks every bit the part: big, busty, and dirty, with a huge mole on one cheek.

"Two pints porter, and stew." Yvaine squeezes my hand. This is the first time a girl's ever squeezed my hand. Even if she's a thief with crooked teeth.

"Have you seen my dad and aunt?" I say.

She shakes her head as I describe them. I know the answer before she says it.

"I only seen two travelers together one time, an' that was an old geezer and his bag. I crawled up from the highlands, maybe two centuries past."

"*Highlander* is one of my favorite movies!" I blurt out.

She takes her hand back and does a really lame job trying to comb out her matted hair with her fingers.

"Yvaine's a Scottish name?" I say to fend off the silence.

"Means evenin' star. Ma was an Inverness lass, but Da was French."

"Are they here with you?"

She bites her lip, then says. "Tick-Tocks got 'em." She used that word before, in the alley.

"The clockwork guy?"

She nods. "If they kill you, you be gone forever. Even if someone goes back before an' changes things, you stays dead."

"Why? What are they?"

She shrugs. "Da told me about 'em, but it was so long ago I dinna half remember. There was a war and the Tocks comed from far uptime. Engines built to dodge and twist around the laws." She shrugs and half smiles at me. "'Tis them against us—"

The wench slams two big mugs and a bowl of brown stuff on the table.

"Tuppence," she says.

Yvaine looks at me, so I take out the purse she stole — but I don't know what a pence looks like.

Yvaine reaches over, takes three copper coins, gives two to the wench, and drops the third down her cleavage.

"Me tip," she says.

I'm more interested in time travel and the clockwork guys. "Other people didn't notice the Tick-Tock was all mechanical. Why's that?"

"Same reason no one remembers us." She reaches under the table and puts her hand on my knee. "If you give me a shilling I'll tell you what I knows."

"Are you crazy?"

"Life ain't never done me no favors."

Her Shrek-girl accent and grin just sell it. I sigh and take out the purse again.

"How do I know that isn't like a pound?" I say when she takes a coin.

"Would I cheat one of me own?" She taps the 'shilling' against my forehead, then leans over and kisses the spot, which tingles. Then she takes a big swig from her mug and uses the single wooden spoon to shovel some brown goop into her mouth. It dribbles down her chin. She pushes a nasty-looking chunk of meat onto the spoon using her filthy hand and offers it to me.

I eye the lump of fat and gristle and find my stomach is growling. When in Rome.

The stuff is tough and tastes like something my food-snob dad wouldn't eat if he were starving. I try to wash it down with the contents of the mug.

CHAPTER THREE: BAR TALK

Which are about the same color as the stew and incredibly bitter.

Yvaine laughs so hard she sprays the table with stew-colored spit.

"Your face looks like a dog with a rod up its arse," she manages in between guffaws.

"Is this beer?" I ask.

"Porter. This is an alehouse, aye?"

I take another sip. The stuff is bitter as hell.

"Can I get some water?"

"You has a death wish? That's a one-way trip to jail fever, dinna you ken!"

Yvaine drains her own cup and pounds it on the table. The wench brings us two more and I pay again.

"What's the mug made of?" It's heavy.

"Pewter."

"Doesn't that have lead in it?"

"An' what if it do?"

Dragging my brain back on track, I realize I half forgot about something huge.

"Back at the church," I say, "that friend of yours, is he *the* Ben Franklin?"

"What of it?"

I might be new to this, but I guess if she's from the past, there are also things I know that she doesn't.

"He's from America, right? A printer?"

Yvaine nods.

Did Dad know I might end up here? He gave me Ben Franklin's book, made me read it twice, even quizzed me on it before he left, even pissed me off by calling my answers *subpar*.

Was this adventure some sort of final exam? That seems a stretch. He gave me books about everything from Archimedes to Zapata.

"Ben Franklin's really important," I say, "or at least he will be. He's one of the founding fathers."

Her blank stare reminds me she doesn't know what the hell I'm talking about.

"When America revolts and becomes its own country, he's like hugely famous," I say. "He's on the hundred-dollar bill. He discovers *electricity*."

"The colonials revolt?" She smiles. "I always know how to pick 'em. Actually, what am I talkin' about? I got the eye for the downy rakes."

This is too weird. "That Tick-Tock came from Ben's house in Philly. Was he chasing him or us?"

"Nobblers!" She spits on the floor. "They kills travelers on sight an' they're always up to funny business, muckin' with time an' whatnot."

"You said they try to get around the law? The one I saw pretended to be a police officer. Are they time cops?"

She laughs again. "I didna mean man's laws. Tocks are fashioned t'dodge the Lord's natural edicts. Like how folk dinna notice us, or we always speak the language wherever we goes."

I wonder what language *she's* speaking.

"How's *didna* different than *dinna*?"

Listening as I talk, I realize I'm speaking with a British accent. The universe sure is crafty.

"*Didna* your mum teach you *dinna* tease a lady?" She winks at me.

"I was just asking."

"Anyways, we live outside history, same as the Tick-Tocks." Yvaine shrugs. "We dinna belong." She winks again. "Regular folk, they find it hard to see us, we find it hard to change things — except each other. An' if we bring somethin' to a time where it dinna belong, that somethin' changes."

Like my phone or my wallet. It's hard to get my head around all this — the spinning room and beer-addled brain aren't helping.

"People see what they expect in us," she continues, "but smart folks notice us more than others. That's why I like Ben. He's sharp as a barber's blade. Still, even he dinna remember me name."

She pauses for a second then says, "Charlie." This time when she puts her hand under the table, it's my thigh she touches.

Which is great except for one thing.

"How do I get home?" I say.

She laughs. "That'll be a trick. Boys only travel downtime."

Panic wells inside me. "There must be a way."

"If I could fan about as I please, do you think I'd be sleepin' in the slummin' rookery?"

"I don't feel so good." In more ways than one.

"Can't hold your drink?" Yvaine just finished off her third pint.

Once or twice I sipped at Mom's pinot grigio, but that's it. Now I've gone and had a mug and a half. I look into the dark amber fluid. God, I really have to pee.

"Is there a men's room?"

"Huh?"

"I have to go to the bathroom."

"You want to take a bath?"

I'm pretty sure my face goes bright red. "I mean, I have to piss."

"Why didna you say so? The alley be most convenient."

I stand, spin away, and find myself face to chest with a burly dockworker dude.

"Watch where y'goin'!" Mr. Twice-My-Weight says.

Yvaine rises and slides between us.

"He didna mean any offense, good sir."

The big guy looks at her and mumbles, "Then 'ave 'im keep outta me way." But he moves on.

"Thanks," I tell Yvaine. "Assuming I make it back from the alley, what's the chance you're still here?"

"Pretty good." She smiles. "I dinna have all your money yet."

It's still drizzling outside, but lightly. I crouch in the space between a nearby pile of garbage and a wall and try to unbutton my pants. Between the beer and the long-instead-of-round buttons, this proves more difficult than I thought.

When I return, Yvaine's where I left her. Thank God. I don't bother to ask about washing my hands.

"Thomas feelin' better, does he?" She eyes my belt.

"Who's Thomas?"

Distant church bells ring, nine times. They remind me of the creepy clockwork guy — the Tick-Tock.

"Donnie be here soon," Yvaine says. "You better hide your coinage."

"First Ben, then Thomas, now Donnie?"

"Donnie deals with the money. I'll tell him you're me cousin from Scotland. You're fast, an' nobody never notices us much. Just dinna let on that you has cole, and give him what he do see."

"What's cole?"

"Rum cole, good money. Queer cole, bad money."

I nod. "You just want me to keep it safe so you can steal it later."

"I like me a fast learner."

Chapter Four:
Donnie

London, Spring, 1725

When Yvaine turns away from me, it feels as if the sun slides behind a cloud.

She watches six or so noisy boys clomp down the narrow stairway from the street. Most range from eight to sixteen years old, but their skinny leader could be nineteen, maybe older. Even with his hat tucked under an arm he's tall, his height enhanced by his cherry-colored high heels and enormous wig of white curls falling onto a peacock-blue jacket offset by a lipstick-pink vest, canary-yellow pants, peach stockings, and the red shoes.

This has to be Donnie. He swaggers over and thunks his lime-colored cane onto our table. His fingers are half-hidden by grungy lace shirt cuffs.

"If it ain't me sassy lassie," he says.

The addition of his ridiculous lisp almost brings my throttled laughter to a boil, but Yvaine kicks my shin.

"Keepin' your seat warm, Dancer," she says.

He taps his walking stick on each of our half-dozen empty mugs.

"A profitable day at your trade, I hope. But who's your friend?" He points the wand-o-green in my direction.

"Me cousin Charlie from Scotland, a runaway 'prentice, maked his way south t'find me."

The rest of the boys drag over a nearby table — hastily abandoned by its previous occupants. Donnie gestures at a teenager with absolutely no neck and an arm that ends in a buttoned cuff. He kicks a stool into place between Yvaine and me.

"Most gracious of you, Stump," Donnie says as he sits and drapes one arm over my shoulders and the other over Yvaine's. "I believe some drinking is in order. Sally!"

The wench rushes over with armfuls of mugs soon lifted to toast.

"To..." Donnie looks at me and blinks. "To a pair of new hands!" He slams his now empty mug in front of Stump. "Some of us be short in that there department."

Stump's red face makes a halfhearted attempt at a smile.

"T'was a bullet aimed at Donnie the Dancer that mangled me hand."

"For which I'm eternally grateful." Donnie reaches across the table to ruffle Stump's patchy crewcut.

Whoever barbers this gang is either blind or suffers from a degenerative nervous disorder — which explains why their leader wears a wig. Several new kids join our group, including two other girls, one raggedy little one and another about Yvaine's age, better dressed and with dark hair peeking from under her bonnet.

"How'd the burgling go?" Yvaine says.

"My dear." Donnie runs a finger down her cheek and around her chin. "T'was before nine, so it was only thieving."

A redheaded boy, perhaps twelve, chimes in. "We gots two silver candlesticks! I crawled in whilst Dancer kept the servants busy, ain't I?"

He stands next to our table, facing away, then bends his torso ninety degrees backward until he lies flat on top of the

32

Two's company, three's a crowd

ale mugs and reaches his freckled hands toward Yvaine, who slaps them and does a bunch of handshakes and slaps that'd make a brother from the projects proud.

"Right proper." She beams. "Carrot always bends to the occasion."

"Indeed," Donnie says, "Ginger here made a fine showing on his belly, more than some do on their backs."

He points his cane at the dark-haired girl, who blushes.

"Which, my dear family," he continues, "brings us to that paying of the piper and thusly rendering of proper and timely tribute. Moreover, to wit, rent be due."

His eyes spar with the dark-haired girl until she pulls a handful of coins from her bodice.

Stump sweeps them from the table — Carrot has rolled off — into a leather purse. One by one Donnie cajoles each of his crew, using a creative mixture of compliments, bluster, and veiled threats to extract what he feels is the appropriate sum. This guy has serious style and I'm thinking Charles Dickens really did know something about the London underworld.

"And you?" Donnie plants a kiss on Yvaine's cheek, which also plants a barb of jealousy in my heart.

She offers him a few coins — all of which came from me.

"Poke me in the peepers," he says, "did me favorite have a skinny day?"

"Me cousin and I were conversatin'."

Donnie squeezes our necks, perhaps a little too firmly for comfort.

"Far from me to discourage familial bonding and all. As I always says, family comes first, and what ain't we, if not one happy family?"

He turns back to me and moves close, his nose not two inches from mine. His breath smells like the cafeteria dumpster. There's a smile on his white-painted face but there's also a hardness in his eyes.

I wrestle out my purse, which he plucks from my grasp. Fortunately, most of my money — thanks to Yvaine's warning — is now in my stockings.

Donnie shakes out what remains and returns the empty purse.

"Still short, but I'll cut you some slack, being your first day and all."

He tousles my hair like he did Stump's and thwacks me on the back for good measure.

"Sally!" he yells. "Another round of ale and some roast beef!"

I was having a much better time before he crashed the party.

As the group makes its way to the neighborhood where they apparently sleep, I question the wisdom of following a gang of thieves to their lair.

But to be fair, I'm royally drunk.

Time moves like Mom's old eight-millimeter films — the ones of when she was a kid — all flicker and choppy bursts. When the alley spins into hyperdrive, I find myself vomiting into a pile of rotting garbage.

Yvaine supports me during this little embarrassment — although I'm not the first of the gang making with the Technicolor-yawn. A younger boy ralphed five minutes ago. Afterward I feel better and she takes my hand. I'm grateful — even if she did steal my money, we time travelers ought to stick together.

We file through a ragged wooden gap into what you might call a townhouse, if you were as drunk as me. We step over sleeping bodies in cramped rooms that reek of piss and B.O. until we descend a staircase so badly built it's a wonder we make it to the bottom without plunging through the half-rotten risers.

Below is a foul little cellar, just big enough for four filthy mattresses. It smells even worse than upstairs, like a whiff of shit has been added to the piss bouquet.

I'm not so sure about bunking with the homies. It's not just the conditions — all of a sudden I'm *really* homesick. Before bed, Mom and I usually curl up on separate chairs in the library and read. I'm too drunk for that but I wouldn't mind raiding the fridge for ice cream.

"Can you take someone uptime with you?" I ask Yvaine. It must be possible; Dad and Sophie go places and come back.

"One person." She shrugs. "An' they has to be our sort."

Like me. I relax a little.

The nasty basement is wall-to-wall kids except for a woman maybe thirty going on sixty, thin as a nail and dressed in rags. She approaches Yvaine carrying a bundle.

"I has the chit — get comfortable, lass," she says, then launches into a coughing fit that sounds none-too-wholesome.

Yvaine is already unbuttoning the jacket-like part of her dress. She throws it in a corner and sets to work on her bulky skirts.

"Charlie, can you unlace me stays?" She presents the row of knots that run down the back of the newly revealed stiff-looking top.

I glance around. Everyone else is half-undressed, even Donnie, who looks startlingly different without his wig — not to mention the outlandish jacket-and-vest combo. His real hair looks more or less like a marine buzz-cut.

I work on Yvaine's laces — easier said than done, drunk — then she makes me help with the bulky cloth and wood things strapped to her hips. When we finish she's wearing only a ratty gray shirt that comes to her knees.

CHAPTER FOUR: DONNIE

"Thanks, Nancy," she says, taking the bundle from the lady.

Only candles light the cramped space, but now I can see that Yvaine's holding a baby. It opens and closes its little mouth like a guppy.

"You hungry, Billy?" she says. "Mama's got somethin' for you."

She tugs open the drawstring of her shirt and presses the infant close.

I'm not sure what surprises me more — that she's a teen mother or that I just saw my first glimpse of tit.

Yvaine, sitting cross-legged in the corner we've staked out, is still feeding the baby. I lean against the wall, hiccuping. At first the hiccups seemed funny, but now I'm dreading each spasm of my gut.

The room is full of smoke. Some boys burn a bit of coal in another corner where a hole in the ceiling serves as a half-assed chimney.

I eye the baby like it's a chinchilla. I've never been this close to one before. Our family is tiny and our friends few and far between.

And I have to pee again. The mechanics are easier this time, but the real problem is the ten other people all within five feet of me. I stare into the piss-pot, as Yvaine calls it. The sight cures my hiccups. Apparently, it's not just a piss-pot.

Donnie is talking to Yvaine when I return to the corner. They stand so close I can't see between them.

"You're a dirty puzzle, sporting your dairy. And short to boot."

"I'll do better tomorrow, Dancer."

He toys with his cane, the green of which stands out against his plain white underwear.

"You saw that Ben fellow again, didn't you?"

Her teeth torture her lip. The other time I saw her do that was when we talked about the Tick-Tocks.

"Of course not, I was with Charlie. Ain't I?"

"All day," I say.

Donnie's free hand draws back and I think he's going to hit her — she flinches — but at the last minute he moves to caress her cheek. He tucks his cane under an arm and takes the baby in both hands and swings him so high his head almost whacks into the low ceiling.

"Me son is going to grow up a right fine lad." He stops with the tossing and starts tickling. "Aren't you, Billy?"

I choke. Donnie's the father? What about Ben Franklin?

I realize my fists are clenched. I have to stop myself from stepping forward. Sure, Donnie's one of those fast-talking types I never liked in school, but he hasn't really done anything — and besides, he's a lot taller and older than me.

He coochie-coos the baby one more time and gives him back to Yvaine.

"But don't go near that prigstar again." He grabs her hair and kisses her roughly on the mouth, then returns to the other side of the room, where Stump and a couple others play a game for money.

I glare after him as Yvaine settles back into her corner, pushing the baby against her breast.

"You weren't kidding about picking the losers," I tell her.

Her eyes poke back at me. "There's worse than him."

"If you include serial killers in the mix," I say. "Has he hit you?"

"He takes care of his own." A tear wells in one of those green saucers. "Where were you last year?"

"Let's go," I say. "The future is great. Women's lib and all. Girls can have the same jobs as guys, lots of them make just as much money."

She scrunches her face. "Why would I want to dig ditches or shovel coal?"

"Not by hand. We have machines for that."

"Machines killed me parents."

Yeah, I wasn't thinking of that. "The future is safer. If you get hurt or sick they rush you to the hospital in minutes."

"Doctors kill you faster than a knife in the gut."

Too bad I didn't script this conversation.

"I'm just not explaining well," I say. "We should go, trust me."

She shrinks back, clutching her baby. "We make of it what we will."

"What's that mean?"

She shrugs. "Something me Da used to say. No one can help. I brought this on meself, now I be mired here."

"You said you've been crawling uptime. What's stopping you?"

She brushes at the baby's wispy little eyebrows. "Not without Billy."

"Why don't you just take him?"

"People remember his name," she whispers. "The only way he's going into the future is one second at a time."

Eventually the candles go out and leave us in the smelly dark. My mind swirls, partly from the lingering effect of the ale and partly from the need to put things together. Obviously, Dad and Sophie are time travelers but my mom isn't.

I realize I don't have a clue what I'm supposed to do. Did Dad plan all this? Did he want me to find him? Or is this the Time Wars and today my personal version of when the droids start leading Luke Skywalker to Obi-Wan?

Except I didn't even get the cryptic recording from Princess Leia.

Yvaine lies next to me. I know she's awake because I hear her whispering to the baby. What she said about him has me freaked out, particularly given my own situation with my mom.

I find her ear and whisper, "You said we don't always have to travel alone."

Her breath is warm against my cheek. "Not always, but we're adrift in a river with two currents. You flow downtime an' I flow up."

The barbed tendril of fear around my heart gives a little squeeze. Grime and stink aside, this has all been fun so far — and I'm smart enough to know the reason why is lying right next to me — but it's not like I want to spend my life in the past. I miss Mom already, and she'll be worried.

I think of the baby and am surprised to find resentment creeping in. If he wasn't here, Yvaine would probably just take me home. It's hardly his fault, though. I guess the children of time travelers sometimes are and sometimes aren't. Maybe it's recessive, like red hair or the wrinkly peas my biology teacher goes on about.

Will go on about. Like two hundred and eighty-five years from now.

"Who's the father?" I ask.

Her lips brush against my ear. "Dinna say anythin', not never."

It better be Ben. He's way cooler.

"Donnie loves Billy," Yvaine continues. "Just don't cross him an' you be fine. He's decent, made somethin' of hisself, even after his parents leaved him to the parish workhouse as a babe. He does right by us, all of us."

My fingers graze the skin of her arm. At least I think it's her arm.

Chapter Four: Donnie

I'm not sure she notices since I hear soft snores from her direction. My own thoughts grow chaotic as I drift into sleep and dream of an outlandishly dressed clockwork man kissing a sandy-haired waif.

Chapter Five:
Training

London, Spring, 1725

I wake with an ache in my head and a foot in my face.

My skull hurts even worse when I bat the leg away and pull myself to a sitting position. A shaft of light from the stairwell isn't doing much to illuminate the dingy cellar, but that's probably for the best. There are still four of us sharing our mattress, but I think that's two less than last night. My nose is so stuffed I have to breathe through my mouth — again, probably for the best.

"When I was a wee lassie," Yvaine says from beside me, "I used t'sleep between the sow and her piglets t'keep off the chill."

"I've hardly ever had to share a room," I say. Hint, hint.

One of the boys on our mattress farts. I tell myself it's just like that Cub Scout camp-out where they fed us canned beans.

"You hungry?" Yvaine asks.

Gross as the idea is, I am. Besides, this is my first hangover, and people on TV treat them with greasy breakfasts.

Yvaine sets the baby down and stands. A cloth-wrapped packet falls out of her open shirt, spilling a bunch of dusty things on the mattress. She kneels and grabs at them.

I pick one up and realize it's a dried purple-topped flower, pressed flat. They're all flowers, just different types.

"Gimme that." She reaches for it.

"My mom used to cut flowers in the yard and bring them inside," I say.

"I told you, I'm not your mother."

Someone woke up on the wrong side of the mattress.

We pick our way over the sleeping masses. She stops near the stairs — and the piss-pot.

"Hold Billy."

He's lighter than I expect, and very warm. Yvaine hitches up her long shirt and squats over the pot. I don't look but I can't avoid hearing the stream.

"I hope you really are a fast learner," she says. "Rent's due and we needs kick up our share."

Someone charges for this pigsty?

"The dollymop's got it right." Donnie, back in his garish blue jacket, steps in so close his breath tickles my hair. "But firstly, empty that there pot and fetch us some proper water."

Another annoying trait — he's obviously one of those people with no sense of personal space. I have to step back just to see he's pointing to an empty wooden bucket near the chamberpot.

There has to be a way to get out of this.

Donny crunches my bicep in his grip, so apparently not.

"Don't worry, Dancer." The redheaded contortionist, Carrot, wraps an ankle behind his neck and cracks some double joint or other. "I'll show the new lad the well."

Yesterday's rain has been replaced by a featureless gray sky. I'm glad for my wool coat, but the shoes still suck. Carrot's a real champ, having volunteered to carry the chamberpot.

44

As he's in front of me, I notice he has this rubbery style of moving — like a beggar boy gummy bear.

"Guess all that flexibility is helpful in your line of work?" I say.

He grins. "Dancer sure thinks so."

We reach the crowded well and Carrot shows me how to lower the bucket. If I'm trapped here, I can invent plumbing and make a fortune.

"Why do they call him Dancer?" I ask.

"On account 'e studied with Mr. James Figg, the bare-knuckle fighter. 'E's impressive fast. Mr. Figg sayed Donnie be one of 'is bestest boxers and bestest fencers."

Not just a trained boxer, but he knows how to use that sword he carries. Great.

As we lug the heavy water bucket back to the lair, Carrot continues, "I sees why Mr. Figg taked a shine to Donnie. 'E stopped a vagabond crew pushin' me li'l brother into Fleet Street Ditch, then taked us in outta the kindness of 'is own 'eart."

"Nice of him." Is he talking about the same Donnie?

"Dancer, 'e don't never like to see the wee ones beaten upon, on account of 'is own upbringin'. In the workhouse they was fierce wont to pick on 'im."

If Donnie really does like kids, there might be a place here for Billy. But how am I supposed to convince a mother to abandon her baby? I'm a lowlife for even thinking it.

At least some of the gang are cool. Carrot hasn't stopped smiling once, which makes it pretty much impossible not to like him.

"Which kid is your brother?"

"None of 'em. The cannikin pox took 'old of 'im a year back and ate 'im all up so as Old Mr. Grim comed and put 'im down for a proper dirt bath."

Foot in mouth much? "I'm sorry," I whisper.

"Ain't no need t'apologize," he says, "Me brother always be sickly, and touched t'boot. I miss 'im, but 'e's better off with our mum and dad in 'eaven."

"I'm sorry about them, too."

He shrugs. "The reaper puts us all t'bed with a shovel."

No break in the smile, not a waver.

Carrot, Donnie, Yvaine. All orphans. I don't think I ever met an orphan back in Philly. Dad might not have been around much, but having some of him and all of Mom sure beat no parents at all. Which just makes me feel guilty about Mom and really miss her. We kept a board with our chores in the kitchen, hers and mine. The last couple years, I erased my name from the board, knowing she'd have to wait for Dad to put it back up.

And the sad part was, once my name was gone, she did my chores for me.

Back in the cellar, I reach into the long coat Yvaine hung on the wall and try for the hundredth time to retrieve the watch.

The bell jingles again.

"That weren't as loud." She's feeding the baby — three-month-olds are always hungry, I guess. "It takes a bloody sight of practice t'master."

I tuck the timepiece back inside the jacket pocket and quiet the little bell she tied to the collar.

"Do I really have to learn this?"

"Only if you needs eat," Yvaine says. "Pretend the coat's a proper gentleman. Swagger an' stride next to him, then just reach — dinna think."

I play her little game, hamming it up a bit, even tip my hat at the jacket while I try to steal its watch. The bell still rings, but I get a laugh from Yvaine.

46

So what if I'm stuck in the past, learning to steal, lusting after a teenage mom with a thing for bad boys. Yvaine's—

"You're fast, Cuz." Donnie has a way of sneaking up on a guy. He takes the baby from Yvaine and tosses him in the air twice.

"Charlie's catchin' on fast," Yvaine says as I regain my composure.

"'E should be ready by this evenin'." Carrot's been supervising from a nearby stool —upside down, since he's in a headstand with his legs wide apart.

Donnie hands back the baby, hops in front of me, then hops back. He twirls his lime-colored cane in one hand and presents my little leather notebook with the other. He must have snatched it, but I didn't feel a thing.

"Let's see how you do against a mark that doesn't hang on the wall." He flips off his ridiculous wig, shrugs out of his jacket, and tucks my notebook inside his waistcoat. Then he drops into a kind of boxer's stance, his fists held in front of him.

"Are we fighting or am I picking your pocket?" I say.

He takes to hopping about on the mattresses. "They don't call me Dancer for nothing."

Thanks for the reminder. I've never fought anyone before, but I do my best to copy his posture.

"You gents 'ave fun." Carrot unfolds from his pretzel pose, blows Yvaine a kiss, and heads for the stairs. "Covent Garden's unsuspectin' proprietors await me tender ministrations."

Dancer gets my attention with a mock punch that passes a millimeter from my nose.

"Donnie," Yvaine says, "he's just a laddie." She holds Billy close.

"Merely seeing what he's made of."

Donnie takes another swing at my face. My heart is racing and I know I should be afraid, but I don't want Yvaine thinking

Boxing in the basement

I'm a wuss. Besides, at least he's not a murderous mechanical cop. So I twist my shoulders and avoid the blow.

Lightning fast, his other fist strikes out and connects with my upper arm. He pulled the punch, because it doesn't hurt that much.

I don't know what else to do, so I jump forward, much like I would in the middle of the triple jump. The move puts me closer and I manage to tap him on the hip.

"Unorthodox, but interesting," he says as he dodges away.

The other gang members in residence gather around.

Donnie comes at me again. I find that if I watch him closely, even fast as he is, I can avoid his blows.

"You're light as a grasshopper," he says, "but you'll just end up tiring yourself out."

He's right. I'm breathing heavily and starting to slow down. Instead of jumping to the side, I twist in the air and come at him. He elbows me hard in the side, but not before I get a hand inside his coat and close it on my notebook, drawing it out as I fall onto a flea-ridden mattress. I lay gasping, the wind knocked right out of me.

Donnie grabs me by one arm and yanks me back onto my feet. I'm still fairly helpless as he puts me in a headlock and gives me an authentic eighteenth-century nuggie.

"Not half bad, Cuz," he says. "In a deuce of years you might give me a proper run for me money. I miss fibbing with ole Stump. That right hook of his could ding a man with just one blow."

The thick boy glowers at his amputated hand. "That's why I gots me knife now."

When Donnie releases me, another boy presses a cup of water into my hand and I gulp it down.

It's not water.

The stuff burns like hell and I choke on it, soaking the mattress. Even after I recover, the bitter perfume taste lingers.

"'E might be quick," Stump says, "but 'e can't 'old 'is gin."

Chapter Six:
Show Time

London, Spring, 1725

"**W**e'll meet up with Carrot, then I'll snatch women's purses," Yvaine says on our way to Covent Garden. "Easier than men's pockets."

"Did you learn this stuff from your parents?"

She shakes her head. "Our farm was a day's walk from Inverness. If you stole somethin', the clan you taked from just beat you senseless, maybe killed you."

"You paint a great picture."

But her expression is wistful.

"T'was great, Charlie. In them times I was loved. Although even if that scaly Tick-Tock hadn't slit me mum's throat and put a dagger in Da's eye, sooner or later I'd have gone by accident."

Way to sugarcoat it. "What do you mean?"

She sighs. "Your da needs his arse whipped for what he didna learn you."

If I ever see him again, I'll be sure to pass that along.

"He made me study history, but he didn't tell me why."

She snorts. "We girls can't even do that — no guides for uptime."

"Why doesn't someone bring back a history book?"

"Me folks tried. The pages went blank. Girls start earlier, too. We travel at seven. For boys it'd be about fifteen."

"Why's that?"

"We be the superior sex." She grins at me.

As weird as things are for me right now, I try to imagine being a seven-year-old girl alone in the world — regardless of the when.

"What was it like?"

"You mean as an unprotected lass, findin' food, shelter, and safety when the only thing I'm good for is me charm and wit?"

"You don't have to be alone anymore," I say. "We can go uptime together." The bizarre image of Yvaine sitting across the kitchen table from Mom invades my brain. "It's better there."

She stops for a second, either because of what I said or to avoid being trampled by a passing six-horse carriage.

"You beatin' that nag again? I told you, I canna never leave little William."

William — Billy. Oh my God! The solution was right there in Dad's last batch of books. I was only kidding myself about Donnie taking the baby. But this, this is perfect.

"Yvaine, Ben Franklin takes William! Raises him as his own!"

She snorts again. "You saw what he thinks of me!"

"I don't know how, but it happens. I read his autobiography — the story of his life — he came to London from Philadelphia to learn the latest in the printing trade, but he only stays a year or two then goes back to start his own business."

"What's that needs do with Billy?"

"When Ben gets back to Pennsylvania he brings an illegitimate son named William home to his wife."

She looks shocked. "Bastard! He's married?"

"Engaged, I think. Debbie's her name."

"Oh."

"That's not the point," I say. "He takes William back to America. Billy grows up to be governor of New Jersey and lives into the next century."

I don't mention that he's a traitor to his new country or that the older Franklin eventually disowns him. Every life has its ups and downs.

"Guv'nor? You sure it be me William?"

"Absolutely." Well, ninety-nine percent sure. "All the details fit — Ben goes to his grave never saying who the mother was."

She's facing me but not really looking at me.

"Ben raises him right," I say. "He becomes a lawyer, hob-nobs with lords and ladies, marries, lives to be an old man. What better can anyone hope for?"

Yvaine wipes at her eyes. "I dinna want to talk about this anymore. I needs think."

In general, 1720s London is far more chaotic than modern Philadelphia or even New York, which I saw on occasional family trips. But Covent Garden makes the rest of it look tame.

Pedestrians, animals, carts, and carriages move in every conceivable direction. The road is paved but no space is sacred. We have to throw ourselves into a doorway to avoid a horseman using the side of the road as an express lane and are nearly clobbered by a pair of carpenters wielding timbers.

Yvaine has us walking back and forth until she spots Carrot, then pulls us both into an alley. Dusk builds murky shadows as the redheaded boy shows off the coins he looted from an unfortunate street vendor.

She nods, looking at me. "Meet back here if there be trouble and never keep anythin' on you but the rum cole, that way if you're caught by the crowd you can play the innocent."

"I imagine that'd be hard with three pocket watches in your shirt," I say.

Yvaine snickers. She seems to take real pleasure in teaching me her thieving arts. It's hard to remember that only thirty-six hours ago my life was normal, if being a hard-to-remember baby time traveler counts as normal.

Getting lost in history is easy, but the details can kill you, Dad used to say when he went into lecture mode.

I guess he meant literally.

"Look!" Yvaine pokes me in the chest. Her smile catches the fading light. "Carrot will draw out the mark. I'll get the swag, then you play the stickman."

"What's a stickman?" I say.

"Sassy'll pass you the goods," Carrot says. "Just slip off into the crowd posthaste."

Yvaine nods. "*Show time* be the signal. When I says them words, it's your turn."

She drags us down a street where marquees advertise theatrical performances. The road is jammed with carriages, elegantly dressed guests, uniformed footmen.

"That one." Yvaine nods at a lady whose green silk dress matches the interior of her gilded coach.

Carrot pulls three wooden balls from his jacket and gives them to Yvaine. He rolls himself into a handstand and she tosses him back the balls, which he actually juggles with his toes while walking on his hands toward the rich woman.

Nearby pedestrians stop and stare at this amazing little feat.

"Stay close," Yvaine whispers. She points at a theater and says, "Show time!"

Show time indeed. I follow her through the crowd. She pretends to watch Carrot and stumbles into the mark.

"Pardon, ma'am."

Something soft presses against my thigh. Looking down, I see Yvaine's arm snaked in my direction, holding a fancy green handbag. I shove it into my rather loose trousers, where it bulges.

"My purse!" the lady screams.

"Grab her!" one of her footmen yells. He starts to pat down Yvaine, who raises her arms and looks indignant. Her eyes flick from me to the street.

I toss myself headlong into traffic, which given a near collision with a pair of horses turns out to be a questionable choice.

"That boy's got it!" a voice yells behind me.

A carriage passes. There's a vertical bar running along the coach's back corner. I grab it, swing hard, and scrabble to gain purchase on the little iron shelf above the bumper.

Mostly this works just like in the movies. My coach cruises along and the green lady's fancy one recedes behind me.

Except for the footman clinging to the opposite corner.

"Thief on me coach!" he screams. "Stop 'im!" He kicks at me.

"This must be my stop," I say, swinging down to an open bit of street.

Looks like I'm in the clear.

"Thief!" a voice bellows from behind me.

I glance over my shoulder to find six people giving chase. Who would've thought Londoners were such good Samaritans!

I'm faster than my pursuers, and this time I keep my shoes on, but a couple storekeepers join in front and try to block a narrow alley. I hop up on a low wall and sprint right by them, leaping over someone's clumsy attempt to grab my feet.

I need to get out of sight so they'll forget what I look like. Ahead is a building under construction, which gives me an idea.

A glance back reveals the crowd is several dozen strong. I put on some speed and snatch up a long wooden pole from the construction site. There's a wall up ahead, about twelve feet tall. I heft the pole into position. It isn't as flexible as I'm used to, but twelve feet is nothing.

I eye the ground, watching for the right distance to plant the pole—

And totally don't see the guy who trips me.

I spill hard into the mud and taste the dirt and blood from where I smack my lip.

The crowd is on me. I don't even make it to my knees before someone kicks me in the gut and knocks the wind out of me for the second time today.

I curl up like Sonic the Hedgehog. As Yvaine said, people see what they expect in us, in this case just a thief in need of a lesson. I just wish the lesson didn't hurt so much.

Then I hear a loud rattling sound and the beating stops. Blue-knickered legs stand beside me. I wipe the mud from my eyes.

My rescuer's face still has that little crack I gave him with the rock. His glass eyes stare down at me and he stops spinning the wooden noisemaker in his hand. As that sound fades I can hear the soft ticking of his clockwork heart.

"Constable!" a man says, out of breath, "this urchin ran off with a woman's purse."

The Tick-Tock reaches down and grabs me by the arm. His grip is like iron. He drags me down the street.

"Don't let him take me!" I scream.

"The magistrate'll 'ave you dancing at Tyburn by Monday!" someone yells.

"But, sir," says another, "don't we needs testify?"

The Tick-Tock spins his head completely around and stops them with a glare.

He's moving fast. I drag my legs against the ground, then

beat my free hand against him, which is like pummeling a parking meter.

Soon he's dragged me several blocks, leaving the crowd behind. We come to a square filled with vendors. He tosses me down into the mud and draws the sword from his stick.

I scrabble backward like a crab as he raises it high....

And points into the crowded market.

I don't stop to count my blessings. I just spring to my feet and run.

Chapter Seven:
Celebration

London, Spring, 1725

Somehow I find my way back to our alley. Yvaine's waiting in the evening shadows.

"You had me worried." She wraps her arms around me. "I've lost too many folk already."

Two beatings in one day makes her hug painful, but I don't care.

"Where's Carrot?" I ask.

"He'll be fine. He was already disappeared when they let me go." She points at my bulging pants. "Is that the swag, or are you just happy to see me?"

I have to unbutton to extract the purse. "One of those clockwork guys caught me. He was posing as a constable."

She freezes mid smirk. "How are you here?"

"He stopped the mob and let me go."

"Tick-Tocks dinna do that. They kills us on sight." She's biting her lip.

"If that's true, we need to move on. To the future."

She scowls. "You can go downtime if it pleases you."

It doesn't.

"How common are they?" I ask.

"I've only seen them thrice, four times if you count yesterday."

"He didn't kill us on sight then," I say. "We ran away and lost him."

"That was different, he had t'go. Once they starts ringin', they dinna stop. Twenty-six seconds, thirteen chimes, and they be gone."

"Where?" I say.

She shrugs. "Some other time. When I saw them before, they'd have killed me if I didna flee uptime."

Gulp.

"How do I do that? Travel."

"Dinna go." She takes my hand. "I didna mean what I said."

Is that a chink in her girly armor?

"We be so rare, Charlie. It could be years before either of us meet another."

"If I go, I can only go backward — downtime?"

She squeezes. "Even if I wasn't trapped, I'd go forward. So stay."

I look into her big green eyes. She's hardly the girl I imagined myself with, and she has two boyfriends already. But I want her, maybe more than I've ever wanted anything.

"If you can't go because of Billy, and I can't go because of you, that leaves us pretty well stuck."

She leans toward me. "Here ain't so bad."

Maybe it isn't.

"Even if I wanted to go, I don't know how to travel."

She cocks her head. "Same as you did yesterday. You'll ken when you've got your strength back."

"Yesterday I used the Tick-Tock's hole."

She braces herself against the alley wall. "You what?"

"The Tick-Tock was doing his chime thing, he hopped down into a hole, and I followed."

"You jumped in his time-hole?"

"It brought me here."

Yvaine scratches her head. I think she might have lice.

"Charlie, you're either the dumbest or bravest cull I know."

"Go with bravest." When she stops laughing I say, "You're sure it's dangerous?"

"Every time I seen someone go near a Tock they ended up dead." She squints, her eyes starting to tear. "Includin' me folks."

"What if that Tick-Tock wanted me to follow?" I say. "You said we could bring one other traveler."

"You needs be touchin' for it t'work. Besides, why would he do that? He tried t'kill you. That's what they always do."

"I wish we could ask my dad. He knows all about this stuff." At least I assume he does.

"But he ain't here, is he?" she says.

"No." I take her hand again, the one holding the green silk purse.

"We needs ditch this." She pulls out the money and throws the bag into the darkness. "Merciful Jesus." She counts out the gold coins. "Fourteen guineas!"

"Is that a lot?"

"Half a year's wages for a master tradesman!"

Yvaine hugs me close and kisses me full on the lips. For a second, shock has me rigid as an I-beam. Then I try to kiss her back — not that my moves are anything but theoretical.

She puts her head on my shoulder and I float upward in a bubble.

"Oh, Charlie," she whispers, "Donnie's goin' to love us to death."

Her words send me crashing back to the cobblestones.

She pats me like a poodle and spirits two coins away to some inner recess of her person.

"We'll keep two yellow boys an' gives the rest to Dancer."

We should keep it all and run to the country or, if we can get Ben to take Billy, the future.

But instead the familiar old Charlie who asked Michelle about the Fourth of July kicks swashbuckling Charlie to the curb.

"Do we need to give him that much?"

She leans against the alley wall, presses herself against me, and tilts her head sideways so we knock temples.

"I am crackin' through your knob-skull." She hands me another pair of coins. "Ten will still send him to heaven."

We find Donnie not far off in an alehouse called *The Rose*, where he's shooting dice with Stump. The game involves a lot of gin.

I punch holes in him with my eyes while Yvaine plops in his lap and counts ten guineas into his palm.

His long face pulls into a creepy smile.

"Charlie was brilliant," she says. "Spinned the mark around six ways from Sunday an' rode out on a coach like he owned it!"

Donnie stands, letting Yvaine down to the floor. He turns to me and pops up into his boxing stance.

I remain frozen like a deer, but he just gives me a couple quick taps, then pulls me in close and presses his lips to my head. Yvaine's kiss was better.

"You're a right proper member of the gang now, Cuz!"

He lets me go and points his cane into the air.

"Leathercoat! A sip of gin for the house, and a private room for us lordships!"

Gin is passed around while the doorman — who, true to local naming conventions, wears a long leather coat — arranges our room. But the celebration's interrupted when a bowlegged gang member waddles into the alehouse.

"Carrot's been habbled," he says.

Donnie sets down his cup. "Where they holding him, Bandy?"

"The King's Head Inn, for lifting."

Yvaine grips my arm hard. Her face is pale.

"Newgate prison be the worst," she whispers. "He must've run another sneak after our lay."

Donnie sighs and offers Stump a single gold coin. "Go facilitate the ginger's garnish and comforts. I'll see to arrangements with Mr. Fusée."

"Dancer, can I go instead?" Yvaine asks.

Their eyes meet and hold, but after a minute she looks away.

Stump leaves and Bandy brings Donnie his jacket and hat, then helps him buckle on his sword. He grabs the gin bottle from Yvaine, drinks, and passes it to me. I can't decide if I should wipe it off because of his spit, or not, because of hers.

"Who's this Mr. Fussy?" I ask Yvaine while we wait.

She snickers. "Mr. Fusée. He works for the Thief-taker General, Mr. Jonathan Wild, the most cunnin' fox in London. That one has his hand in every theft, an' every magistrate in his purse."

I hate to think about cheerful Carrot in Newgate. I've never read anything good about it, in any century.

"How often is one of you arrested?"

"Every couple weeks, but they mostly come back."

"Mostly?"

"Donnie will see to Carrot, buy him an alibi. He takes care of his own."

Dancer and Stump return just as Leathercoat shows us to our room.

The place must have been nice once, but after who-knows-how-many parties most of the paintings are torn, the mirror cracked, and the effort to sweep the last group's trash from the floor lackluster at best.

Stump takes a seat next to Donnie, who overturns the chair with a laugh.

"Place of honor's for Cuz tonight." He presses a full gin bottle into my hand and massages my shoulders.

There are only five of us paying customers: myself, Yvaine, Donnie, Stump, and Bandy, but we're joined by a mysterious gaggle of elegantly — or at least boldly — clad young women.

No one seems to mind. The one sharing my chair keeps pouring gin on her neck and trying to get me to lap it up.

Food comes in plenty, and I tear into it. Roast beef, pies filled with meat, boiled vegetables, potatoes, pickled fish, oysters.

Yvaine sits next to me, on Donnie's knee. I tug my chair as close as I can.

Donnie pours gin into his glass and mine, and we raise them in toast. He leans in, his face so close I can count nose hairs.

"To whatever in the world you desire most dearly."

Him to disappear and me to bug out with his girl?

"Dancer," Yvaine says, "what'd the Thief-taker General's man say about Carrot?"

Donnie takes a puff from his long clay pipe and another swig of gin.

"Boy's good as free. Innocent as a babe. Mr. Fusée arranged a plumper to vouch for his whereabouts."

"I see'd to 'is residential comforts," Stump says. "Bought 'is fetters off, gin and grub." He deals a hand of cards.

One of our merry female companions makes territorial claim on Donnie's far knee, causing Yvaine to scoot onto my

The back room at the Rose Tavern

lap. I pull her close and she shoves the girl with the wet neck onto the floor.

Yvaine stares down after her. "Why dinna you let Stump there give you a hand?"

Everyone laughs hard enough that gin splatters against the cards.

Stump holds up his shorter arm and unbuttons the cuff to reveal his namesake.

"Don't mind if me do, lass."

The girl on the floor, too drunk to stand, crawls around and he helps her up onto the table.

Donnie is making out with his wench, who I think might be stealing his watch.

Yvaine gulps some gin, grabs my cheeks, and pinches my jaw open. She leans over and lets the booze drool from her lips into my mouth. I watch the ruffled lace on the front of her dress heave.

Her mouth is so close. I want to pull her down and kiss her.

CHIME. I startle. Her eyes go wide.

CHIME. She topples off my chair.

CHIME. She's laughing on the floor.

CHIME. Donnie lays off kissing the girl on his lap. "Sassy is a crazy mort."

CHIME. I spot the source of Yvaine's mirth — a grandfather clock against the wall.

CHIME. I wait till it rings eleven and stops. Tick-Tocks go to thirteen.

Yvaine rises and shoves Miss Friendly off Donnie. I reach for her arm but she peels off my fingers and shakes her head. After that, she won't meet my gaze.

I'm the drunkest I've ever been but I gulp more gin and the recently evicted Miss F. takes the bottle and settles for me. Soon we're kissing, but as I watch Yvaine toss Donnie's wig into the corner and run her hands through his short hair, I wish the sword he threw on the table was a little closer.

"I'll go with you if you like," Miss Friendly whispers in my ear.

"If you can say my name," I whisper back.

Leathercoat comes in with a huge silvery plate and a candle, both of which he sets on the table. One of the girls takes off most of her clothes and gets up there. I can't even figure out what I'm seeing.

Stump points at Bandy, snoring in his chair.

"He always wanted t'see a posture-girl, but drink hath foiled many a man."

Stump and I play cards and drink. I don't know the rules, but we're past caring. I distract myself from Yvaine kissing Donnie by counting Stump's missing teeth.

I've held my bladder so long I think I might explode. Stump leads the way by sweeping aside the cards, standing on his chair, and pissing against the wall.

The room spins and spins. I crawl up on the table and lie down. The flickering chandelier moves in figure eights. It reminds me of last year when I had the flu, but Mom isn't here to take my temperature and ply me with ginger ale.

The lights dim. I try not to listen to what Yvaine and Donnie are doing in the corner.

Chapter Eight:
Hangover

London, Spring, 1725

A herd of hippos invades my skull. Someone rocks the concrete pillow under my head.

I open my eyes and focus on a long, ugly face. It's Leathercoat's, and he's pressing a mug into my hands.

"Breakfast time, young sir."

I'm thirsty so I take a long pull... of beer.

The doorman moves on to try and wake Bandy, half upright in his chair. The effort doesn't go well.

My second sip brings on a surge of nausea, followed by an agonizing stomach spasm. I stare down at the nasty puddle I've deposited on the floor.

"That'll warrant extra tip," Leathercoat says.

Sunlight creeps in through shuttered windows. The girls have vanished like wood fairies, except for Yvaine. She and Donnie are unconscious in the corner.

I have to get out of here.

On the street, the sun shines for the first time since I arrived. The weather is warm and I'm still drunk enough not to need my jacket. Still, the air clears my head.

Making out with that girl last night should have been a highlight of my young life, but instead the memory makes me shudder. What fun there was in this little travel adventure is gone. I've got to convince Yvaine to get us out of here, not just for me but for her, too. I think of her alone as a little girl, alone now as a young mother, and alone with Donnie looming over her in the basement. She needs me. Fate — or the Tick-Tock — threw us together, and together's the only way we're going to get out of this place.

And I need her. It's more than just her big eyes and crooked smile. Yvaine not only remembers my name, she *sees* me.

I've been wandering aimlessly through the morning streets and come to a wall where a rickety stair leads down to the river and a row of boats. There's a black iron cage mounted here. The wasted and rotting limbs of some poor fellow jut from the bars. Crows fight over the scraps of his flesh while flies crawl across flaps of skin.

I'm done with messing around and going native. This isn't Michael J. Fox playing the prom, but just the same, I need to get back to the future, and I'm taking Yvaine with me.

My pounding head throbs its way into a plan — although I'd hardly call it a well-thought-out one. I stumble back to our cellar, where Nancy swallows hook-line-and-sinker my story about Yvaine needing me to take the baby. But finding the church with Ben Franklin's print shop isn't so easy.

Billy starts to cry as we wander about, but I soothe him with a finger. His little hands bat at my bigger one as he sucks. He'll be better off with his father. Dad made me read those books for a reason. This is what history wants for Billy. Yvaine and I don't belong, but he does. Anyway, if he stays in that basement he'll probably just catch whatever nasty cough Nancy has and die.

Chapter Eight: Hangover

I make my way to the alehouse where Yvaine and I first talked then try to retrace my steps. This leads me to the cloth seller's street and finally the church. There's only the one door, but it's standing open.

The front room is filled with shelves of books and papers. It must be the shop, though I have no idea what it's doing in a house of worship. There's a curtain hiding a busy-sounding workroom.

"May I help you?" a middle-aged clerk asks.

"I need to see Ben Franklin."

"Journeymen aren't to receive visitors."

"It's really important."

"Very well." He parts the curtain and shouts, "Mr. Franklin!"

When Ben arrives, the eyes behind his thin round glasses squint at me.

"Do I know you?"

"I'm Yvaine's… cousin. I've brought Billy, your son. You have to take him."

Ben grabs my arm and drags me out into the churchyard.

"I don't have a son."

So much for my best-case scenario.

"His name's William," I say.

Ben Franklin looks at the baby, then wipes his glasses and puts them back on.

"I've seen you before, with that girl."

"Yvaine. She asked for your help."

He scratches his head. "I warned myself. No good comes from associating with women of low character."

I kick at one of his boots. "She's not of low character."

He scoots back and I practice anger management.

"Look," I say. "He's just a baby. You're his father. And there's no way his mom can take care of him."

"William." He sighs. "The child looks the very image of my sister Jane as a baby, so I suppose the girl has the right of it. How about a quarter quid each month?"

The nasal way he says *quarter* makes him sound like Ben Affleck.

"Yvaine doesn't need your money," I say. "She needs you to take the baby."

"Have you considered that as a young man just mastering his trade, I mightn't make a most congenial father?"

"You'll be fine. Listen to me, I'm from the future."

"Is that a town?" He rubs his forehead. "What do you mean?"

"The future, as in next year and the years after that. You have a son named William, you bring him back to Debbie, and you raise him together. It's what happens, so you have to do it."

"How do you know about Miss Read? Has Ralph been talking to you?"

"Who's Ralph?" I say.

"Someone else of low character."

The words just spill out of me.

"I know what I'm talking about. You're Ben Franklin. From Boston and Philadelphia. You love to swim. You do the whole kite and lightning bolt thing. You're one of the founding fathers of the United States, the new country formed when the colonies fight the Brits and win. You're even on the U.S. hundred dollar bill!"

He's looking at me really intently.

"I do like to fly kites."

"See!" I'm almost bouncing up and down. "You fly a kite in a storm, to prove lightning is electrical."

"Electrical fluid can be generated by rubbing different surfaces together." When he looks off into space, he reminds me of my dad. "I'll have to devise an experiment."

I hold Billy out to him. Time to get down and dirty personal — I did read his autobiography, after all.

"Take the baby. You can't walk out on this the way you did with your brother."

The color drains from his face. Ha! He skipped out on working for his brother and called it 'the first errata' of his life. I remember because I needed to look the word up on the Internet.

He slowly raises his arms toward the baby.

"How did—"

Billy is snatched out of my hands, but not by Ben.

Yvaine clutches him close to her chest, then kicks me in the balls. I hunch over in agony and rock back and forth.

"Damn you, Charlie! What were you thinking?"

"I was just trying—" But a wave of pain silences me.

"Me cousin's crazy, Ben," Yvaine says. "He shouldn't never have taked the baby."

"Is this Future in Scotland?" Ben asks. "Londoners use the word 'Scot' to mean someone rash and temperamental."

I peer up through tears. Yvaine doesn't look so great either. Her face is red and her eyes redder. And she seems mad as hell.

"You sorry stall-whimper!" she screams. "He *is* yours, you know."

"William," Ben says, as if in vague confirmation.

The commotion has brought Ben's co-workers to the door. He glances over at them and slinks back into the building.

"What kind of fool by-blow are you?" Yvaine screams at me as I limp out of the courtyard after her.

"It almost worked."

"What? Stealing me baby? That's rich."

"He's supposed to be with Ben. History says so."

"Yeah, well, history ain't our friend."

"What do you mean?"

"You can't tell someone about travelin'. They'll only hear what time wants 'em to hear."

"How does time want anything?"

"Time certainly dinna want us," she says. "Not here, not nowhere."

"That's why we need to stick together!"

She stops her headlong rush and jabs a finger at me.

"Go find your own history!" she says. "Jump downtime into some medieval dungeon for all I care."

I chase after her again as she works her way back into the crowd.

"You told me I shouldn't go." It sounds so lame. Guess stealing her son really wasn't the best approach. Mom would remind me that I *act rashly!*

"I changed me mind!" The way she shoos me off is more painful than the bruised gonads.

"You need me."

"I dinna needs anyone."

"What about Donnie? I saw what you two were doing!" The team of horses across the street couldn't pull my mouth shut.

"Is that what this be about?"

"Do you love him?"

"I do what I needs do t'survive."

We reach the rickety gap that leads to our cellar.

"Charlie, get out of here. I dinna want t'see you."

I follow her anyway.

Donnie's waiting in the lair. "Sassy," he says, "I told you not to see that printer fellow again."

"I see'd you in that there churchyard," Stump says. He's picking his teeth with his knife.

Yvaine turns on him. "You followed me?"

"Actually," Stump says, "I followed your good-for-nothin' cousin."

Donnie slaps Yvaine hard across the face. "You know not to test me patience." He punches her in the gut.

She doubles over gagging, nearly drops the baby, but Donnie takes Billy and hands him to someone else.

Something in me snaps. I leap at him as he punches Yvaine in the side.

"Not so fast." Stump steps in front of me, his knife held low.

I don't think, just strike out at his wrist. He drops the blade in surprise and I dive for it.

He kicks me in the ribs but I get my hands around the knife and roll away and into a crouch.

"Now there, Cuz," Stump says, "gimme back me knife and I'll go light on the beatin' I owes you."

In the background, Donnie is hammering the crap out of Yvaine. She's on the ground now, but this doesn't stop him. The way he's going at her, he might even kill her.

I spring toward him, intending to do a kind of double jump and stab him.

But the oddest thing happens. During the first jump something — and I mean something I can't see — turns me in the air. I land wrong, my ankle bends under me, and I drop to the mattress.

Stump grunts and throws himself at me. I twist and get the knife between us. He can't stop himself and he comes down fast, blade pointed right at his heart. I feel an odd wrench of the handle and hear a metallic snap.

Surprise widens Stump's already puffy face as he thumps into me. We're face to face for a second, then he rolls off, clutching at his chest.

I glance down to find I'm holding the bone handle of the knife. The blade has broken off and slid into my lap.

What?

Stump can't seem to believe it either, because he pats his vest.

"I guess you be just dumb unlucky." He clocks me in the jaw.

Stars shoot across the cellar.

Donnie catches the next fist that comes at my face.

"You don't need to drub a fellow for defending his family," he tells Stump. "That's just loyalty."

Chapter Nine:
Nursemaid

London, Spring, 1725

It takes Yvaine almost a day to regain consciousness. In the meantime, the gang leaves us to our own devices — and our own mattress. When I'm not checking on Yvaine, I keep an eye on Stump and Donnie, who like to return my glares with cheerful waves.

"Water," is her first word back in the land of the living.

I squeeze some onto a rag, really grateful for what I take as a good sign. She just has to get better — not only because I need her to go home, but because my old life and new both feel like a blurry dream. Yvaine's the only thing in focus.

I press the rag to her mouth, then use the damp cloth to wipe away a bit of dried blood I missed earlier.

"Billy?" she mumbles.

"He's with Nancy," I say. "Try not to speak."

How could I have been so stupid as to take the baby? Jealousy and gin obviously make poor bunkmates.

"At least they didna throw us into the gutter," she says.

I should apologize, but "It'll all be better soon," comes out instead.

"It won't never be better." Her face and arms are purple and yellow, but her eyes are clear. "These be the good years for my sort."

"It doesn't have to be that way," I say. "We can go somewhere safe."

She moves her arm toward mine and winces.

"You're sweet. I saw your mill with Stump. You shouldn't
never have used the knife."

"What's the knife have to do with anything?" I ask. Odd
to think she was watching me while Donnie beat her.

"We—"

She starts coughing. It looks painful and I offer her a sip of
water when she settles.

"We can't never kill nobody," she whispers. "Would
change time too much."

I think about the weird push I got in the air and Stump's
lucky break.

"That's why the blade snapped?"

She nods and grimaces. "Time fights us." Her tongue is
red with blood. "Every step of the way."

"I'm sorry," I say. Finally.

"It dinna no longer matter for me," she says. "Soon enough
you'll be lookin' for a new girl to take you uptime."

But Yvaine doesn't die. By the next day she's hobbling around
and the day after that, while her bruises look even worse, they
don't seem to hurt as much. She stops calling me Charlie and
christens me Lack-wit, Fool, Bite, Moron, Simkin, and Cully,
which I take as further sign of her improved spirits.

No one offers us any food so I go out and buy some. I
exchange one of my gold coins and hide most of the change.

When I get back, Stump stops me with his hand out.

I swallow my pride and give him some of my money.
Yvaine suggested 'pinching' handkerchiefs and told me
where to 'bank' them, but I'm done with stealing.

"Good thing Donnie likes you," Stump says, fingering his new knife, "'cause this ain't but a part of what you owes me."

"I'll get you the rest soon."

I've learned my lesson. Next time I act, I need a solid plan. Stump is hardly real anyway — if I take Yvaine back home, he'll be just as dead as if I stuck the knife between his ribs.

"Wakey wakums." A boot prods my side.

Donnie towers over Yvaine and me. She yawns and stretches stiffly.

"Where's Billy?" she says.

My head is still groggy, but I'm pretty sure the baby was with her during the night.

"I set *me* son up with Nancy, somewheres safe," Donnie says. "Sorry I lost me temper, luv."

He hands Yvaine a paper-wrapped package. She takes it, but I see her teeth gnaw her lip, still swollen from his 'temper.'

Inside is a dress made of green velvet.

"Lifted it from a house off Whitechapel last night," Donnie says. "Had your name written all over it."

"What *is* me name, then?" Yvaine says.

"Don't be silly, Sassy." His smile looks too wide on his narrow face. "Cuz, I got something for you too." He hands me a leather case. I open it to find a bone-handled knife.

I stare at him.

"Take it. I knapped one for you and Stump each, seeing as you both got all broken up over the last."

He's obviously not embarrassed to laugh at his own jokes.

"Thanks," I say, not knowing what else to do about this latest take on bizarro world.

Yvaine lays the dress down and struggles to her feet.

"You dinna take a baby from his mother, Dancer."

"They giveth me to Parish before I was weaned." He shrugs. "Besides, you can earn him back on me generous terms." His grin grows even wider.

"Terms?" I say.

"Whilst I parleyed with Mr. Fusée concerning Carrot's release, he revealed that Mr. Palmer — your Mr. Franklin's boss — has himself a bit of a contract with Parliament. Printing special notes of credit. I hear the man is right skilled, best at making the highest quality, right impossible to forge."

I have a bad feeling about this.

"Me darling." Donnie pokes Yvaine with the green cane. "You wants to see your little chit again, you're going to introduce our gang to dear Mr. Franklin. And you," Donnie taps me with his red shoe, "are coming along with us."

"What are we going to do?" I whisper to Yvaine when the Lord of All Evil leaves the cellar.

"What do you mean?" she says. Her bruises have faded to an ugly yellow-green. "We do what we should've done in the first place — what Dancer says."

"How can you defend him?" I say. I screwed things up — royally — but still.

"I've lived in three centuries, and nothin' I seen was much better."

I want to grab her arm and shake some sense into her, but since that would probably just make her whimper in pain, I keep my cool.

"But it does get better! In my time, kids don't work, and everyone goes to school until they're eighteen."

She rolls her eyes. "I'd rather work in a mine than listen to some preacher's wife with a ruler."

Maybe I better stick to the here and now. "Helping Donnie rob Parliamentary bank notes from Ben Franklin is a *really* bad idea —"

A commotion by the stairs draws our attention.

"Welcome back!" someone says.

I catch a glimpse of red hair as Carrot descends into the room.

"I didn't even needs the plumper for me alibi," he says, still smiling big after days in jail. "The gager I hoisted didn't never press charges."

He makes his way through back claps and shoulder squeezes to our corner.

"Girl, what 'appened t'your face?"

Yvaine struggles to rise. She hugs him so hard she seems almost her old self except for the bruises. I'm not even jealous. I like Carrot — it's his boss, my rival, that I want to see bite the big one, or as Donnie himself might say: croak, dance at the sheriff's ball, stretch out for the morning drop, do the dismal ditty, and ride the gaoler's coach to Peg Trantums!

But back to reality. "What's a plumper?" I ask.

"You sure be the country cull." Carrot mock punches me in the arm. His spirits seem high, even if he looks thinner than I remember and his wrists are red and raw. "A plumper's a git Mr. Fusée paid to say I was with 'im instead of liftin' that shop."

"This Fusée guy is the mob boss's man?"

"Tight as a pigeon's arse with the Thief-taker General," Carrot says.

"He's the one that told Donnie about Ben's paper money," I whisper to Yvaine.

"I didna never meet him." She gives Carrot another hug. "I'm just happy to see you alive and free."

"You needs not 'ave worried about me." He clasps his arms behind his back and raises them up above his head, twisting his wrists back on themselves. "I didn't even 'ave to spend me money on me irons, wiggled out meself."

"It's great to have you back." I step behind him and put an armlock around his neck, but he twists out of it like an eel, his grin so big I can see his not-so-healthy looking gums.

"This new lay could change everything," he says, "make us rich forever. Dancer's a genius. First 'e gets me off, then this plan!"

"A right genius," I say.

In the days that follow, Yvaine refuses even to discuss alternatives to Donnie's lunatic plan. But her health improves to the point where she can go out pickpocketing again.

As much as part of me wants to spend the time with her and Carrot, I can't bring myself to join their little crime sprees. Instead I wander the streets. A row of jars in an apothecary window gives me an idea. I have to use my second gold coin to buy what I need, and I set to work in a little abandoned space upstairs from our cellar, not even big enough to lie down in.

A glass jar half-filled with river water, a bit of foil, some brass rods, and two disks of leather and glass. It takes some trial and error to get it working, but by spinning the leather against the glass I can use friction to build up a charge between the foil wrapped around the jar and the brass rod in the middle. This is the experiment we did just last month in Earth Science, the one I read about it in Ben Franklin's autobiography. I'm building a Leyden jar, which will be invented in seventeen-forty-something. About twenty years from now.

I ground myself on the brass rod I've rammed through the cork in the jar's neck and receive a satisfying jolt.

Time isn't half as clever as it thinks it is.

Chapter Ten:

The Heist

London, Spring, 1725

I crouch behind a stack of barrels in the darkness of the churchyard and watch Yvaine approach the building's single door. She's more or less fully recovered — physically — but I can sense the hesitation in her step. As for me, my guts feel like an ogre is kneading them into a ball of pizza dough.

Donnie squats so close to my right that I feel the barrel of his belt pistol pressing into my leg. He holds another gun in his right hand, a third is tucked into his sash, and of course he didn't leave his sword at home. Stump's also got at least one pistol. Even Carrot is armed with a makeshift club.

Yvaine pounds on the iron-banded oak door. She carries a small lantern, the only real light in the courtyard. The door's set into a huge arched entranceway. In the old days, the whole thing probably opened, but now most of it's been bricked over except for the little door.

A small window in the middle slides open to reveal a candle and half a young face.

"We're closed." A boy's voice carries across the fifteen feet.

"I've business with Ben Franklin," Yvaine says.

"At ten at night?" The boy starts to close the window.

"I'll make it worth your while," I see a glint of copper in her raised hand.

He snatches the penny and the window slams shut.

A few minutes later, it opens again and Ben's bespectacled face appears.

"Can I come in?" she says. "I needs talk to you."

"I'm working late as it is, I don't want it to be any later."

"Please." Even in bad light, the look she gives him would make me do anything.

The window shuts. I hear the scraping metal-on-wood sound of the door being unbarred. It swings open.

Donnie grabs my arm and pulls me up with him.

Carrot's shrouded by darkness, but I know he's slinking toward the door.

My heart is pounding so loud in my ears I can't hear what Yvaine and Ben are talking about. But I don't have long to wait. Carrot's shadow leaps out of nowhere to shoulder the half-open door.

We're on our feet now, closing the short gap to the entrance.

Ben pulls Yvaine inside and struggles to get the door closed, but it's big and heavy and Carrot starts it swinging in the other direction.

Stump is inside before Ben gets it under control and Donnie puts his pistol to the head that will eventually grace the hundred-dollar bill.

Once we're in the shop, I hear shouting and scrambling from the workroom behind the curtain. Stump in action.

"Mr. Franklin," Donnie says, "you may close that there door now." He thumbs back the flint-tipped hammer of his bulky pistol.

A pale Ben complies, then sees me standing there.

"Aren't you with the girl?" he says.

Donnie pistol-whips him across the back of the head. Ben collapses.

84

"They both be with me," he says. Not that his victim, unconscious, can hear him.

"Dancer, you didna have to hit him," Yvaine says.

"Sassy, help me move him. Cuz, you get that door bolted, and don't let anyone leave. If they do, I won't go easy on her like last time."

Yvaine takes one of Ben's legs and they drag him across the room, Donnie smiling the whole way.

"I hear Mr. Franklin's a smart man. Seeing as I be the only one allowed any smart ideas tonight, mum's the word for him."

They pull Ben through the curtain separating the store from the workshop. I could use a bright idea myself.

When they're gone, I look around for anything useful. Ever since Donnie put us up to this insane plan, I've been trying to figure the best way out. So far I've only come up with two choices:

Go along with the heist, hope no one gets hurt, and pray Donnie gives Yvaine back her baby.

Or try and sabotage things, hope no one gets hurt, and pray the situation becomes so desperate Yvaine is forced to hop with me to a different time.

Neither plan strikes me as a winner. The first just seems like aiding and abetting, and the second leaves Billy at the mercy of fate — and Donnie.

Anyway, the boy under the table tips me toward Plan B.

Out of the corner of my eye I see him crawling through the shadows toward the entrance. He might even be the same boy that answered it a few minutes ago.

I haven't bolted it yet so I kick it open and wave him through.

His eyes go wide but he darts forward and out into the night.

By the time I secure the door and enter the workroom, the bad guys — that's us — have won.

The space is cavernous, surprisingly hodgepodge, with the printing presses clustered in a side vault. The rest of the room is strung with twine from which newspaper-sized squares of paper hang to dry.

Donnie is leafing through papers while Carrot and Stump finish tying two prisoners to chairs. Ben is still unconscious, but the other, a teenage employee, is alert and unharmed.

If you don't count the bloody nose and missing teeth.

"This is what them notes look like," Donnie says, holding up a sheet of paper. "But these here be missing half the words."

He takes the paper over to the conscious prisoner, draws his sword, and places the tip against the boy's throat.

I try to edge closer to Yvaine, who stands like a statue off to the side.

"Where be the proper notes?" Donnie says.

"T-two pass job." The boy's so terrified he can hardly speak.

"That ain't me question." Donnie drags his blade across the boy's neck. Red blood dribbles onto the white ruffled collar.

"In the crypt, sir."

"Thanks and wine." Donnie points the sword at me.

"Cuz, with me to the crypt. Stump, you be captain in me absence. Locate anything else worth taking."

Books are stacked everywhere, and the shelves contain rows and rows of lead type and little pots of ink — which I don't think is what Donnie has in mind.

He waves his sword again and I follow, our footsteps echoing in the big space. I doubt it's been used as a church in a long time. At the end where I suppose the altar stood, a huge anvil lurks half buried in a mess of hay. Nearby a makeshift chimney of red brick stands out against the blackened, decrepit stone walls.

Walking behind Donnie, I twist my fingers into an imaginary pistol and practice shooting him in the head. Maybe I can figure out some way to lock him in the crypt, or push him down the stairs and hope luck and time knock him out cold.

But he stops.

"After you, if you don't mind." Donnie uses his sword to indicate a dank stairway between the entrance and the altar. He thrusts a candelabrum into my hands.

So much for the push-him-from-behind idea.

The temperature, never that warm to begin with, drops sharply as we descend the stone steps. Donnie is so close behind he's literally breathing down my neck.

At the bottom of the short flight, our way is blocked by a heavy wood door with a small barred window.

"Light," Donnie orders.

I hold up the candles and he fusses with the door. There's a bulky padlock, but even though it's open, the door refuses to budge.

"It's bolted from inside," a young voice calls through the window.

Donnie puts his sword away, takes the light from me, and shoves it up to the small opening.

"You there inside, open up."

"Don't think I'll do that, sir. Me master'll whip me good."

Donnie rattles the door again.

"He don't even pay you 'prentices. Let us in and I'll give you ten guineas."

"Show 'em to me," the boy says.

Donnie fishes in his pockets and holds up some gold coins.

"That be only two, sir. Not enough for breakin' me oaths."

Donnie holds the candelabrum up to the hole again, draws a pistol, shoves it through the bars, and fires.

The blast sets my ears ringing. I put my fingers to them, not that it helps after the fact.

"You missed!" The boy's voice is muted by my diminished hearing, but I have to give him points for bravery.

Donnie kicks the door, then waves the candles over the

surface. It's pretty hefty, made of thick planks banded in iron and set deep into the stone walls.

"I'd get to confessing," he calls through the window.

"Boy needs a little incentivizing," Donnie tells me as we climb back to the others.

"I don't see how we can get inside before morning," I say. Not that there's much chance of him giving up on his dreams of paper riches, but at least he's stalled for the moment.

"Leave that to me."

"Dancer," Carrot says when we return, "I got me some news most unfortunate."

Donnie pulls off his hat and wig and throws them onto a printing press.

"What now?"

Carrot indicates the shop area where Yvaine's standing at the front door. The only door.

"Stump, stay with them prisoners," Donnie says as we walk over to her.

She's peering out the head-sized view hole. I hear people in the courtyard beyond.

Donnie shoves her aside and looks for himself.

"Buttock and Twang!" he says. "How'd them find us out?" He storms back into the main room.

Yvaine's face is pale under its usual layer of grime. I glance out the window myself to find twelve or fifteen Londoners holding torches. A boy amongst them is waving at the church.

The boy I let out through the door.

"What will they do if they catch us?" I ask Yvaine.

"If we's lucky — and I means really lucky — they'll turn us over t'the magistrate."

"And what's the punishment for..." Breaking and entering, kidnapping, and who knows what else.

"Same as everything else." She holds a fist up to her neck, tilts her head, and sticks out her tongue.

In my mind, I hear my Dad saying, *Man is not God. All actions have consequences.*

"We could just—"

Donnie returns dragging the bloody-necked printer boy at gunpoint.

"Journeyman, tell 'em t'go home." He shoves the boy up to the porthole. But the kid starts ratting Donnie & Co. out at the top of his lungs.

"Burglars! Five—"

Donnie slams the boy hard into the door then punches him in the gut. He falls to the floor.

"That was awful stupid." Donnie adds a kick to the face by way of punctuation.

Yep. *All actions have consequences.*

For a while, we hear heavy thuds against the oaken front door.

"Get back," Donnie says. "They're right outside."

He drags his prisoner over to the curtain separating the shop and the church proper. The rest of us trail behind.

"Boss, what we goin' t'do?" Stump says.

"We ain't stolen nothing yet," Carrot says. "We lets them in, they just give us a beatin' on the way t'Newgate."

"Stop your blubbering!" Donnie fidgets in place, then snatches up a nearby lantern and hurls it at the front door.

The glass shatters. Burning oil explodes across the wood.

"What you do that for?" Stump plunges his knife into one defenseless book after another.

"I ain't going back t'Newgate." Donnie's voice is cold as a Vermont mountaintop. "Ole Half-Deaf will have his retributions from me in pieces."

I glance at Yvaine.

"The second time he escaped," she whispers, "he bited off a sub-warden's ear."

Wonderful. The whole door is now coated in flames. Thin tendrils of smoke curl upward.

Outside I hear voices, then shouts.

"Fire! Fire!"

Carrot cradles his head in his hands. "I should've stayed in jail."

Dancer sighs. "Don't be such rank culls. This caper's been proceeding at a toddle. A bit o' fire under our bums will provide right proper motivation."

"But that's the only door!" I must be crazy to draw his attention.

"Cravens." Donnie gestures at the group. "There be an old chimney in the nave, at the other end of the church."

"You know me dislikin' 'em 'igh places," Stump says. "Ain't goin' up no chimney, not never."

"You prefer burning to death?" Donnie flops a loop of rope over Stump's head and shoulders. "Take Carrot. And think, you might make the papers: 'One-handed thief climbs to safety!'"

Stump goes, grumbling.

Donnie pulls the journeyman boy to his feet, forces him through the curtain, then yells for Yvaine and me to follow them to the big room.

He wrests the boy to the top of the crypt stairs, in sight of the door below.

"You there! 'Prentice in the crypt!" he yells.

"I see you," the voice calls back up.

Donnie has his sword out now, the point against the journeyman.

"If you don't open up, I kill your friend."

"I don't believe you," the boy says.

Yvaine and I stand close to Ben. We hear a cough behind us and I glance back to see him lift his head from his bound chest.

CHAPTER TEN: THE HEIST

"Yvaine, we have to do something," I say. "Donnie's crazy."

She's biting her lip again. "I'll distract him. You try an' untie Ben."

"What do we do then?"

"His temper," she says, "his anger makes him reckless."

In my book, a guy wearing scarlet high heels is reckless any time of day.

"Last chance, 'prentice!" Donnie says. The poor journeyman is sobbing in Donnie's arms, but he just raises his blade higher.

"Let him go, Dancer," Yvaine calls out. "They'll give Billy to the parish if we dinna get outta here."

He looks at her, then back toward the front of the church. The fire from the door is now browsing through the nearby bookshelves.

He grunts and pushes his rapier into the journeyman, just below his shoulder blade. The boy's eyes go wide in surprise as the front of his blouse tents outward and darkens with blood.

"You're next, 'prentice!" Donnie yells. He lets the boy slump forward and slide off the sword.

Time grinds into slow motion as I watch the body flop down the stairs. The world dims a little. *Oh my freaking God. He just killed him! Killed him dead and —*

"Now!" Yvaine whispers, a sharp hiss that jolts me to my senses.

She runs at Donnie.

I force myself to turn toward Ben. I feel caught in molasses, unable to process what I just saw. It's all I can do to place one foot after another.

I've never even seen a dead body before, much less a kid killed in cold blood. I try to blink away the image of the journeyman's face.

I hear Yvaine yelling behind me.

"Dancer, you idiot cove! What will happen to Billy when they hang us all at Tyburn?"

I kneel before Ben, pull out my knife — the crazy gift from Donnie — and start sawing through his bonds. I smell smoke, hear the crackle of the fire, feel it biting back the chill.

"Mr. Franklin, you all right?"

His eyes are glazed, but he nods and moves his legs to expose the ropes, making it easier for me to cut.

Behind me, Yvaine and Donnie scream at each other like some quarreling sitcom couple.

"How did the building catch fire?" Ben says.

"Our criminal mastermind has a death wish," I say.

"Look at the papers," he says. "The flames are consuming the air, creating a vacuum that lures them in."

Sure enough, the hanging sheets are fluttering. But who thinks about that while tied to a chair in a burning building?

"Fires are a source of great devastation in all cities," he continues, "but London has an unprecedented level of organization regarding—"

I feel the bite of steel against my neck.

"I think you owes me one of these." Stump takes my knife and pulls me to my feet.

Ben struggles against his ropes, but I only managed to free one arm.

I stomp on Stump's foot and try to twist away but he only laughs and tightens his grip.

"Stump," Donnie says, "this bunter has run rusty and ain't worth the air she breathes."

He approaches, dragging Yvaine by the hair with one hand. When she claws at him, he gives her a good smack with the other.

I lunge forward, but Stump's knife only cuts deeper into my neck. I can barely draw breath for fear of killing myself.

CHAPTER TEN: THE HEIST

"No need for that," Donnie says, using the hand he just hit Yvaine with to push away Stump's blade.

I gasp for air as his fist rises to strike.

Chapter Eleven:
End Game

London, Spring, 1725

The world swims as I come to my senses. Moving brings on a wave of nausea. My jaw seems to have grown an egg-sized tumor, a really painful one at that.

"Dancer," Stump's voice says, "Carrot got 'isself 'alfways up that there chimney, but I comes for more rope t'make me 'arness. Not that I'd 'ave to if you 'adn't set the place on fire."

Donnie snorts. "Fusée gave me the idea. When they find a bunch of smoking bodies and burnt-up paper they won't come looking for us. Besides, the big one might be docking me girl."

Stump starts to cough.

"Anyways," Donnie continues, "gimme your powder horn. I needs finish this charge."

"But the fire be spreading to the rafters."

The air is hot and smoky. I inhale and rattle my bruised brain with coughing. I hear shouting from outside, but if they're trying to put out the fire they're doing a terrible job.

I open my eyes.

Stump has his pistol pointed at Yvaine, who glares at him from the floor nearby. Donnie has a teapot he's filling with dark powder from a little horn. What'd he call it? A powder horn.

Gunpowder.

Damn. A few lazy sparks flit about the room.

Donnie caps the teapot, grabs some loose paper from the presses, and twists it into a cigar-like wick.

"I'm going to set this," he tells Stump. "Keep your peepers on them three."

He dashes off toward the crypt stairs. I try to sit up, but Stump steps on my chest.

Back in two minutes, Donnie throws himself under a heavy table. I have the sense to clap my hands over my ears.

KABOOM! The explosion is like a weird pop. It starts loud and then cuts off. The air in the room constricts around me. A new cloud of smoke, dust, and bits of stone rolls our way.

Stump mouths something, but I can't understand. I force a yawn to clear my ears. Moving my jaw hurts like a mofo.

"Rope… Carrot!" Donnie yells as he crawls from under the table, but it sounds like a whisper.

Stump's foot lifts from my chest. He grabs up the rope they used to bind the poor journeyman and bolts off.

I manage to get to my knees in time for Donnie to crawl over and poke me with his sword.

"Cuz, go down to the crypt and bring me the money."

I shake my head. No way I'm helping this crazy-ass dude.

He tips the sword over toward Yvaine.

I go.

But first I notice a jar of pens and some buckets of water by one of the presses.

"Can I take that?" I yell. "In case I need to put out any fire."

Dancer looks up at the burning rafters and nods.

Using a single candle for light I pick my way down the stairs, hard enough thanks to all the rubble, and nightmarish when I have to step over the boy Donnie murdered. I don't see any sign of the teapot bomb, but the door's blown off its hinges and the wood's scorched.

The crypt is filled with paper, some of it charred but mostly just all over the place.

"Is that water?" The voice is quiet as a ghost.

The apprentice is surprisingly intact, considering that blood runs freely from his eyes, nose, mouth, and ears. His skin looks like half-cooked steak.

Feeling hollow inside, I kneel, scoop up some of my water with the jar, and press it to his lips. I see little tendrils of blood mix into the clear liquid, then he coughs. He tries to sip. Tries again. Stops. I can't see his chest moving and I don't want to touch him to check.

Over by the door, I can make out a shadowy hint of the other dead boy on the stairs. God. Two bodies in one day.

Yvaine, though, she's alive. For now.

I try to hurry, but my hands shake as I take the Leyden jar parts from my jacket pocket. Some of the bucket water goes inside the former pen container. I fit the foil around the jar and fix the brass rod inside. Last, I rub the leather pad against the glass like crazy. Static pops and crackles as the charge builds.

Having wasted as much time as I dare, I gather up the scattered paper sheets. About the size of copy paper, they're printed with a fancy two-color job — well, fancy by local standards.

On my way out, I pause near the apprentice's still form.

"You were brave to the end," I say.

He doesn't answer.

I didn't kill these boys, but as I hustle back to Donnie I have to wonder if they might still be alive had my choices been different. The muscles of my jaw spasm uncontrollably, my body's way of letting me know I'm scared out of my gourd. I struggle to balance the messy heap of crumpled bank notes in my arms while clasping — and hopefully hiding — the Leyden jar underneath.

Donnie sits on a press and nurses a gin bottle, but he has Yvaine throwing water onto spots of flame. I'm just happy he hasn't killed anyone in my absence. The whole scene is surreal in the extreme. The walls of the church are all stone, but the roof above is crawling with flame. The hanging papers flutter, some sucked upward into the inferno.

I guess Ben Franklin knew what he was talking about.

Donnie hops down from the press and shatters his bottle against the wall. He has the big leather bag we brought for the loot.

"About time, Cuz. Stump and Carrot be on the roof already."

"Maybe he'll have himself a Stump roast," Yvaine says.

I hold the pile up to Donnie.

"Here you go, Dancer. You've murdered us all for your money."

He bends to take the papers. I jam the brass terminal of the Leyden jar into his hand.

There's a spark and an electric pop as if he shuffled his feet around on a shag carpet for an hour before touching a doorknob. His eyes go wide and he jumps back. The papers fly everywhere.

He's probably only stunned. The Leyden jar is a high voltage capacitor, but I'd have to be damn lucky to stop his heart, and time doesn't seem to favor me for that kind of luck.

"Did that jar just make a spark?" Ben says.

The curious mind is always at work.

"Yvaine, untie him!" I scream.

I'm on Donnie before he can recover. I drop everything in my hands and punch him in the balls as hard as I can. Then in the gut.

He doubles over, and I slam both my fists into his head.

He falls to his knees, an agonized look on his face, hands clutching his groin. I reach for the hilt of his sword and he's too stunned to resist as I pull it free.

For an instant, I consider just running him through, but just for an instant though I know he deserves it. For one thing, I'm not sure I could do it. For another, time might just break the blade or something. Instead, I slide the sword across the floor to Yvaine.

I grab for Donnie's guns next. The first two I get free and throw into a stream of fire along a nearby wall.

CRACK! CRACK! Two small explosions blast even more papers around. Too late, I realize tossing metal tubes stuffed with gunpowder into a fire might not be the best idea.

His third gun is caught in his belt. While I struggle with it, he grabs my thighs and throws his weight forward, carrying us both to the ground. As I go down, I see Yvaine hustling to free Ben.

I kick furiously, but God, Donnie's strong. We roll around in the pile of bank notes. He gets his pistol free and I grab at it. He boxes me hard in the side of the head, puts the barrel to my face, and pulls the trigger.

CLICK! I'm still here.

"Lucky cull!" He tosses the gun away.

I thank the patron saint of time travelers that flintlock pistols misfire easily. Then Donnie punches me in the head again. His face is a furious mask.

My brain feels too big for my skull. I hadn't even recovered from when he uppercut me the last time. He raises his fist again.

"Billy's not your son," Yvaine yells from behind him. "You was too much the capon, so I found me a toffer. Mr. Franklin."

Donnie's face goes Looney Tunes angry and he pops up and off me. I sit up to see him charging at Yvaine and Ben, now just getting free of his chair.

I scramble to my feet as the three of them collide and Donnie locks his hands around Ben's neck.

"You wanking bunter!" he screams. "No one bucks me."

Yvaine beats her fists against him — like a girl.

I scoop Donnie's sword up off the floor and line myself up for a good poke, but they're hardly making it easy. Donnie's choking Ben so hard, the founding father's face looks like an eggplant.

I lunge forward with the blade, but my foot twists on some crap littering the floor and I stab a table instead.

"Dancer!" Yvaine screams. "Let him go. He's not supposed to die."

I yank the sword free and try again.

A burning beam falls from the ceiling and cascades downward. I'm forced to throw myself to the side to avoid being battered and burnt alive.

Foiled by time again. I throw the sword to the ground and look around for something a little less lethal.

CHIME!

A man climbs out of the hole in the floor. The swirling whirling hole that wasn't there a second before. The man who isn't a man.

My good friend, the Tick-Tock.

He dusts off his blue suit and saunters on over.

Even Donnie notices. "Mr. Fusée?" He drops Ben to the floor. "What are you doing here?"

The clockwork man opens his mouth but says nothing. Instead, he draws his weapon.

Donnie snatches up a fistful of bank notes, shoves them in his vest, and flees into the smoke and darkness of the burning church.

Yvaine kneels by Ben, lying motionless on the floor.

"We've bollocks'd it all." Her hair is everywhere and wet trails streak her sooty cheeks.

I grab the sword I dropped and step between her and the clockwork man.

"Charlie, Ben still be breathin'," Yvaine says behind me.

The Tick-Tock lunges at me. I clumsily bat away his blade.

"Can you drag him toward the back of the church?" I ask Yvaine.

My opponent stabs again. I've never actually fenced before but I'm pretty coordinated, and *The Princess Bride* is one of my favorite movies.

His parry is lightning fast and I almost lose my grip on the blade. He pokes me on the arm of my jacket with the dull edge, then opens and closes his mouth.

I'm pretty sure he's laughing at me.

Yvaine drags the unconscious Ben by one leg. She's grunting and not moving very fast. I have to stay between her and the Tick-Tock.

I grab a burning bit of wood and throw it at him.

He skitters away.

I drop the sword and grab two more fiery brands. "Can't take the heat?" I say.

He clicks his jaw at me again but backs away.

I may not have his fencing skills, but I do know how to throw things. I grip one plank like a javelin and throw the other at him. When he moves out of the way, I toss the remaining one right into his chest. His suit flares and he starts dancing around, beating at his breast, limbs moving sluggishly, as if sunk in Jell-O.

I run to Yvaine and grab Ben's other leg. Together we drag him as fast as we can toward the back of the church. There's less fire there, but even so, the air is freaking hot. Smoke swirls around and we have to dodge piles of flame. Burning bits of ceiling rain down on us. This place won't last much longer.

I don't know how we're going to get him up the chimney, but we're out of options.

After a minute or so, the Tick-Tock gets his fire problem under control, but he takes his time following us. He walks around a perfectly good patch of floor, then watches as a huge beam falls upon it. Turning back to us, he resumes his slow-motion pursuit.

We reach the chimney by the anvil.

"There's no rope!" Yvaine screams. "When you was in the crypt, Donnie pulled me over here, an' there was a rope hangin' in the hearth."

I drop Ben's leg, step into the huge fireplace, and look up. I see stars, but no rope.

"Donnie must have taken it," I say.

"Bastard!"

That I knew.

The Tick-Tock closes on us. We duck and shield our eyes as the front half of the church roof collapses into a curtain of flame behind him. He pays it no notice, his mechanical form silhouetted against a wall of fire.

He's too close now, sword drawn. I grab Yvaine's arm and pull her so the anvil squats between us and our assailant.

"What about Ben?" she screams.

"You said the Tick-Tock couldn't hurt normal people!"

The Tock takes something from inside his jacket, a shiny brass thing about the size of a paperback book. I've seen it on him before, when I first met Ben, and now at close range I think it actually is some kind of book. Made of metal, like the one my dad had back in Philly. The Tick-Tock looks at it, kneels, and presses one gloved hand to Ben's neck. He nods his head and makes a mechanical clicking noise.

When he looks at me, the only thing I can read on his ivory face is amusement.

I study the walls for any other exit, but there's nothing.

Tick-Tock TLC

The narrow stained-glass windows are at least twenty feet off the ground.

Sword in hand, the Tick-Tock leaps across the room to crouch on the anvil. He was playing with us all along.

We're trapped.

Yvaine grabs my hair with both hands.

"Charlie, I hope you dinna make me regret this."

She gives me a quick, fierce kiss, and we're sucked upwards like a ping-pong ball becoming the lucky number.

Chapter Twelve:
Thistles

France, uptime

If time traveling involves any actual *traveling* — the passing of real time *in-between* sucking out of 1725 and landing wherever we land — it's not the kind of thing the human mind can grasp all at once. I sense we're falling upwards through the void, the same empty swirling of minced-up stars that was inside the Tick-Tock's time-hole. Lights flash around us and I cling to Yvaine as if my life depends on it—

We pop up out of nothing, and the top of my head slams into something hard. Yvaine and I clutch each other, but the space is too cramped to sit all the way up. My forehead knocks into her nose and she grunts. We're under a table.

Someone shrieks high enough to break glass.

"Shit, woman!" A man says. "Don't fart lead."

A dog is barking. Knees and feet ring us in. Some wear leather shoes, some are barefoot, all are muddy.

Ruddy arms pull me out into the room.

"What kind o'devil are you?" The man's thick and round and red-faced and funny-bearded. And he shakes the sense out of me.

The room is small, showing green trees and blue sky through a hole in the stone wall that only the charitable might call a window. I count four children and a woman as red-faced as the big man.

"Witchcraft!" The woman crosses herself.

I feel a deep bass rumbling, sense it in my bones. The floor vibrates, a silent tremor that grows until I can barely stand upright. I sway and Yvaine grabs my legs.

"Get down!" she yells. "Timequake!"

The earth pitches and heaves as the family becomes transparent, fading with each passing moment.

Yvaine kneels right through the table and tugs me to the ground. Her head looks normal but her body is obscured by a see-through slab of wood. A slab that fades along with the people, the roof, and half the walls.

When the shaking stops, we're kneeling inside three ruined stone walls, only two reaching full height. A carpet of moss and mud has replaced the straw and dirt floor. Outside, downy green fields stretch into the distance, crisscrossed by thick lines of darker trees and dotted with bright flowers.

"God only knows what we done." Yvaine's whisper is loud against the soft chirping of birds and insects. She wears a new dress — new as in different, not as in clean — with a top almost like overalls over a puffy white blouse and a lace thing covering much of her hair.

But evidently, we haven't gone far enough into the future for her to get shoes.

"What happened to those people?" I say.

She shakes her head. "We changed somethin'. It caught up with us, an' those folk weren't here no more."

I think about the Tick-Tock gloating over the still form of Ben Franklin, fire blazing all around. I definitely didn't read about that in his autobiography.

The adrenaline rush from the church wears off and exhaustion smacks me like Mike Tyson's fist. I slump against one of the rough stone walls and reach for Yvaine's hand, soft against my palm. The air feels humid. While the smell of char and smoke lingers in my nostrils, the weather here is warm and breezy, scented with flowers and herbs and trees and all sorts of things not found in Ben Franklin's London.

In short, it smells great.

"When and where are we?" I say.

"I couldn't think what else t'do, so I bringed us to me da's." Tears trickle down Yvaine's cheeks. "It feeled like a long way, too, further than I ever gone in one hop."

"Scotland?"

She shakes her head. "France. In the last months before they was killt, we fled here t'escape the Tocks." She's sobbing now. "I'm not goin' t'see him never again."

I scoot closer and put my arm around her.

"Billy?"

She shoves my arm away and stands up.

"You gots what you wanted." Her voice isn't loud, but her tone is as cold as the stone wall against my skin.

She staggers out the gap in the walls where the door was five minutes ago, squares her shoulders, and strides across the field.

I drag myself to my feet and follow.

"I didn't want it this way!" I yell.

"I be doin' fine before you an' that there damn Tick-Tock dropped into me life," she says. "Almost wish you hadn't."

At least I rate an *almost*. I follow her swaying blue skirts through the emerald sea dotted with violet flowers.

I have shoes, but they're knee-high boots now. Not to mention the high-waisted white trousers, short jacket, and vest. Something not unlike the knife I had in the church is thrust through my belt.

Yvaine seems to know where she's going. We march across the big swath of high grass. To our left the field rolls upward and at the top of the little hill, perhaps a mile away, is an enormous house, four or five stories tall, with gray conical turrets on top of a white stone facade.

We come to a row of trees and the banks of a sluggish river, perhaps thirty feet wide. Yvaine wades right in.

She pulls her dress, then her underthings, over her head and throws them onto the bank. Then she turns to me, knee deep in the water and stark naked.

"Is this what you want, Charlie?" She claps her hands across her breasts, then between her legs. "Come take your victory prize!"

I'm frozen. Shock, horror, lust — I don't know which. I feel like two different animals in the same body. The lizard part of me coils underneath my trousers. The monkey in my head chatters senselessly.

"Not this way." Although I can't help but notice she has a little peanut-shaped birthmark on her upper right thigh.

She steps backward into the river until it rises to cover the mark. Rises across her hips and navel and —

"Take me here." Her voice is bitter. "Like a water nymph carried off with heather in her hair." The tears are back.

I don't really know what she's talking about, but I wade in myself, boots, socks, pants and all. The water is warm, but Yvaine is shivering. I pull off my jacket and hold it out to her.

She doesn't take it but neither does she resist as I drape it over her pale shoulders and walk her toward the shore.

"You've freed me an' binded me both as sure as with tartan an' ring," she says between sobs.

When we reach the bank, her jaw is chattering even though the air's nice enough. I rub her shoulders through the thick wool.

"You should be happy now," she says.

Then why do I feel like such a shit?

CHAPTER TWELVE: THISTLES

Yvaine's outspoken insanity is as brief as her nudity and she maintains a sullen silence until the hazy sun drops below the walls of the ruined farmhouse. She hasn't moved in hours but sits against one stone wall with her skirts wrapped around her knees and her bare toes half buried in the dirt.

"Welcome home." I've had hours to work on this opening.

My pithy remark garners a weak smile, so I follow up with the brilliant, "Will it get cold at night?" Plus my stomach's growling.

She surprises me by answering.

"I'm guessin' it be June, maybe July, so we ain't gonna freeze."

"How do you know?"

"The cotton thistle be in bloom." She rolls forward and crawls to a cluster of the violet blossoms. As she does, I can see her legs to just above the knee. My imagination, amply fueled back at the stream, fills in the remaining inches.

"Me mum brought them here t'remind her of home." She plucks a flower. "Seems they like it."

She holds one out and I take the spiky green bulb with the feathery purple top. It looks like one of those kooky troll dolls.

"I'm sorry," she says. "I shouldn't never have teased you."

"Does that mean you aren't mad at me?"

"I know it ain't *all* your fault. But your comin' changed everythin', twisted me on me ear."

"You scared me back at the stream," I say.

The light is almost gone now, but I still see her scowl.

"You can't save me, so there's no use worryin'."

"Maybe you can save me," I say.

"I couldn't even save me own baby." Her face is wet again. She fumbles inside her dress and takes out the little cloth-wrapped bundle I saw her drop in the London cellar. She sorts through her flowers for a particularly ratty one, just a bit of gray with a lone strand of purple.

"Me mum pressed this for me," she says, holding it alongside the fresh one I've got. "It comed from this very place. Long ago."

I want to comfort her but sense she's as skittish as a mouse in the kitchen.

"And you kept it with you all those years, through how many jumps across time?"

"Eight. Maybe ten. Flowers be safe. Time take no issue with 'em." She puts it away and rewraps the bundle. "She an' Da always bringed me a lil' gift whenever they comed back."

Clueless as I am, I get that she just cracked open a door for me.

"May I put my arm around you?"

"I tupped me share of gentlemen but no one never asked me that."

I cringe. "Maybe they weren't gentlemen."

"Maybe not."

I sit close with my arm behind her back. The temperature is dropping, but she's warm against my side. I notice the stars for the first time. Really notice the stars. They speckle the sky like jewels, a hundred times more of them than I remember.

"I love the smell of this place," she says, and I have to agree.

I'm suddenly aware she's not speaking English but some alien and prettier tongue — which somehow I understand.

"What language is that?" Listening to my own words, I realize I'm speaking it too.

"French, I suppose," she says. "Time makes sure we fit in."

The sunset has left me with a deep sense of sadness. And guilt.

"Do you think Ben Franklin is…" I can't even say it.

"I'm pretty sure we killt him, if that's what you askin'," she whispers.

Wow. She knows how to get to the heart of it. My stomach makes like a fish on the dock.

"I so didn't want that," I say. "Not any of it the way it happened."

Except for her.

She shakes her head. "Not me neither, but it happened."

"What's it going to mean if he's dead?"

"You be the one from the future. But things have changed, that timequake be the universe's way o' letting us know. And it be the biggest I ever felt. We mightn't now find history what you expect."

I'm still confused. "What's a timequake?"

She sighs. "If history gets changed — and that ain't never easy — it makes a quake. Like ripples flowing uptime, bringing the changes. The bigger the change, the bigger the quake. Only travelers notice 'em. And Tick-Tocks, I suppose."

"And we caused it?"

"Methinks."

That flopping fish in my gut, I think it's one of those spiky pufferfish types.

"How do we even find out what year this is?" I say.

She giggles. "Walk up t'someone and ask."

"Tomorrow?"

"Don't be in such a hurry. The past an' the future ain't goin' nowhere."

I guess once you acclimate to the idea of time travel, it's hard not to think of different times as different places. My mom might be crazy-worried back in Philly, but so long as I pop back the same day I left, she'll never even know I was gone.

"If we don't get some food soon," I say, thinking of the gnawing pain in my belly, "you might start to look like lunch."

There's a rustle in the darkness and one of her legs flops into my lap. "Here, have a ham hock." She tugs her skirt up to her knee.

I feel hot in the face and tight down below. My heart is

pounding, but my head is all confused. The situation is so serious, yet here in my little *now*, it's hard to focus on the grand sweep of history — even if it may now include an American Revolution without Ben Franklin.

"Are you teasing me again?" I jiggle her legs with mine.

A brief glimmer of teeth. "You'll just have to find out."

If she's testing me, which move is right? I touch my index finger to her shin and draw gentle figure eights. Whenever shaving became popular with the ladies, it was after Yvaine's time.

She adds her other leg to join the first and lies back.

"That's nice," she says. "Travelin's like bein' borned anew. Every time, me old life fades like a dream."

I wish mine could — my recent old life, anyway. Letting the Tick-Tock skewer us or Donnie's fire burn us wouldn't have helped anyone, but all the same I know my hands aren't clean.

But rubbing Yvaine's legs is a terrific distraction from shame and guilt.

I must've dozed off, but a dull boom in the distance wakes me.

Yvaine stirs. She's still draped across my lap, cuddled against me for warmth.

More of the big sounds echo across the countryside, like distant fireworks. The first hint of dawn edges the sky, and a flash lights the tree line. More booms follow half a minute later.

"What are those noises?" I whisper.

"I dinna ken. But they seems far off."

She stretches and rolls on top of me. Suddenly her face is in front of mine and her hands are holding my head. Then we're kissing.

"What are you doing?" I say.

She stops for a second. "Charlie, do you want to talk or do you want to…" She goes back to kissing me.

I don't complain again. I have to pee, but no way I'm getting up now, and so between the full-bladder feeling and the snuggling I'm… well, I believe the eighteenth-century expression is piss proud.

Yvaine keeps rubbing against me. She nips at me like a puppy. I slide a hand down her soft cheek to her neck.

"That feels nice," she whispers. "I needs feel somethin' nice."

She takes my hand in hers and slides it lower. Things are soft. Real soft. She presses herself against me.

We grind lips and hips. She starts unbuttoning things — a lot of things — then rolls on top of me. She undoes her hair and I feel it on my face, on my chest, everywhere.

Chapter Thirteen:
Lessons

France, uptime

The early morning sun illuminates our little ruin. My head is clear, which feels odd, since I've been hungover practically every morning since I met Yvaine.

I'm especially glad I'm sober, otherwise I might think last night was a dream. Given the general disarray of our clothes, I'm pretty sure it wasn't, and pretty psyched, a sentiment shared by the birds chirping their little hearts out.

Yvaine's hair covers her face. I try to brush it back behind her ears without waking her. Fail.

She yawns and stretches. "Mornin'."

I kiss her, hoping she'll be up for more — I know I am — but she pulls back.

"One tumble an' the laddie gets all lovey dovey."

"Shouldn't I?"

Her grin would put the Wicked Witch of the West to shame. "T'was nice, just a little overeager, quicky sticky."

This is *not* how I imagined the conversation going.

"Don't give me the long face." She pulls down the blanket, offering a good view of her marginally dressed state. "That ought t'cheer you up."

"I just thought—"

"We needs go back and help Billy, and save Ben if we can."

I try to focus. "For sure." But going back to change something in our own timeline... "What happens if we meet ourselves?"

She shrugs. "I never gone but one direction. Da tried to explain, somethin' about ghosts, but I was too young to understand. This much I know, you can't change your own past."

"So how do we save Ben — and Billy?"

"We gots to think of something." She walks to the window and starts untangling her hair.

"What if we go forward in time?" I say. "We'll find my dad. I told you, he knows everything. He can help us fix this."

Her hair-combing speeds up, her fingers ripping out knots rather than untying them.

"That be far uptime. Months each way. We goes back now."

"I don't even know how," I say.

"I'll learn you."

On that, at least, we agree.

"We almost died in that church. I say we go uptime."

She stomps her pretty little foot. "Downtime."

I step forward again. She backs up. I maneuver her into a corner.

"Uptime." I put my hand on her breast, which is pretty darn cool — and not in a temperature way.

She removes it. "Downtime."

"Uptime." I kiss her.

"Downtime." She whispers into my mouth.

Breakfast a-la-Yvaine is four tiny bird eggs for the two of us and all-you-can-eat blackberries. The eggs come raw.

We picnic in the field. The distant pops that woke us during the night continue in fits and starts.

"Those booms sound like artillery," I say.

"Cannon?"

"At least they aren't getting any closer." I nod at the big house, which in my mind translates as *chateau*. "What's that building?"

She snickers. "That center stone tower be part of an abbey when I's last here."

"Won't they notice us camping on their front lawn?" I say.

Yvaine stands. "The first time is the hardest." She points right at my crotch.

I glance down. Truth be told, I'm pretty sore—

She punches my shoulder. "Openin' a time-hole, you dolt."

Oh yeah. That. "How do I do it?"

"If you be ready to travel, you'll just feel it." She grabs me and squeezes. *There.*

I stifle a squeak. I feel it all right. Last night was great, but this seems more like coughing for the family pediatrician.

"I'm ready." Which, sore or not, is true.

"We'll see about that. Before you open a hole, you needs learn where t'put the other end."

"I managed last night."

She grins. "You've still a thing or two t'learn."

Low blow.

She continues, "But I means where in time and place we be wantin' to go."

Now I imagine dumping us out in the middle of the Atlantic or above a lava crater in Hawaii.

"Your hole will open at your feet," she says. "Downtime holes be underneath."

"Is an uptime hole different?" I ask.

"It's above me head — goin' up, silly."

"It was so crazy in the church I didn't even see it," I say.

She smiles. "That be because I was kissin' you."

"Yeah, that too."

"But anyways, our holes open and close much faster than a Tock's, so you never sees it when you travel, only when you stays behind. The moment it opens, you're gone. So dinna ever do it unless we're holdin' hands or kissin' or skin to skin one way or another — or you'll be gone downtime and me caught in your future with no way t'ever meet."

I grab her hand. "Skin to skin!"

"You be likin' that a wee bit much." But the crooked smile is on her face and she squeezes my hand. "First, you must needs conjure in your head an image of where and when you wants t'go."

"A place I can understand, but how do I think about a when?"

"Once we start fallin' there be a sense of time rushin' backward. The longer you hold the picture in your mind, the further you go until you release an' pop out."

"So it's like staying on the train until you get to your station, then stepping off?" I say.

"What's a train, Charlie?"

"Forget the train. Riding a carriage in a straight line, then deciding to hop off?"

She nods. "Just like that. But you can't turn around, an' each of us can only go so far. It be different from traveler to traveler. I dinna ken how far we come yesterday. My longest be thirty-one years, but travelin' with you felt queer."

This makes me chuckle.

"What happens if you don't get off at the end?"

"You just pop out, can't go no further. That usually not be the problem. If you pay close mind when you're in that no place, you feel time pass."

"The *in-between* place? The one with the spinning lights?"

She nods. "The light be the sun, not as it spins around the earth each day but as the seasons orbit the year. Once around per annum."

"Doesn't that make it hard to arrive at a particular day?" I ask.

"A day, yes, but time be strange in this *in-between* of ours. The spinnin' sun speeds an' slows as you will it. It has a way of workin' out. At least for me. I heared it telled different by others I met."

Sounds oh-so-scientific.

"So where and when are we going?" I ask.

"Here."

I give her a funny look.

"This be deadly business," she says. "If we go somewheres dangerous we could die. You needs hold a portrait in your head of this here place." She waves her free arm to indicate the ruined farmhouse and the gentle fields. "We go maybe one orbit of the sun. One year. Best to pass our same selves long by. From the look of things, this place been empty some considerable while."

I open my mouth but she presses two fingers to my lips.

"Let's practice." She grips my hand hard and points at my groin again. "Find the feelin' inside you and pull down. Like wanking."

One thing about Yvaine: she isn't coy.

"What makes you think I wank?" I say.

"All boys wank."

Got me there.

Two hours later, after countless futile attempts at *pulling down*, sweat beads my brow and I feel a headache coming on.

"It ain't so easy the first time." Yvaine rubs my neck. "But I needs show you somethin' anyways."

She leads me across the field, past the cottage and onto a wooded knoll. Halfway up, she stops to pick pink flowers off a shrub growing from the rocky soil. When we reach the top, we find a sloppy ring of mossy gray stones.

"Just after me seventh birthday," she says, "Da was teachin' me how to travel. He bided me tiptoe into the future but stay in the same place."

"What if you'd gone too far by accident?"

"He comed with me just in case, but we only traveled a week or so. Ma was much relieved when we showed up. My reach only be a few decades, but I gots more control than most. Da could go over a hundred, but hearing him talk, he'd be walkin' as many miles and waitin' as many days to get where he wanted."

"What happened after that first trip?"

"Da saw a Tock at market day in Inverness. After that we comed here. Everythin' be good for some months, then he found us."

She paws at one of the waist-high rocks. Purple-topped thistles grow about its base.

"The Tock taked Mum first," she says.

Although the stones bear no markings, now I can see them for what they are: graves.

"He comed out of nowhere with twin dirks of brass." Yvaine pauses to wipe her eyes. "Held one to her neck. Da went for him but the beast hurlt a second blade into his eye. Killt him so fast his clothes fell to the floor empty. Nothing left even t'bury."

"And your mom?" I say.

"The Tock sliced her throat, opened her up like a hog, then she too be gone."

I put my arms around her, holding her tight. "I'm so sorry."

"I be hidin' in the loft." She leans into me. "I never did nothin' to stop him."

"What were you, seven?"

"After, I taked their clothes an' the small things that mattered an' buried them here in the old circle."

"What were their names?" They aren't written anywhere, but names are important to us travelers.

"Phillipe an' Heather," she says, patting first one stone, then another.

"Did you have a surname?"

"De Verge. Me da sayed his own da was no traveler — like your mum — so he used me grandmum's name an' heraldry."

"Yvaine de Verge suits you."

She watches the breeze ripple the wildflowers. "Time's taken everyone that matters. First me parents, now Billy."

"I'll stay with you. Trust me."

She rests her head on my shoulder, looking me in the eyes.

"Can I? Someday, they'll take you from me or me from you."

This makes me mad. Not just Mom-grounded-me-for-something-I-didn't-do mad, but really mad.

"Not if we stop them first. I know it hurts, but can you remember anything else your parents said that could help us? Anything about this place?"

"This just be where me da was born."

"In the past?" Which I realize is a useless term for us.

"We was here in Tudor times, but me da, he was born uptime somewheres."

She scrunches her nose and leans against a stone, thinking. Then her face lights up like a cartoon lightbulb just appeared over her head.

"In the church," she says. "The Tock, he held that brass thing, the little square!"

"I remember. Same as the day we met, at Ben's."

Her lips curl into a wicked smile. "Me da had one of them brass pages too. At night he'd sometimes sit by the fire and read it."

Like the shiny book on Dad's desk. Pages from a time traveler manual?

"What happened to your dad's?" I ask.

"You be standing on it."

I look down at the green between the gravestones, then drop to my knees and start pulling up the moss.

"Stop!" Yvaine kneels and grabs my hands.

"You said there aren't any bodies."

She shakes her head. "It ain't right. Their ghosts might come for us. Da said travelers has ghosts."

She crosses herself.

"But it might help us!" I say.

She chews on her lip again. "It ain't right."

We end up by the river, at a place where the water forms a pool by the bank. Our feet dangle in the not-so-cool water. Under the surface, Yvaine tickles my toes with hers.

The thunder-like sound has been going on all morning, but it's pumping up the volume, which I mention.

She shrugs. "Try travelin' again when you be ready. One of these years you'll get the knack for it."

"You always give me a hard time."

She snickers. "Me mum warned me that travelin' couples be bound tighter than regular folk, that no matter how we argue we gots t'stick together."

I elbow her. "That's a good reason not to argue."

"She also said I be a most disobedient child, full of piss and vinegar."

Seeing her impish expression, I want to throw her down on the riverbank and do everything we did last night and then some. But memories of the burning church overpower such thoughts, and anyway Yvaine is lecturing again.

"After we travel, we has t'recover. The period be different for each of us, but until the power returns, no time-hole."

"If this were a video game," I say, "that'd be called a *cooldown*."

She pats my pants. "Cooldown, that sounds about right."

"I mean the length of time between using your super power." My face feels hot.

She scrunches hers.

"How long is yours?"

"Seventeen days," she says.

"So we have to wait sixteen more before we can go into the future?"

She nods. "When both our... cooldowns are finished, we'll see about moving on. That way if we lands somewhere dangerous, the other can pull us back t'safety."

I have to admit, she's pretty clever about this stuff.

After I tug on my shoes and socks, I make sure my knife is secure. It looks different, longer, with a leather-wrapped handle.

Yvaine says, "Try to—"

"Shhhhh."

Men in colorful uniforms erupt from the tree line across the river and plunge into the shallow water, rifles held high above their heads as they splash across. They're wearing fuzzy hats, red jackets, and green plaid skirts.

"Those be me countrymen," Yvaine says, "Highland Dragoons!"

A few carry flagpoles with a Britishy flag, but I don't waste time asking her what Scottish troops are doing in France. I grab her hand and run back toward the field and the chateau.

The fireworks have gotten all too close. I hear a whistling noise familiar from countless war movies.

Then the world explodes.

Brown geysers erupt all over the lawn. Sod and earth fly everywhere. The air chokes with smoke and the rotten-egg smell of gunpowder.

And the day started out so well!

Through the haze I hear excited yells, then see a red, white, and blue army pour across the field. Little white flashes and continuous popping erupt like Chinatown fireworks.

What the Military Channel calls small arms fire.

I throw Yvaine to the grass.

"Charlie—"

Another artillery barrage ripples across the battlefield to collide with the second army. If the noise weren't so deafening I'm sure I'd hear screaming. Instead I only see men — and parts of men — hurled every which way.

A nearby soldier clutches the stump where his leg used to be, which spurts red blood onto the yellow flowers.

I never in my life more wanted to be somewhere else.

The weirdest feeling comes over me, sort of like finding an extra arm I can move inside myself, sort of like a switch deep inside my... groin.

The sun goes behind a cloud. I feel Yvaine's hand pulse hot in mine.

Suddenly we're falling.

My brain claws toward an understanding of the *in-between*. Maybe I'm getting used to time traveling, or maybe it's because I made this trip happen myself.

I clutch Yvaine's arm as we tumble down through the awful emptiness. The sun hangs in the void, a bright spot on a field of bright. I feel it turn just a bit—

Is that artillery fire?

Chapter Fourteen:
Chateau

France, 1807

We tumble onto the grassy field. In front of us, the chateau windows reflect the sunset. The balmy air smells like it did this morning — better, even — and the rich smell of the soil mixes with the perfume of flowers.

I feel totally spent, but I did it! I traveled back in time on my own power!

"Merciful Jesus in heaven," Yvaine mutters, her head in her hands. She looks exactly like she did before the battle, only more frazzled.

"You aren't hurt, are you?" I ask.

"I dinna think so. You?"

I pat myself down. My ears are ringing worse than when Dad dragged me to a Pink Floyd concert, but otherwise I seem intact.

"How far did we come?"

She sniffs the air. "A month or two. That was mayhap late June or July, this be spring."

I sit down, then lean back onto the grass. My eyes almost close themselves. A nap would be—

Yvaine kicks me gently.

"I dinna hear no cannons, but methinks this time we inquire with the neighbors. We dinna ken how long before you be ready t'travel again."

"What about you?"

"I telled you. Seventeen days, less the one we spent a wee bit uptime. When we both ready, you takes us back to Billy."

She kicks me again.

Up close the chateau looks a bit decrepit. The bushes need trimming, rust stains drip from the iron railings, and cracks mar the white marble facade.

"Where are you going?" Yvaine asks.

"The front door?"

"Tsk tsk. Our sort dinna never enter that way," she says. "Follow me."

The building is big enough that walking around back takes a while. And I'd pity the guy who mows the lawn, except he seems to be on vacation.

Yvaine leads us to what's obviously the kitchen, a multi-chimney wing protruding from the back of the house. It smells like bread and onions, which reminds me that I've eaten only two bird eggs and some berries since leaving London.

Yvaine taps the side of the door, left open in a half-assed attempt at ventilation.

"Madame," she says, "mighten two orphans beg a wee bit of food?"

Inside a skinny girl in a grubby dress chops onions under the watchful eye of the cook, a short, wide woman who clearly enjoys the fruits of her labors.

"We got no use for beggars," she says.

I notice a newspaper covering something on a nearby counter. While Yvaine continues her pitch I creep over.

Determining the date is difficult — the paper being stained with grease and written in French.

I parse out May 20, 1807, and something about Paris and the war effort before the cook — armed with a knife — takes notice.

"Get your grubby paws off the veal chops," the mistress of the kitchen says.

"I was just—"

"Madame Fournier?" a male voice says from across the room. "I'm aware the war ministry has left you little in the way of meat, but must you butcher a young man for tonight's roast?"

"Monsieur!" the cook says, retracting the point of her blade a smidgen. "These two were stealing."

"Is that so?" The speaker is a balding gentleman of about sixty, dressed in a somber suit with a white cravat.

"Sir," Yvaine says, holding her hands out, "we be but two hungry orphans, driven from our homes by the war."

The man has an intense stare. He focuses it on Yvaine so long that she squirms.

"What's your name, girl?"

"Yvaine."

The way he's looking at her, I almost expect him to repeat it back. But he scrunches his face, then approaches to take Yvaine's chin in his hand and tilt her face.

"Do I know you, chérie?"

"I dinna think so."

"Madame," he says to the cook, "give them the bread and the cheese, at least. And a spot of the wine. Lord knows it'll go sour before I finish it all alone."

"Very well, monsieur." The fat woman sheathes her weapon and gets some plates for us.

The gentleman plops himself into a wooden chair by a small table, uncorks a bottle, and pours several glasses of wine, filling his own to the brim.

"Sir," I say, taking a seat, "what are the soldiers in red and green doing here?" Sure, that hasn't happened yet, but he might know whom I'm talking about.

"British troops? I'm surprised scouts have made it this far." He takes a sip of wine. "General Bonaparte has them fairly well bottled up."

"Napoleon Bonaparte?" I say. Not a big surprise. It *is* 1807 France.

"The king's first minister." He sighs. "Popular or not, the man's *petit conflit* has dragged on nearly a decade."

"That king shouldn't exist," I whisper to Yvaine. "I remember a revolution, a Republic, then lots of head chopping. Liberté, fraternité, and all that jazz."

"How far we come from 1725?" she says.

"Eighty-two years."

"I warned you things would be different," she says. "An' that be like thrice as far uptime as I ever go before."

"What did you say?" the old man asks. "My hearing isn't what it used to be."

"Just wishing the king good health." I tear into the hard bread and pungent cheese the cook sets on the table.

The man raises his glass. "Vive le roi! Vive Louis XVII!"

Louis Seventeenth?

"Pity he takes after his late father," the man continues, speaking as much to himself as to us. "Queen Marie-Antoinette is the brighter of the two for certain."

"She's still alive?" I'm pretty damn sure Louis XVI and Marie-Antoinette lost their heads a decade earlier during the revolution.

He gives me a funny look. "Did I tell you I'm making a watch for her? Not that she's likely to pay me with the war and all, not to mention I'm about twenty years behind schedule. Still, it's splendid."

"May we ask your name, good sir?" Yvaine says.

"Forgive me. I get so fixated on my work. Abraham-Louis Bréguet, pleased to meet you."

"Yvaine," she says, "and me cousin Charlie."

It's my turn to glare at Yvaine, for not promoting me beyond *cousin*. But Monsieur Bréguet takes to calling us *chérie* and *garçon*.

"Your house, sir," she says. "Did it once belong to the Franciscans?"

He looks surprised. "The oldest wing. But my late wife's family built the rest. Did you grow up in the village? Or Chantilly?"

Yvaine shakes her head. "Me da did. He taked me here when I was young. But he died."

Monsieur Bréguet looks morose. "I'm sorry. The long war has cost us all a great deal."

"We make of it what we will," Yvaine says.

"What did you say?" the Monsieur asks.

She shrugs. "Thank you for the food." We polished off two loaves and a cheese, not to mention Yvaine's three glasses of wine. "But we best be off."

Monsieur Bréguet is still giving Yvaine the stare-down.

"Do you have somewhere to go?" he says.

"In a couple weeks, Charlie's takin' me t'find me only survivin' relation." She elbows me.

"My family's all gone too, Chérie," he says. "Perhaps I'm merely hungry for new faces, but I'd be happy to have you as my guests."

Staying in a nineteenth-century French chateau is a tad surreal. I could live without the gold paint, fine china, and fabric colored walls, but slumming in London has given me new appreciation for beds, baths, and windows — not to mention regular meals. And the house is nearly deserted with all the servants off to war. Monsieur Bréguet and I are the only men left, and he spends most of the day locked away in his workshop.

Which leaves us plenty of time to think. The battle and the downtime hop distracted me, but my brain keeps going back to Yvaine's mysterious brass page. I know she wants to leave it buried, but I can't help thinking we need all the help we can get.

At dinner, Yvaine shows up wearing a pink dress and white ribbons in her hair.

"Where'd that come from?" I ask.

"Monsieur Bréguet asked Mademoiselle Brigitte to fit it for me." She twirls around so it lifts. Still no shoes.

"I didn't know you liked that kind of thing."

"All ladies like dresses and ribbons." She beams at me.

"My Aunt Sophie doesn't."

The Monsieur pats Yvaine on the head. Unlike Donnie's attentions, these don't bother me in the least. It's nice to see her acting the girly girl, and the old man treats her like a daughter.

"Yvaine," I say, "we need to dig up that—"

"Not at dinner," she says.

Afterward, our host lights his pipe and offers us some *marc*. Yvaine — no surprise — is partial to the brandy.

"Are those your sons?" she asks of a big portrait showing a younger Bréguet with two boys, one in his twenties and the other in his teens. The older looks like his father but the younger is blond and — oddly — turned away from the viewer.

Our host nods. "My oldest, Louis-Antoine, followed me in my trade, but I sent him away to Geneva for safety."

"Why is your other son facin' backward?" Yvaine asks.

"He wasn't when he sat for the portrait, but the painter, David" — he says the name in the tone one reserves for Picasso or Rembrandt — "insisted that was the only way he could complete the composition."

"What was his name?" she says.

"David," Monsieur Bréguet says. But I'm pretty sure Yvaine meant the boy, not the artist. "He was frightfully expensive, too, but that was before the war ruined my business."

"Your younger son doesn't live here?" she says.

"He's grown now, married a Scottish Catholic...." The watchmaker shakes his head, looking down. "He visits every few years."

Yvaine's looking at him funny. "What was his name?" she asks again.

The Monsieur scratches his head. "My wife chose it. After her great uncle. *His* portrait is over there."

We follow his finger to find a swishy-looking French guy, facing sideways, his face mostly covered by the most ridiculous gray wig imaginable. The brass plate beneath reads, *Phillipe en 1694*.

Yvaine looks ill.

"Your son was also named Phillipe?"

"Of course," Monsieur Bréguet says. "I must be getting old. It slipped my mind."

"Does this mean what I think it means?" I ask Yvaine as soon as we're alone.

She nods. "The Monsieur. He be my... my grandfather."

"So this is when your dad meant, being born *here*, uptime?"

"I suppose."

"Heavy," I say. "The blond son in the portrait —"

"Is me da."

"No wonder the Monsieur took a liking to you. His wife must've been the traveler — you probably look like her."

The next morning, Monsieur Bréguet and Yvaine are like peas in a pod at breakfast. He keeps opening different flavors of jam for her to try and she literally eats it up.

I keep thinking about Yvaine's dad's magical brass page.

"What if it's a time traveler handbook?" I tell her.

"I told you, ghosts!" Her stare stops me cold.

Later, instead of working — and to the amazement of the servants — Monsieur Bréguet volunteers to teach Yvaine backgammon. I don't appear to be invited.

I wander outside and head down the slope toward the cottage and the river — the Monsieur called it the Oise. I make my way up the knoll to stand before the gray-green stones.

It's for the best, I tell myself as I pick at the ground, first with my knife and then with a shovel-like strip of bark from a nearby tree. As Yvaine herself might say, *we make of it what we will*, and I just can't leave the proverbial stone unturned.

The ground is soft and seven-year-olds don't dig very deep. It takes me less than an hour to find what I'm looking for.

A single brass page about the size of a paperback book is buried with scraps and bits of other stuff, rotted or turned to dust, but the page itself looks fine. Maybe it's even made of some time traveler metal: the surface seems more focused, more real, than the clumps of ordinary dirt that cling to it.

Engraved across the front are lines of tight text. My adrenaline spikes — this looks like the secret cipher dad taught me.

But before I get any further, the page is snatched out of my hand.

Chapter Fifteen:
Whirlwind

France, 1807

Yvaine looms over me, clutching the page. Her face is pink and flushed.

"How dare you!" Her voice is a hiss.

"I'm sorry," I say. "But—"

She bolts off, crashing into the brush.

"Yvaine!" I yell. "We have to talk."

I understand she's superstitious — hell, she was born two centuries before the Salem witch trials — but the needs of the living have to come first.

She doesn't stop, and I have to chase her down to the ruined cottage, where I'm forced to tackle her.

"You just be lucky I canna travel yet, Charlie!" she says. "I might've gone where you canna follow."

She has a point.

"I just couldn't let a clue rot in the ground—"

"This be just like when you taked Billy! You said I could trust you—"

I tell her the page might help us save Ben and Billy. She whacks my head with it — I'm lying on top of her, but I neglected to pin her arms.

"Ouch!"

"You be frightful rash."

"I know. I love you."

She blinks.

"You dinna know what that means."

I let her squirm out from beneath me and run off, then I slump against a nearby tree. I'm still pretty sure I'm right, but that doesn't mean I don't feel like shit. Yup. Frightful rash.

I wander the woods and fields. The weather is gorgeous, but I don't care. When the sun touches the horizon, I drift back to the cottage. The place is pretty and forlorn, the lush French vegetation having made a good go at reclaiming it. I contemplate the corner where — a month or two from now — Yvaine and I slept together.

The cynical devil-voice inside my head, the one that can't accept my own failings, wonders if she's using me like she used Donnie and even Ben. Or because I'm the only time traveling boy within who knows how many miles or years.

But if that were the case, she might not be so mad at me.

The first of the purple thistles are blooming. I take one, and when I get back to the house, find a dusty book, and press it between the pages to dry.

At dinner Yvaine ignores me completely. And at breakfast Monsieur Bréguet remains oblivious to the tension and the two of them chat like a pair of schoolgirls.

At least *he* answers my questions.

"Who are your clients?" I ask.

In theory, there's nothing wrong with making watches, but after our dose of Tick-Tock loving, I can't say I'm a big fan of anything that needs winding up.

"With all the death and disruption," the Monsieur says, "there's not the demand for fine timepieces there used to be. I still file my patents and build my prototypes, but few can afford such luxuries. If it weren't for my patron, the Marquis de Messidor, I'd even have to sell the estate."

"It was better before the war?" I say.

"I was Horologist de Roi to the late Louis XVI."

Somehow, I never put two and two together about my last name. *Horologe*. French for clock.

"It must be nice to be so *respected*," Yvaine says.

The Monsieur puffs his pipe. "The old king's son prefers cannons to clocks."

"*Deplorable*." She refuses to meet my gaze. "Can I see your work?"

Monsieur Bréguet checks an ornate pocket watch tucked in his vest and nods.

I stop Yvaine on the way out of the room. "You're going to have to talk to me sometime, you know."

She pries my fingers off her arm — a response of sorts! — and follows him to the workshop.

It isn't big, but then neither are Monsieur Bréguet's creations. Little bits of steel and brass and copper cover the workbenches, gears and springs and wires and whatnot. Tools and parts hang from every surface.

The Monsieur is like a kid in a candy store. He hands Yvaine a pocket watch the size of a bagel.

"This is the prototype for Marie-Antoinette's timepiece. I'm still working on the movement. It has every known horological complication!"

It does look complicated.

"It's a perpetual watch," he says, "one of my earliest and most reliable inventions."

"I'm sure it's most *trustworthy*," Yvaine says.

He moves the watch back and forth, looking at is as if it had done something astonishing.

"Everyday motion winds it. Just carry it around in your pocket, and voila! It's always there for you."

"More than I can say for some people," she says.

"The Marquis de Messidor is most interested in the mechanical arts," Monsieur Bréguet says. "And a loyal patron."

"*Loyalty* is hard t'come by," Yvaine says.

"The marquis gave me the idea for this." He holds up a tiny knot of twisted metal. "My springtorb. It stores mechanical energy at high efficiency. A springtorb watch needs winding just once a year."

"My Seiko needed a new battery after two," I say.

"But my most famous creation is the whirlwind." The French word he uses is *tourbillon*. "Which counteracts two of the three forces of gravity on its escapement."

He searches through the pile of parts and hands me an open pocket watch. Inside is a creepy rotating mechanism whose gears crawl around in a hypnotic little march.

"One thing about having so few clients and a generous patron, it frees up my time for the inventing. I've almost completed a new gyroscopic *tourbillon*. It rotates in all three dimensions, but the marquis thinks even that can be topped!"

"How so?" I say.

"Bear in mind he has a little of the crazy." Monsieur Bréguet winks at us. "But he's convinced it's actually possible to counteract four dimensions of gravitational force. Imagine that. Four dimensions — what exactly would the last be?"

I think I might know.

Time.

Yvaine has almost two weeks before she can travel, so I suffer through a few more painful days of evil eye silent treatment before I confront her again.

"I'm sorry," I say, walking on my knees into the snazzy drawing room where she likes to hang out.

The Monsieur's toys

"Good." She's sprawled in a chair that probably costs $10,000 back in Philly. "But I'm still not talking to you."

"Don't Monsieur Bréguet's inventions bother you?"

"You bother me."

I swallow my pride. "There's no question he's one of those geniuses — like Ben Franklin — who sees us better than most. But his work seems really Tick-Tocky, particularly that *tourbillon* thing."

She stands and puts her hands on her hips and glares at me.

"The Monsieur has nothin' to do with the Tocks. He be a good man."

"You said that about Donnie." I crawl closer before the sneer becomes a retort. "But I agree. He *is* a good man. But that doesn't mean the Tick-Tocks aren't up to something. I've been reading the newspapers and questioning the staff. Something's messed up here."

She's still glaring — and sneering.

"I don't remember all the details," I continue, "and the Napoleonic wars are complicated, but Mr. Short and Bossy isn't doing as well as he used to. Lord Wellington landed an invasion force on French soil last year and has Paris under siege. Not to mention the French Revolution never happened."

"When we go back to help Billy, none of that will matter."

At least she hasn't written me off completely.

"How will I know when I can travel?" I say.

"You'll just feel it. Then downtime. For Billy."

I grope around for the weird space where the time travel muscle lives. It's there, but unresponsive.

"Look," I say, "we have no idea what's really going on. Bréguet's patron, this marquis? He reeks like a clockwork fish. We need to go uptime and find my dad. I'm telling you, he knows everything about history —"

"You promised we'd fix things for Billy."

CHAPTER FIFTEEN: WHIRLWIND

"We will, but we need help. We don't even know what the Tick-Tocks want. And in my time, research is way easier. We can find out exactly what happened to Ben and Billy *before* making a move. You can't think the Tock went to London just to kill two underage time travelers — he went to Franklin Court first, then back to find Ben himself. That can't be coincidence. If we just head downtime without a plan, things could get even worse."

She doesn't embrace my brilliant logic, but I can tell she's thinking about it. I'm thinking about Doc Brown's warning: meeting yourself could unravel the very fabric of the space-time continuum. I'm also thinking how dubious it is taking advice from a fictional character who drives a flying DeLorean.

"Have you tried reading your father's page?"

Yvaine sighs. "I dinna read so well, an' I've not never seen them funny letters."

"Let me try. My dad taught me that alphabet."

"Why should I?"

"Because if I'm right — and you know I might be — it's the best clue we've got."

She gives me a long, hard look, then pulls the page from her dress.

"You swear on the life of your mum you'll give it back if I ask?"

"I swear."

She hands it over. "An' dinna think this means I've forgiven you."

Yvaine and I have separate rooms in a quiet wing of the big house. When we arrived, I considered this a major bummer, but things between us being as they are, it allows me to concentrate on the page.

I stay up all night studying by candlelight, work all morning, collapse the next afternoon. Then again the next night, and the next.

The symbols might be familiar, but damn if I can make any sense out of them.

Assuming it's a simple substitution like the one Dad taught me, I count the number of uses of each letter. Vowels should be more common. It takes a while to write this down — feather pens are really hard to work with — but I don't make any headway until I realize the page is written in Latin!

It's also obscured by some kind of complex sliding encryption. My first breakthrough comes when I identify several of the seven-letter words as all being different encodings for *Bréguet*. The only other useful word I decipher is *tempero*, which a book downstairs translates as *regulator*.

A few days later, I'm forced to admit that I've done all I can. I need my dad's help — or maybe a couple years.

That night, lying in bed, the weird time traveler part of me feels all awake and perky. It's hard to describe yet obvious, like an itch that's ready to be scratched. I can travel again! And Yvaine's cooldown should be up in a day or so.

But how in the world am I going to convince her to take me uptime?

Chapter Sixteen:
Looped

France, 1807

Early morning light and dull booming sounds drift through the open window to wake me.

"In the interest of full disclosure," I tell Yvaine at breakfast, "I can travel again. I felt it come on last night."

She menaces me with a butter knife. "You be takin' me back to Billy, then?"

"I said I'd tell you everything. Not do everything."

She snarls at me. But it's a cute snarl.

"When can *you* travel?" I ask.

She pats her belly. "In a few hours, methinks."

I offer her the shiny brass page. "I can't fully translate it but I can tell it's all about your grandfather."

She takes the metallic rectangle. "Humility be a start."

"Will you take a walk with me?"

I'm surprised when she agrees. We wander down the beautiful slope toward her old home.

This morning I retrieved the now dried thistle I shoved inside a book. I offer it to her, pressing it into her hand.

"I made this for you."

I half expect a wisecrack, but she looks pensive.

"Don't all ladies like flowers, Yvaine?"

Boy, did I miss having her smile at me.

"We do." She adds the flower to her private stash.

I put a hand on her cheek and use the other to brush a strand of hair behind her ear.

"I wish I knew more about Monsieur Bréguet's real role in history," I say.

"He's quite famous," she says "He's been to balls at Versailles."

"History's changing around your grandfather, Yvaine. There's talk that Lord Wellington might break through Napoleon's lines, and Parisians have been rioting over food. And that page of your dad's might explain why or how."

"But you sayed you dinna understand it."

"No, but my dad will. He comes to my house in the future twice a year. We can go there and find him. Then I swear on my life we'll take care of Billy."

Yvaine eyes me warily. "I'm not sayin' I'll do it. But I needs details, so I can pictures the place."

I describe Independence Hall. It's near where I left, walking distance from my house, distinctive, and, since it was built before 1800 not unlike buildings she's seen before.

"Your da," she says. "We can trust him? He'll help us fix things for Billy?"

"I think so. And if he doesn't, I will."

"I still say we goes downtime."

We reach the old cottage. The floor is covered with foot-prints: Yvaine's little barefoot ones and my not-much-bigger booted ones.

"It rained yesterday," I say, "but those footprints are new. Did you come here before breakfast? I didn't."

"Charlie, Charlie, Charlie." She pokes my shoulder with her chin. "What am I going to do with you?"

"Forgive me?" I say.

She sighs. "It be hard to hate someone so earnest."

"I make mistakes."

"I abandoned me own son." Her lips are pressed thin.

"As long as we're alive, we can fix it."

"We make of it what we will."

"What does that even mean?"

"This place an' time isn't important," she says. "Livin' be important. Billy be important. Even you be important."

It's true that the nineteenth century doesn't feel any more or less real than the eighteenth or twenty-first. I guess life is more about who you're with than where — or when — you are.

Yvaine leads us down to the river. The artillery's distant pounding is louder the closer we get to the water.

"When we came here the first time," I say, "you're sure it was late June or July?"

"Cotton thistle ain't never in bloom before then," she says. "At least in Scotland — quiet, now, someone's up ahead."

I hear a girl's voice: "One of these years you'll get the knack for it."

"You always give me a hard time," a young man says. Also familiar, but weird-sounding. Really weird.

I pull Yvaine behind a tree and peer around.

A girl and a boy sit next to each other by the stream. She's wearing a puffy white blouse beneath her dress and her blond hair is tucked up under lace.

It's Yvaine, but not.

I mean, it looks exactly like her but it doesn't. She has none of Yvaine's shiny in-focus quality. And behind her is some other *me*, eying her like a dork and looking ridiculous in a too-short jacket.

Yvaine was wrong — we only traveled back a few weeks! Those footprints were ours. Sort of. On the bright side, Doc Brown was wrong too — the fabric of the space-time continuum seems intact.

"You fool," the real Yvaine says in my ear. "We shouldn't never have comed down here."

Meeting Mr. and Mrs. Fake

"Hey, I followed *you*!"

By the stream, fake Yvaine snickers. "Me mum warned me that us travelin' couples be bound tighter than regular folk, that no matter how we argue we gots t'stick together."

Fake Charlie elbows her. "That's a good reason not to argue."

"Piss and vinegar," I whisper to real Yvaine, who crinkles her nose at me.

Fake Yvaine comes in on cue. "She also sayed I be a most disobedient child, full of piss and vinegar."

Real Yvaine has her hands over her mouth and is snorting, the way people do when they're trying not to laugh. Somehow this makes her sneeze.

"Who goes there?" fake Charlie says. He sounds like videotape me, the me from Mom's home movies. If they were in French without subtitles.

Yvaine and I freeze. Fake Charlie and fake Yvaine leap to their feet, and the four of us face off.

Our previous selves look puzzled, not a glimmer of recognition on their faces. But again, glass being half-full, the universe doesn't implode.

"Did you come from London?" I ask.

"I'm no foreign spy," fake Charlie says, looking confused.

Trust me, real Charlie is just as baffled.

"You didn't just come from the church?" I say.

"I took Mass last Sunday, what of it?"

Weirder and weirder.

"What're your names?" real Yvaine asks.

Fake Charlie really looks stumped this time.

"Everyone calls me Garçon," he says finally.

"And I'm Chérie," fake Yvaine says. "Nice t'meet you."

Real Yvaine looks from her to me and shakes my arm.

"The war's comin'. We gots t'get back to the house and warn the Monsieur."

"Let's stay a minute," I whisper. "We can learn something."

To the fakes I say, "And you work here?"

"Up at the chateau," fake Charlie says, "doing... work."

They have this vague way of talking, as if they aren't entirely here.

"They be like ghosts," real Yvaine whispers.

Like her father said: time travelers have ghosts. But they look solid enough — neither time-traveler sharp nor translucent — just ordinary.

"Last night be our honeymoon." Fake Yvaine slips her arm through fake Charlie's and they kiss passionately.

I elbow real Yvaine. "See, we were good together."

Explosions rock the tree line, much closer.

"Me grandfather!" she says.

"Take cover!" fake Charlie yells. "The English are coming."

How does he know? We didn't, at least not then. Two weeks ago. I mean now. I mean the first time it was now.

Real Yvaine and I pound full tilt up the hill toward the chateau.

The full-on attack hasn't started yet but dozens of troops in red, white, and blue uniforms gallop across the field. Fortunately, they're French and don't seem to care about us.

"Hide this in your jacket." Yvaine passes me her father's shiny page as we run. "You be right. We dinna ken what we're dealing with. Ghosts for sure." She crosses herself again.

"They belonged to this time," I say. "Maybe the universe covers up for us when we're gone, puts the ghosts in to fill our places in history. You heard them at the beginning — they repeated our exact conversation but probably had no idea what they were saying!"

"Time's the lazy cull. Doin' whatever be easiest."

"This is really important," I say. "When we go back and fix things with Ben Franklin and Billy, ghost Yvaine and ghost Charlie will be there too. And if I were a gambler, I'd say they'll think they're members of Donnie's gang. Regular citizens of the London underworld."

"I needs say goodbye to me grandpapa before we go."

Artillery continues to pound the field. As we run to the chateau we pass some of the war's handiwork, like Monsieur Torso, a soldier who's missing just about everything from the waist down. The poor guy waves his arms at us while his guts pool on the ground like sausages.

"And I used t'think," Yvaine says, gasping for breath, "that I did too much runnin' away before we meeted."

Two uniformed French soldiers are waiting on the gravel driveway with three horses and a cart. We blow right by them and plunge inside the house. Half a dozen crates are stacked in the foyer. Bréguet is usually in the workshop, so we head there.

But we find only the youngest servant girl and Brigitte, the housekeeper. Both are shoving watches and tools into crates.

"What's going on?" I say.

"The Monsieur's patron arrived to relocate us!" Brigitte says.

"Where's Monsieur Bréguet?" Yvaine asks.

"Packing the library with his lordship."

Yvaine runs and I follow.

More shells explode. The chandeliers rattle.

The library isn't far and the huge double doors are open already. We tear into the two-story room. Bréguet is facing us, packing watches and clocks from the display cases into a crate.

"Chérie!" he says.

The Marquis de Messidor has his back to us. He stands tall and thin in his blue and red jacket, white pants, and high black boots. A long rifle hangs from a pale leather case across his back, and his hat is one of those sideways Napoleon-type jobs.

He pivots as if standing on a turntable. He's super in focus, and I know what he is before I see his face.

Chapter Seventeen:
Longshot

France, 1807

The new Tick-Tock — and he *is* different, at least a foot taller — gives us the evil eye. Literally. He's got goggles built into his ivory mask, ringed cylinders like brass telescopes. One of them extends to focus on us. Colored glass in the other lens flicks from green to red.

He crouches and springs high into the air, back-flipping like a circus performer to land fifteen feet above us on the upstairs balcony. Silently, he whips the big rifle from its holster and brings it to his shoulder. A freaking clockwork sniper!

He aims at Yvaine.

I force us both to the ground.

BANG! Something whizzes past to strike the parquet floor and throw up a puff of sawdust.

What are the odds Mr. Longshot keeps missing? I scramble to my feet. I know we should run, but we watch in horrid fascination as NRA Tick-Tock reloads his gun. He winds and cranks. I've never seen a weapon like this, long and brass and covered in gears and levers.

My hand grabs Yvaine's. "Time to go. Uptime!"

"Not till we help the Monsieur!" she says. "Try to distract the Tock."

And this one has a rifle!

CHAPTER SEVENTEEN: LONGSHOT

Oh, God, what is she getting me into? I snatch up a heavy bronze bookend and shot put it at Longshot, who lays off his winding to hop out of the way. Next, chucking all caution, I make a running jump onto the balcony ladder underneath him. It slides sideways on its little track and I climb.

The rifleman — or is that *riflemachine* — circles the balcony to get a bead on me. He resumes his reloading efforts.

I reach the top and grab another pair of bookends.

"Marquis de Machine!" Yvaine hollers up.

She's standing below with Bréguet, holding two of his *mécanisme spécial*. She dashes them to the floor, where they explode into a billion pieces.

Machine and inventor both howl. Bréguet's is a pathetic gasp of human loss, Longshot's a high metallic whine. He was aiming to shoot me in the head, but now he turns toward Yvaine. He pulls back the bolt on his rifle.

I hurl one bookend then the other. The first misses but the second is mega-lucky and knocks his gun askew just as he fires.

BANG! The bullet blasts into a bookshelf.

He swivels back to me, causing those gold ropey things on his uniform to flap. Telescoping lenses whirl and contract. He rotates back to Yvaine and gets to reloading.

I get to collecting bookends. Yvaine gets to smashing.

Bréguet gets to howling. "Non! Non! Chérie—"

The chateau shudders like a dollhouse under assault by a jealous younger brother. The chandelier sways to the accompaniment of titanic booms.

"Timequake?" I yell.

Yvaine shakes her head.

I realize she's right. Timequakes — and I've only experienced one — feel different, like the universe is shaking. Plus they don't really make any sound. This does. Booms, thuds, cracks, groans.

Duh. There's a war outside. The army is shelling the house!

More explosions rock the ceiling. The balcony pitches and tilts while I cling for dear life. Plaster and wood and who knows what tumble toward the floor.

The world clicks into odd slow motion. Yvaine and Bréguet are standing not far from each other, separated by a crate. Both look up, both faces terrified.

Across from me, Longshot sheathes his gun and leaps. At first, I think he's coming for me, but he sails out into space and comes down right on top of Bréguet, straddling him like an enormous spider.

Yvaine hops away — into the middle of the room!

"Take cover!" I scream.

I'm drowned out by the wrenching sounds from above.

Track and field star or not, jumping down to Yvaine won't work — unless I want to break both legs.

As the chandelier, the gold-painted wooden ceiling, and pretty much everything else breaks loose, I take a deep breath and pull down.

I let go the instant I'm *in-between*.

And grab the doorpost to the library to get my bearings. Part one of my desperate plan came together perfectly. I just pray the whole time-ghost thing works like I think it does.

I shrink back and peer into the room.

"Chérie!" Bréguet says.

The ceiling's perfectly intact and he looks perfectly normal. Fake Yvaine and fake me are walking into the room. And the faux Marquis that turns to greet them seems human enough. He's still tall and thin, and his face is long and fleshy with a honking Gallic nose and bushy sideburns.

One inventor, three ghosts, and a time traveler.

The Marquis's eyes widen on seeing the fakes. He bolts across the room, leaps to grab the balcony, and flips himself up. It's impressive, if not equal to Longshot's unnatural gymnastics.

Fake Charlie grabs at fake Yvaine. "Time to go. Outside."

"Not till we help the Monsieur," she says.

I watch my fake climb the ladder and get into a weird object-throwing match with the faux Marquis. He never draws his gun. I have to assume this ghost-theater is what normal humans see — a sanitized version of our time traveler reality.

My cooldown's burned so I only have one shot at this. I suppose I could jump in there now and grab fake Yvaine, but since I don't know if that will work, I bide my time.

And it isn't long before the house is shaking and the ceiling threatening to fall. I'm running for Yvaine when the faux Marquis does a suicidal swan dive toward Bréguet. Just as I reach her, she shimmers, blurs, and sharpens into hyper-focus. We collide, and my momentum drags her across the room until I drop to the slick wood floor and pull us underneath the Monsieur's enormous desk.

The last thing I see before ten tons of debris cover the room is the Tick-Tock. He's caged Bréguet with his own body, and his emotion-free mask of a face is back. The head swivels toward me. The weird goggles pulse and his mouth cracks open in what I take for a snarl.

Yvaine and I clutch each other as chunks of building pound the desk above. Dust pours into our little cubby until we can hardly breathe.

But the French build furniture to last.

"You traveled t'save me?" she says when the rumble subsides. There's dust in her eyes and she rubs at them, turning herself into a gray raccoon.

"Just a short hop. Worked like a charm." Actually more like a bizarre undo button.

"You just wanted t'burn your cooldown so I has t'take us uptime."

But she gives me a deep kiss. Dusty but so worth it.

"Is yours ready?" I say.

She nods and we struggle to push aside enough debris to reach the surface. Amazingly, most of the balcony is still intact. But four stories above I see sky!

"Where's Grandpapa?" Yvaine says.

"Under there somewhere." I nod toward the rubble.

"We needs get him—"

More explosions rock the house, but there's not much left to cave in on us.

I sigh and help Yvaine over to where I last saw Bréguet, keeping a firm grip on her hand.

"If things get nasty," I say, "it's up to you to lift us out of here."

"Monsieur!" Yvaine calls.

There's a feeble reply. He's trapped under the chandelier and a big beam, but at least he's alive.

CHIME. The nearby rubble shudders and settles.

CHIME. "The Tock," I say. "He's under there somewhere. We need to leave!"

CHIME. "Grandpapa first," Yvaine says.

CHIME. "I hate to say it…" But I'm going to. "The Tick-Tock wanted him alive. His research, it's wrong somehow."

CHIME. She starts tossing debris to the side. "I dinna care."

CHIME. I try to see what the Tock is up to. One of his booted feet twitches under the wreckage. He must be trapped, but not for long. Who knows where or when he's about to go, but I can't imagine it's good.

CHIME. Yvaine's making some progress. With a sigh I start helping her.

CHIME. "If we get Bréguet free, can we please go uptime and let my dad sort it out?"

CHIME. Her smile's cute even under the grime. "Deal. But I'm still holdin' you to your Billy promise."

CHIME. "Fair enough."

CHIME. Yvaine screams. A battered riding glove grabs at her ankle.

CHIME. I jump on the hand, trying to wrestle it loose. I feel the unyielding gears under the leather. It twists in my grasp, snakes into my jacket, and gropes for the brass page. I bend the fingers backward.

CHIME. Through the gaping ceiling, the sun dims. A time-hole opens beneath the Tock, who tumbles into nothingness. As it closes, I can't help noticing the bits and pieces of debris don't follow him down but settle into his now vacated space.

We pull Monsieur Breguet out of the rubble. I think the old watchmaker broke an arm, and blood is smeared across his battered face, but he'll live.

"Thank you." He glances around. "Where's the Marquis?"

"He's history," I say, "but unfortunately, history repeats itself."

The room — or what remains of it — is in shambles. Through a half destroyed pair of French doors I see the garden choked with powder smoke. Bodies are all over the boxwood paths, but a handful of living men crawl amongst the corpses.

Yvaine wraps Bréguet in a hug. He grimaces in pain but forces it into a smile.

"No need to torture yourself over smashing my mechanisms," he says. "Whatever the reason—"

"Your younger son, Phillipe," she says, "he was my father. So you—"

CHIME! CHIME!

The sound comes from outside. Two figures stride from the carnage.

Longshot looks like he stopped for a tune-up, his uniform repaired with spit and polish, his rifle cradled in front. Next to him is the shorter Tock, the one from London. His sword is in one hand, so my comic-book brain can't help but rechristen him

Rapier. His cracked face turns to us, then to what he holds in his other hand, a shiny brass page.

Not one Tick-Tock, but two. If my mom hadn't taught me better, I'd be summing up the situation with a word that rhymes with *trucked*.

"We have to go!" I yank Yvaine back, keeping a firm grip on her.

She glances from the Tocks to Bréguet and back again. The older man seems confused by the sudden return of his patron — as well he should be.

"It's us they want to kill!" I point at the watchmaker. "Him, they like!"

Yvaine reaches out with her free hand and touches Bréguet.

"Goodbye, Grandpapa," she says.

His eyes widen just before she grabs my hand and we're sucked up *in-between*.

Chapter Eighteen:
Sideways

Philadelphia, uptime

As we fall upward through the *in-between,* I realize the light of the sun orbits around us. Bright on bright, it stands out against the galactic tapioca smear of stars behind. Its feeble warmth weaves through the distant swirling, turns from warm to cold, into green glow and back to reddish brown then chill white and back into green.

I count the years as marked by the rotating light — 1808, 1809, and so on — but when I get to 1900 I'm frazzled and I think I missed or skipped some. I expect the trip to be over but it keeps going and going. At 2000, Yvaine's expression grows unnervingly intense.

She winks at me.

We pop out onto the Philadelphia street right in front of Independence Hall, which looks more or less like it should except it's grungy and covered in graffiti.

The park is much smaller than I remember, but the familiar short brick structures of old Philly crowd around us. The skyline looks weird and it takes me a second to realize why: no Comcast Center. No Liberty Place towers. There's only one building more than ten or fifteen stories, and it stands about twice that height, a Big-Ben-shaped

Can this be Philadelphia?

monstrosity. It's not a stone tower, more like a metal cage filled with gears and clock parts so big I can see them a mile away. Scrawled across the big dial at the top is a huge logo: *Edison-Bréguet Engine Company.*

I take Yvaine's and my hands, still clasped, and raise them toward the tower.

"If it makes you feel any better," I say, "I think your grandfather did just fine after we left."

She stares and stares.

"That weren't here before?" she says.

"Never even heard the name Breguet until two weeks ago," I said.

Yvaine looks different too. Her hair is cut short in a punk style, different lengths on each side, with a cluster of hot pink dreadlocks on the right. She's barefoot as usual, but wearing a skintight dress with a skirt so short that an inch less might get her arrested. It's ornate, too, with all sorts of buttons and a high frilly collar. The real shocker is the color — exactly the same shade as her weird bundle of hair.

Bizarre as the look is, it suits her. She looks neater. Hot. Well, she was always cute, and now, after ignition followed by two weeks of pressure buildup, everything about her is habanero hot.

She notices me noticing her.

"The front of your hair be orange!"

So are my jeans.

A peculiar horn honks and a unicycle whizzes past us. I spin around. The park is full of unicyclists. Yeah, that's right, at least a dozen wannabe clowns, minus the white face paint and red noses.

"Do you know what year it is?" I say.

Stupid question. Of course she doesn't.

"Before meetin' you, thirty-one years be me limit," she says. "But somethin' about travelin' together changes the rules."

Things look — and smell — all wrong. The air is sooty, gross, worse even than stinky London though in a different, more industrial, way. This Philadelphia is filthy for the most part, even the park full of litter.

I chase after a page from a newspaper the breeze is toying with.

It's the *Philadelphia Inquirer*, Wednesday, March 23, 2011. About eight weeks after the fateful field trip to this same park.

The version without the circus sideshow cyclists.

Gulp. Another bike passes close. This guy's riding a two-wheeler, but it's one of those old-timey ones with the giant wheel in front and the little one in back. He looks freaky tall up there in his Abe Lincoln-style outfit and stovepipe hat. Except the whole thing is turquoise — and so is the guy's beard.

Hmmm. I glance back at the paper. The left headline says, "Mine strike spikes coal prices." On the right a black and white photo — the *Inquirer* I knew has a color front page — shows a handsome black man being dragged up a set of stairs by official-looking types. "ARA leader, Joe Fairfax, apprehended by Crown Red Coats," the caption reads.

Crown Red Coats?

"What's it say?" Yvaine asks.

"Aided by an anonymous tip," I read, "Crown forces capture CRC's number one most wanted, the alleged leader of a murderous American Republican Army cell."

I glance at the flagpole by Independence Hall. Three standards flutter in the wind. A navy blue one I don't recognize, another with a red lion on a yellow field, and the familiar double cross of the Union Jack.

The British flag.

"Between us letting Ben die and the Tock's private funding for your grandfather's research..." I can't even bring myself to finish.

Yvaine leans against me. "At least we both be alive."

I give her a quick hug — every cloud does have its silver lining. But we need to figure this out, which I have a horrible feeling I already have.

"Let's go inside," I say.

We're about halfway to the entrance when she yelps, balances on one leg, and picks at her foot.

"What's wrong?"

"Stepped on somethin' sharp."

I didn't notice before, but mixed in with the papers and trash are empty glass cylinders about half the size of a roll of dimes.

"Dinna worry yourself." She tugs me forward. "I've got tough feet."

It occurs to me that Chestnut Street with its carts and carriages in some ways looks more like eighteenth-century London than the Philadelphia I remember.

Then again, maybe not.

A few carts are drawn by horses but most seem to be pedaled. They look like what you'd get if you mated a pickup truck with a bicycle, except the drivers seem to be pedaling really fast and easy, like a ten-speed going downhill. Which must have something to do with the gears, because these bike-trucks and bike-cars have lots of those. Gears, cogs, belts, whirling things — you name it, they've got it.

Most people are dressed *Titanic* style but in bright colors, and both men and women wear hats. The younger ones dress more like Yvaine and me, rejects from some Italian runway show mixing period and punk.

"Amazin'," Yvaine says. "I've never seen the like."

"Me either, and this is my hometown."

There's a big tricycle parked nearby. The brass clockwork engine block mounted behind the seat is engraved with the same *Edison-Bréguet* logo as the giant tower.

This place is way weirder than the past. Sure, Ben Franklin dying is a big deal, but that and a few watch inventions couldn't make all this happen. Could it?

Man is not God, my father would say, but that just leaves one question: who *is* God, and why'd the creator allow my little screw-ups to change everything?

A deep rumble and a hideous clanging siren knock me out of my thoughts. What I can only describe as a fire-truck-cum-steam-locomotive shoulders its way onto the street. The smaller vehicles flee in apparent terror. The thing is huge, about the size of a hook and ladder truck, and it is painted red. But the front is all train, down to the cow-catcher grill, cylindrical boiler, and belching smoke stack — although this last is ringed by red and blue lights.

Another whistling blast, and a column of white smoke streams skyward. Uniformed red figures cling to the sides.

"What in hell is that?" Yvaine says.

"Police, fire truck, military," I say. "I've no idea."

"Then we ain't wantin' t'find out."

I nod and lead her up the steps to see if Independence Hall is still open to the public.

Inside, the hall is lit by flickering yellow lamps. It's still a museum, but there the resemblance to the one I remember ends.

I stop at a painting of George Washington offering a sword to a fattish older man in red. Yvaine reads the little plaque next to it with the diction of a fourth grader.

"A victorious Lord Cornwallis accepts the surrender of General Washington at Yorktown, 1781."

"It was the other way around," I say. My sinking feeling hits rock bottom.

"With this crushing defeat the traiti...traitorous colonial rebellion begun in this room came to an end. His majesty King George III later elevated Lord Cornwallis as the first Duke of Virginia in gratitude for his services."

The next painting shows fifteen or so men hanging from the gallows.

"The signatories of the so-called Declaration of Independence," I read, "are executed here in Philadelphia after being convicted of treason. King George graciously commuted their sentences from drawing and quartering to hanging. From left to right: Thomas Jefferson, John Adams, John Hancock..."

No Ben Franklin, of course. In this world, he didn't live to sign — or rather, be hung. It makes me sick to my stomach. Call me a sappy patriot, but I was proud to be born in the country those guys made, and hell, I liked Ben before I met him. Knowing I screwed the whole thing up really bites the big one.

"This is all so wrong," I say. "We won this war. America is a free country. A democracy with no king."

"That not be what it say here."

She points at a big glossy photo of a middle-aged man in an ornate suit holding a crown and scepter. His hair and jacket are dyed red, white, and blue in the pattern of the British flag!

"His majesty Charles III," Yvaine reads, "King of Great Britain, Ireland, Scotland, America, India, China, Australia, New Zealand, South Africa, and Ceylon, head of the Commonwealth, Defender of the Faith."

I recognize Prince Charles from the tabloids. I guess he got to be king after all.

Back to the plaque. "The exhibits in this chamber commemorate the divine right of the Kings of Great Britain, and illustrate the folly of radical and democratic socialism. By the wisdom of the people and the grace of God."

Thank God there's no more to read. I press my thumb and forefinger against my eyelids. "Even in the movies, no one screws up this bad," I mutter.

"Dinna think that way." Yvaine draws my hand away from my eyes and kisses the tips of my fingers. "Your da will know how t'fix it."

I don't know if she believes that or if she just wants to.

"Need some juice?" A whisper from the shadows startles me.

Standing by the wall is a young guy wearing a dark suit with a scarlet tie that more or less matches his red mohawk and ruby nose ring. A fancy brass pocket watch dangles from a chain on his vest.

"I said, want some juice?" He holds out two tiny glass cylinders of brown liquid.

I know a drug dealer when I see one.

"We don't have any money," I say.

He looks us over. "You're a pretty one, miss. Ditch the loser and maybe we can work something out in trade. I'll even throw in a pair of shoes."

I step between them. "Hey—"

"Show time!" Yvaine whispers.

I flail around for an idea. All I can come up with is the bit from *The Princess Bride*.

I point and shout, "What in the world can that be?"

He twists around. Yvaine darts forward, slams into him, grabs the vials from his hand and the ring from his nose.

"Run, Charlie!"

We do. His screams fade behind us.

My eyes contract from the sunlight as we bolt out the hall door and around the building into an alley, where we find a big dumpster to hide behind.

Trash in bizarro Philadelphia smells exactly like trash in regular Philadelphia.

A few seconds later, the drug dealer lurches into the alleyway holding his bloody hands to his bloody nose, looks once in our direction, then keeps going.

"Clean getaway," Yvaine is squatting on the asphalt next to me.

"That was kind of mean." He isn't going to die or anything, but I'm not sure he deserved a trip to the emergency room.

"Also kind of necessary. I filched his purse." She opens the wallet to show bright-colored bills. "Damn the cull! No coin."

"We use paper currency now."

I pull out the money. There's been some inflation. King Charles glares from a ten-thousand pound note. And while I don't see any credit cards, the wallet holds a brown tinted photo of an older woman. I guess even drug dealers have mothers.

Yvaine pockets the cash and tosses the billfold into the alley.

"Good," she says, "the fool without a penny be the fool indeed. Besides, that man wanted your miss, so you should hate him."

As usual, she has a point.

"Are you my *miss?*"

She settles herself onto my lap and wriggles to make herself comfortable, which feels *really* good.

"Everythin' else be torn from me. Me folks. Billy. The grandpapa I almost had." Her big green eyes are only a couple inches from mine. She has her arms tight around me. "I'll hold onto what I got, if you dinna mind."

I don't.

We start kissing. Not the most romantic spot, but—

BING! Soft yet unmistakable. We look behind us.

A small creature is inspecting the wallet Yvaine threw away. Except it's not exactly a creature, and now it's eating the wallet. The thing rolls on six little wheels and looks like a cross between a Frankenstein Roomba and one of those floor robots Chewbacca barked at on the Deathstar.

BING! It makes a high-pitched bell noise, much softer but all too reminiscent of a Tick-Tock's chime. The little robot doesn't have any skin or shell. Gears and other mechanical bits whirl around inside the metal frame of its body.

"What in God's creation is that?" Yvaine asks.

"I don't know, but I know I don't like it."

We run down the alley, giving the mini-tock a wide berth. I didn't get a chance to look, but I'm betting somewhere inside that thing is a *Bréguet* logo.

Chapter Nineteen:
Changes

Philadelphia, March, 2011

We make our way toward my house, but after Yvaine steps on another bit of broken glass I pull her inside a J.C. Penney crossed with Old West general store.

"No shoes, no service," a clerk says, none too nicely.

"That's what we came to buy," I say. Yvaine wiggles her toes and gives him a smile that would melt the heart of a Tick-Tock if he had one.

The clerk shrugs and points.

While Yvaine browses the shoe department — if you can call a ten-foot aisle a department — I interrogate the boy who works there. He looks like he's in junior high, awfully young for a job in retail.

"So what's the deal with that Edison-Bréguet tower?"

He shakes his head. I think I'm being pitied.

"Pretend I'm from Mars," I say.

"Jolly. It's their regional corporate headquarters," he says.

"And they do what?"

"Besides being richer than the king? Make all sorts of machines. Like Identikeys and Springtorbs. Always have. Fine quality, too. E.B. stuff almost never breaks."

"Does the Edison stand for Thomas Edison?"

"Yeah, doofus. He invented Audiocyls, then merged with the Bréguet Engine Company." He pronounces the silent T at the end, so the word rhymes with suet. "Only the East India Trading Company's bigger."

Yvaine waggles a pair of leather-soled moccasins at him, hot pink to match her dress.

"What size?" he says.

Yvaine glances at me, but I'm no judge of girl feet.

"Can you measure her?" I say.

"Jolly." The boy fetches a wooden ruler from under the try-on bench. "I ain't apprenticed to a storekeep for nothing."

"Everything's so different," I say when he goes to fetch the shoes. "And it's all our fault."

"Mostly yours," she kicks at me playfully.

Way to make me feel better. "How does apprenticeship work?"

"His parents, or mayhap the parish, sell him to the master. He learns the trade, but mostly the one be concerned with losin' a mouth t'feed and t'other with workin' him for free."

"He doesn't get paid?"

"Usually only in beatings," she says. "You still gots me da's page?"

I open my jacket to show her. "Arm-wrestled Longshot for it. I won."

She snickers as the shop boy returns with pink moccasins tucked under his arm. No shoebox. Funny, these little changes. But I'm sure we'll still have to pay.

We're not three minutes out of the store when an explosion across the street nearly knocks us off our feet. The pop of the blast is all too like Donnie's teapot bomb. There's no fireball, just a gout of glass and wood and smoke that used to be a storefront.

There's a moment of silence, then the screaming starts. People run every which way. Vehicles squeal and smash into each other.

"Damn terrorists!" a pedestrian yells. "Second bombing this week."

"The owner'll be a Tory," another says. "Royalist scum ought to crawl back up the king's arse."

The shouting is interrupted by the noisy arrival of another steam-powered train-truck.

Yvaine grabs at my arm. "We dinna want to be caught up in this."

Agreed, but I can't get the screaming out of my head. Is everything bad that happens in this history my fault? No. I have to treat this like some other place or time, not really my old home at all.

Yvaine's new shoes pay for themselves as we scramble across a sidewalk covered in broken glass.

"I dinna like all these engines." She points up at the ominous tower. "Particularly that Tick-Tock cock."

I can't help but smile. "Even if it's got your family name on it?"

"We take our names from the travelin' side — *de Verge* and proud of it."

That earns her my best smile. And a pronouncement.

"The clockwork tower, the Tiny-Tock in the alley, the funny cars... I think the Tick-Tocks want it like this."

"Maybe they plays at being God, Charlie. Creatin' things in their own image."

Man is not God.

We turn off near my house.

It's still there, looking more or less the same. It's grungier, but the building was on the old side anyway, a brick duplex we shared with the Montags — the family that includes Michelle, who provided all fifteen seconds of my pre-Yvaine love life.

In my day — lacking a better sideways-universe term — the front door opened into a little hall with mailboxes and separate entrances to the units. It was usually unlocked.

Not so here. And there's no buzzer, so I have to rap on the door.

My apprehension mounts with each passing second.

"No need to break it down," a man says from inside.

I hear the sound of one bolt sliding, then another, until the door swings open to reveal a pot-bellied man in a wife-beater undershirt and suspenders, from which dangles a brass pocket watch.

"Hi, Mr. Montag," I say. "Do you know if my mother's home?"

"Who the hell are you?"

"Charlie Horologe." He won't remember the name, but he knows vaguely who I am. "Renni Horologe's son."

"Huh? The only Renni here's Renni Montag, and she ain't got no son."

My stomach clenches. Everything clenches.

Yvaine squeezes my hand.

"Can I see her, then?" I say, even though I'm terrified of what this might mean.

"Just a social call," Yvaine says.

"How I know you ain't ARA?" He snatches up his pocket watch, flips it open, and presses something that emits a loud BING! "Lemme check your Identikeys."

"Um…"

"No Identikey, no entry." He makes it rhyme.

Then slams the door in our faces.

Another round of pounding gets me nothing but a threat to call the police.

I lead Yvaine around to see if I can get at the tiny area we called the backyard. In this version of 2011, it's fenced in with barbed wire and strung with clothes lines, but a girl's there, leaning against the back porch and dragging on a Cruella de Vil cigarette.

No wonder I didn't recognize her at first. It's Michelle, but her eyebrows are scarlet, her hair is dyed black, and she's wearing a red dress so tight it must hurt. Combined with the cigarette it lends her a Shanghai opium den look. Well, except for the flip-flops.

CHAPTER NINETEEN: CHANGES

"Michelle, can I talk to you?"

Her crimson brows furrow, but she slinks over and toes open the gate in the fence.

"How come you know my name?"

Closer, she doesn't look so great. She has a lot of makeup on, what my mom calls cover-up, and it's doing a piss-poor job of covering a patch of bruises and scabs on her neck.

"I just want to talk to my mom. She used to live here, her name's Renni, brown curly hair, hazel eyes."

She licks her chapped lips.

"Sounds like my step-mom, but she never mentioned any kids. You scamming me?"

Panic is edging in. Step-mom? And where's my dad in this picture?

"Can you ask her to come out?"

Michelle shakes her head. Slowly. She seems to have trouble remembering the question.

"She never comes out," she says finally. "And why should I help? I feel like crap." She knocks the cigarette to the ground and takes out a device the size of a ping-pong ball. Two needle-like prongs project from one end. She winds a knob and presses it. CLICK!

"I'm jolly squeezed out." She winds the knob again. I hear a soft ticking, just like a mechanical watch being wound.

"It's probably an Edison-Bréguet," I whisper in Yvaine's ear.

"Not my fault," she whispers back. "We dinna choose family."

"What are you two talking about?" Michelle says.

"Inside joke," I say.

I could have told her anything. She grabs my arm and says, "I need some juice. Take you inside if you have some."

From the look of her, what she needs is an intervention.

"These?" Yvaine hands Michelle a vial of brown liquid.

"No!" I say. "Don't give —"

I'm too late. Michelle has already snatched the vial out of Yvaine's hand. She slams it into the bottom of the little clockwork thing and punches the needles into her neck—

And drops like a stone. Just drops her ass onto the pavement. I catch her shoulders before she can hit her head.

"What'd I do?" Yvaine says.

Twin trickles of blood snake down Michelle's neck. Her eyes roll back. Drool oozes from her mouth.

"Don't ever give an addict drugs," I say. "I hope she hasn't OD'd."

"What be an addict? Do she need medicine?"

How to explain?

"It's like those beggars with the shakes outside the gin houses. She needs the stuff in the little bottles."

"Then why shouldna we give it to her?"

I sigh. Yvaine's world is a long way from 'just say no.'

"It's bad for her, could even kill her. Never try this juice stuff, or anything like it. Not even once. It's deadly."

"Feels so good," Michelle mumbles.

At least she's conscious. I use her sleeve to wipe some of the drool off her face. Too bad it doesn't wipe off that creepy smile.

"Yvaine, look at me." She looks. "Promise me you'll never use this stuff — or anything like it."

She glances at the girl on the ground, then at me. "I promise."

I pry the little clockwork thing out of Michelle's fingers. The tiny cylinder embedded in the end is empty now. The prongs glisten with blood. As I thought, the device is built like a watch, all gears and little rotating parts. I can't see any battery or electronics, but I see a spring. Carefully I turn the knob she used to wind it. The spring coils and tightens.

"Look at this." I hand it to Yvaine, who studies it for a moment.

"Like the Monsieur's pocket watches."

"Or a really crude Tick-Tock."

"Bugger them!" She drops the device to the cement and stomps on it with one of her new moccasins. There's a satisfying crunch.

"My juicer... no...." Michelle says. But she doesn't look too stressed about it. She doesn't look too stressed about anything.

"Now take us to see Renni." I feel bad, but if I can find Mom maybe I can find my dad, and maybe down the road Michelle can go back to being the straight-A student who snubs me at the park.

Chapter Twenty:
Mom & Dad

Philadelphia, March, 2011

Between the two of us, we manage to get Michelle up the steps to the back door.

"Need the key." Her voice sounds weird.

"Where is it?" I say.

"Necklace."

There's a thin black cord around her neck that goes right down into the low collar of her dress. I reach in this general direction—

"No you don't." Yvaine slaps my hand away and lifts the cord-cum-key over Michelle's head.

I'm feeling pretty stoked that I managed to make my *miss* jealous when a whirling series of clicks and a BING unlocks the door. The room is dark, but where the light switch used to be I find a round knob. I give it a little twist. A really pathetic light flickers to life.

It's creepy, being inside my own house like this. The washer-dryer is gone, the place smells funny, and a tiny Asian woman in a ratty blue robe covered with even rattier dragons is folding laundry.

"Who's that?" I whisper to Michelle.

"Don't mind Sung," she says, "Renni's family has owned her forever."

The eyes in Sung's toothless walnut of a face never rise from her folding.

"Owned her?" I hear the quaver in my own voice.

"House drudge, duh!" Michelle moves into the hall.

With a final glance at the old lady, I follow.

Both halves of the duplex look to be combined now. We come to what still seems to be the living room, but the furniture is brightly colored velvet and the knob on the wall turns on two lame gas-powered overhead lanterns.

Mr. Montag drifts in, drinking beer from a bottle.

"You two again? How'd you get in?"

"They're with me, Dad," Michelle says. "Wanna see your wife."

"Ren!" he hollers, "you got visitors." He slumps into a violet velvet armchair and takes another swig from the bottle.

Mom rolls into the room in a wheelchair. It's all I can do not to run to her. She's wearing a frumpy pink nightgown and she's lost weight, a lot of weight. Her stick-figure legs are twisted at a funny angle. It hurts to think of all those afternoons I spent at the racquet club, reading on the side-lines while her tanned, muscled legs raced across the court underneath that short white skirt.

Her eyes are the same, though, and even her hair isn't so different, though it could use a wash and cut. It's not even dyed some funny color.

"Mom?"

She spins a little mechanical wheel on the arm of the chair and it drives forward. The carriage beneath is filled with gears and cogs and a huge spring.

"What's this git's game?" Mr. Montag says. "Playing at being the son of a barren woman!" He drains the last of his beer. I look down at my mom.

"What happened?" I say softly.

She doesn't even remember

"Could be worse," she says. "Polio put thousands in the brass lung."

Her gaze meets mine. It's sad, sympathetic, all the things Mom always is. But those aren't the eyes of a mother who's been missing her son for two months.

"Are you friends of Michelle's?" she asks.

I can't help myself now. I step to the chair, kneel, and take her hand.

"You don't know me?"

Behind me, Mr. Montag belches. "This is rich," he says. "Michelle, hon, get me a beer."

Michelle zombie-walks toward the kitchen, but as she passes the wheelchair my mom grabs her by the hand.

"Honey," Mom says. For a second my heart surges. "Have you been juicing again?"

Mom has always been big on the hand-touching. I can almost feel her fingers on the back of my own hand.

"Of course not." Michelle turns her head to hide the raw marks on her neck.

My mom pinches her wrist.

"Ouch," Michelle says after a second.

"If you were sober," Mom says, "you'd have slapped me for that."

I know that tone. It's the you-lied-about-doing-your-homework tone. I'd give anything to hear it directed at me right now.

Michelle laughs, a slow-motion sort of giggle.

"Duh, bitch, but I'm too stoned to care."

"Don't talk to your mother like that," Mr. Montag says.

Michelle looks at her dad. "Just because you married her doesn't make this withered husk my mom."

I'm starting to breathe fast and heavy. My head feels light.

"These be bonny flowers." Yvaine's over by the window fingering some crocuses in a china vase. She gives me a sad little smile, but everything is somehow made worse by the fact that I know Grandmom left Mom that vase, and the flowers come from her garden.

Michelle tries to go, but my mom still has her wrist. Michelle tugs and the heavy clockwork wheelchair rocks.

"I know I can't replace her," Mom says, "but I do love you."

I can't help it. I make a squealy sound — like a Yorkie that's been drop-kicked.

Michelle pulls free and stomps off.

"You two should leave," Mom says. "You clearly haven't been a good influence on Michelle."

I try to take a deep calming breath but find I can't draw in any oxygen.

Yvaine says, "Charlie tried to stop her. Be nice t'him."

Whoosh! Now I'm breathing too fast, and it hurts. Mom looks at me again, more closely this time. Is there a flicker of recognition in her eyes? A whiff? I don't care how faint it is.

"Thank you." She's talking to a stranger, which kills me. "But I think Michelle needs to be alone right now."

"And if I find out you're the ones that juiced her up..." Mr. Montag makes a little boxing motion with his hands, one of which is still holding the empty beer bottle.

I have to get out of here. I bolt through the back door, the clotheslines, the gate, and into the alley.

I mash myself into a corner of the alley and drop, pressing my back to the rough brick wall, the pavement hard beneath my ass, hoping the discomfort will distract me from the pain that drove me out of the house.

Up to now, I'd say this whole adventure has been sometimes scary, sometimes smelly, sometimes painful, often exhilarating, but overall? Fun more often than not. Like a weird summer camp where one of the campers even knows my name. That's the part that makes me feel like a dick-wad — the fact that I destroyed the free world while I was having a good old time farting around with Yvaine.

I've screwed things up so bad I don't even have a home. I've deleted my life, my parents' marriage, my whole freaking country — the democratic version, anyway.

"Charlie? Charlie!" Slowly the voice penetrates and I feel the hands shaking my shoulders.

I look up. Yvaine has tears in her eyes.

"Stay with me," she says. "You promised."

"My mother doesn't even know me."

She kisses me — on my eyelids. It might be the sweetest kiss I've ever had.

"At least she be alive, Charlie. Tick-Tocks left me only empty ghosts. You can save her."

She presses something dry and scratchy into my hands. The thistle I gave her in France.

"Us travelers only has each other." She closes her hands over mine and the flower. "For us, normal folks canna never be enough."

The world behind seems lost in a blur, but her face stands out crisp and focused. Real.

"What about your da?" she says.

"That wasn't him," I say. "Here my mom married the loser neighbor." Although, to his credit, in my time Mr. Montag is a computer contractor who probably wouldn't be caught dead in a wife-beater.

"Wherever your da was, the timequake would've left him alone. History changes around us. Unless the Tocks got him, he remembers you still."

BING! We startle. Another of those clockwork garbage-eating robots is right next to us. A little panel on its head opens to reveal a round keyhole just like the one on Michelle's door.

BING! It scuttles back and forth on its toy-sized wheels, gear-guts whirling.

"What do you think it wants?" I ask.

"Nothin' good." She lunges at it. My girl is *brave*.

The Tiny-Tock scoots back, spins around, and whizzes across the alley, right into an eight-inch hole in the wall. Yvaine runs over and squats to look inside, but it's vanished.

"There be all sorts of gears an' stuff in there," she says, "but I don't see—"

The alley rocks and sways beneath our feet. Not for long, and not too hard, but there's no mistaking it.

Timequake.

I hear the sirens in the distance and feel the tingle of fear in my veins.

"Are you thinking what I'm thinking?" I say.

We're both standing now.

"That running away sounds—"

"Young master?" The voice comes from the yard behind the house. The old Asian house slave.

She holds a small lacquered red box out to me. It's covered in dust.

"This for you."

The sirens are getting louder.

"What?"

"Master Li give to me in Shanghai when I young girl. He say give to boy who come in year of rabbit. Boy who say he Ms. Ren's son."

I take the box, which weighs almost nothing. She hurries away without a word.

Inside is a folded sheet of rice paper. The letter is written in my dad's cipher.

Dear Charlie,

If you're reading this, you must know what we are. I'm sorry I was unable to tell you myself on your birthday. Sophie and I overshot — something she's prone to do — and arrived to find you gone and your mother in a tizzy. But as you're probably aware, she isn't fretting about it anymore. We hope you weathered the big quake safely. It caused more than a little excitement for Sophie and me, and unfortunately one of our metallic acquaintances forced me to undertake an unexpected journey without her.

I find myself alone and writing this letter in a Shanghai guest room, June 10, 1948. They speak more English here than I remember, so I plan to stay for a bit, hoping you might join me. Desperate times call for desperate measures, and so I arranged for little Sung to be sent to your grandmother with very specific instructions. Sad business, really, but trust me, she'll have a better life in Philadelphia than here.

On the first of every month, I'll visit a place in Shanghai we once spoke of, the old place where your mother might find her favorite beverage. Look for me there.

But first, find Sophie. She should be close, in a timely way, to where we last met.

Remember, Man is not God,
Your loving father

"Charlie!" Yvaine shakes my arm.

I've been so focused on the letter that even she ceased to exist. But I look up to see red and chrome fill the mouth of the alley. Sirens blare over a high-pitched hissing whistle. Steam fills the air.

We turn the other way only to see men in long red coats hustling toward us.

"Crap!" I pull Yvaine back into the yard.

"We be stuck here on cooldown for two weeks," she says.

I start pounding on the door to my house. There's no answer.

"You two!" One of the officers waves a billy club. "Lie down on the ground and spread 'em."

The letter is still in my hand, but I can't let anyone else get it. If a Tick-Tock finds it, he'll know where to go.

So I eat it.

I'm swallowing the paper when the burly men in the round red caps force us to the ground.

One of them grabs my hair and pulls my face toward his. "This is them."

He's holding a paper of his own. On it is a blurry photo of Yvaine and me looking down at something. Underneath, the caption reads, *Wanted for High Treason.*

Chapter Twenty-One:
Bighouse

Philadelphia, March, 2011

"**N**ame?" the booking officer asks, his fingers poised over a manual typewriter straight out of a movie featuring a hard-drinking and suicidal depression-era writer — if it then went and mated with an alarm clock. "Name?" he repeats before I can even answer.

The big cop who holds me in a vise grip — as if the steel manacles around my wrists and ankles aren't enough — punctuates the question with an elbow to my kidney.

"Charlie Horologe." It never hurts to be honest with the police.

The desk guy squints at me then taps the keys, hunt-and-peck method.

"John Doe. Charge: high treason." His eyes narrow again. "Officer Roberts," he says to the vise grip at my elbow, "how would you describe the male suspect?"

Officer Roberts tugs on my arms and twists me around to face him.

"Ordinary."

The pencil pusher nods, then consults his pocket watch.

Yvaine — Jane Doe — is processed the same way except for one difference.

Description: attractive.

Taking our mug shots is quite the procedure.

The camera is roughly the size and shape of a jukebox. It rolls around on shopping cart wheels and has — surprise! — lots of cogs and levers. The backplate reads: *Eastman Dry Plate Company, Daguerreotechnic series V, powered by genuine Edison-Bréguet Springtorb.*

The photographer wears a green visor. He spends a few minutes winding the camera with a ridiculous oversized key. An officer jams me into a stiff wooden chair. Another turns some knobs on the wall, and the gas lamp's flames leap higher.

"Hold still," the photographer says.

As if Officer Roberts leaves me any other choice.

The photographer loads a soda-can-sized wax cylinder into the side of the machine and spends an awfully long time alternating between adjusting his knobs and dials and peering through what must be the viewfinder. The thing must be a son of a bitch to focus.

Yvaine is being held a few feet away by a female officer I christen Big Bertha.

"Is time making it hard for him to take our picture?" I ask her. Yvaine, not Big Bertha.

"I dinna ken—"

She gasps when Officer Roberts smacks me upside the head so hard I see stars.

"No talking."

I blink and lift my chained hands to my face.

The photographer presses a button. "I've got it." CLICK! Yellowish bulbs flash and the camera gears whirl. We hear a ratchety clacking noise for a good two minutes as the protruding wax cylinder rotates. Finally, the machine rings like a kitchen timer. The photographer pulls out the cylinder and examines it.

"Perfect."

Interesting. He pressed the shutter at the exact moment my hands were cradling my face. And he doesn't take Yvaine's photo until Big Bertha has a momentary urge to stand between her and the camera.

The fun stops when they shove Yvaine through one door and me through another.

I protest eloquently but Officer Roberts is unmoved. They even take Yvaine's dried thistle from me, crumbling it into a trashcan as I watch. But on the plus side, they don't know what to make of her dad's brass page. They let it clatter to the floor and don't even notice when I grab it up and shove it into my scratchy new set of striped pajamas.

We traitors have our own cell ward. Or at least male traitors, because there's no sign of Yvaine. Her absence after our weeks together is like a stone on my chest.

I glance around. A single concrete wall forms the back of all the cells — no windows — and the other three 'walls' are just rows of iron bars. The door is more bars, with a big solid lock. Not that opening the cell would do any good, since the short hall leads to another door thick enough for a bank vault. The only furniture is a stained mattress and a steel chamber pot. Unfortunately, I'm now an old hand with chamber pots.

"Are you okay?" the man in the next cell asks.

I lift my head to see the handsome black guy from the paper, the supposed murderous terrorist leader. He sure doesn't look homicidal. In fact, with his little round spectacles and short beard, no doubt due to lack of a razor, he looks like my seventh-grade math teacher.

"Not really," I say.

"Joe Fairfax." He offers his hand through the wall of bars between our cells.

"Charlie Horologe."

His grip is firm but gentle.

"Would that we met under better circumstances."

"Are you really a rebel leader?" I ask.

He laughs. "I'm a Republican, and an American, and a colored man, but a free man. If that makes me a rebel, then I'm pleased by the label."

"I'm a fan of due process and government by the people myself," I say.

"You look young for all that, but looks can be deceiving."

"What's going to happen to us?" I'm hoping the write-up and mug shots indicate at least some kind of justice system.

"They'll try us," he says, "find us guilty, and if we're lucky, hand us off to the firing squad."

"What if we're innocent?"

"The Court of High Treason isn't familiar with that term."

"How long does this take?" Hopefully, longer than I have left on my cooldown.

"Justice is swift. Less than a week."

That's bad, but it isn't what bothers me most.

"I was arrested with a girl," I say. "Do you know where they'll have put her and what'll happen to her?"

"Same charge?"

I nod.

"She'll be in the female wing of the facility," he says, "but the good news is they don't usually execute women."

"They keep them in jail?"

He shakes his head. "The colony can't afford it. They're sold and someone pockets the silver."

Whichever movie character said prison time is slow time was right. I have a lot of time to think about Yvaine and entertain Joe with stories about a 'hypothetical' United States of America, complete with separate executive, legislative, and judicial branches, elected presidents serving no more than eight years, and all the rest.

To say he's interested is an understatement.

"For your age," he says, "you've an unprecedented level of political scholarship."

I shrug. "Just kind of absorbed it bit by bit. How's your knowledge of history?"

"I read my share." He pushes his glasses up on the bridge of his nose.

"You know what happened to Ben Franklin?" I ask.

"Who?"

I guess dying early didn't do for him what it did for Tupac Shakur.

When I grill Joe about the broad strokes, it turns out the French economy never rebounded after the Continental Wars, and the stinking Brits — his words, not mine — have things so buttoned up that European politics are totally different.

Which has at least one upside: The Germans are still a bunch of tiny kingdoms, and Joe's never heard of Adolf Hitler.

Our on-and-off dialogue continues for what I think is two days, but it's hard to tell. The only thing that breaks up the monotony is the periodic arrival of really awful food.

Eventually we turn to topics of a more personal nature.

"You're clearly in love," he says after I finish an enthusiastic monologue about Yvaine.

I guess I am.

"It feels like fate threw us together for a reason," I say. "Like a one in a million shot in the dark that just has to be."

"When it's right, it always feels that way."

My lawyer comes the third day. He's fat, he has on a ridiculous wig, and his suit is canary yellow.

"I'd recommend a guilty plea," he says. "The evidence is rather damning."

He holds up a little wax cylinder, pretty much a miniature version of the one the photographer used in the camera.

"What's that?" I ask.

He shrugs, inserts the cylinder into his double-sized pocket watch, and presses a knob. An eerie little voice recording plays, full of static.

"This office has incontrovertible evidence that the suspect, one Charles Horologe, is part of a conspiracy to assassinate his majesty. Verified, supervisor for the prosecution, under-secretary Fusée, office of the Lord Proprietor of Pennsylvania."

"There you have it," my lawyer says.

"But none of it's evidence! No jury would buy that."

"Jury?" His wig bounces. "Parliament abolished juries over a hundred years ago. The magistrate will have no choice but to convict on this basis." He shakes the cylinder. "Undersecretary Fusee is a very important man." He pats my shoulder through the bars. "I sympathize. I really do, but I'd plead guilty."

"Is there any other way to plead?"

He looks confused.

"What was *my* name on that recording?" I say.

"John Doe, of course."

Only a time traveler could remember my name long enough to record it. My favorite crack-faced Tick-Tock made that cylinder — and he even signed it.

"It's funny that the Lord Proprietor's office should accuse you of plotting to assassinate the king," Joe tells me after the lawyer leaves.

"It won't be so funny when they shoot me and sell my girlfriend into slavery."

"True, but with a little luck, I intend to do just that."

"Shoot me and buy my girlfriend?"

The flickering gas lamps gleam in his dark eyes.

"No, my friend. I intend to kill the king."

Chapter Twenty-Two:
Unexpected

Philadelphia, March, 2011

Lying on the smelly prison mattress, I dream Yvaine and I get frisky on a bearskin rug in front of a roaring fire. The James Bond theme song blares out of nowhere — Tick-Tocks burst into the room and suddenly we're on snowboards, hurtling down an alpine slope with the Tocks in hot pursuit. They're on gear-and-cog snowmobiles, blasting away at us with clockwork Uzis —

I wake in my cell. In the low-burning gas light I see Joe sitting cross-legged on his bed, eyes fixed on the ward door.

What I don't see are any guards.

The distant popcorn sound of gunfire is punctured by a bigger explosion. The floor vibrates ever so slightly. Sirens begin to wail.

Joe walks to the door of his cell and rattles it.

Suddenly someone else is in his cell. Someone in a tan uniform with knee-high boots who flies up out of the floor, back-flips through the air like an acrobat, and slams face-first into the wall of bars separating us. The impact knocks a military-style cap off shiny blond hair. A thin pink scar runs across a sharp-featured face I'd recognize anywhere.

"Aunt Sophie?"

Aunt Sophie?

"Charlie, what the hell are you doing here?"

"Major?" Joe says. "Where'd you come from?"

Sophie ignores him. I feel almost naked under the gaze of someone who really sees me.

"God, Charlie! What luck! I thought you were lost down-time for sure."

"How —"

"You two know each other?" Joe says. "And how'd you get the ward door open? I thought it would take explosives."

"It will, Colonel." She slips off her backpack and hands it to him. "Four sticks of dynamite and detonators."

Two big pistols are tucked into her belt. She pulls one out and hands it to Joe, butt first.

"Let me get to work on this lock."

She unzips the backpack, removes a soft leather case full of tools, and kneels before Joe's cell door.

"Aunt Sophie, you came for him?"

"Don't worry, I'll get you out too. But I have to open this door before the guards come back or the Tocks find us."

She works two metal sticks into the lock and wiggles them around. If we survive, I have to learn how to do that.

"Thanks for the uniform, Major," Joe says, pulling a red jacket from the knapsack.

"Charlie, you know about us, right?" Sophie says. "Did you only hop back a short way? You don't look much older."

"London, 1725," I say. "But I met a girl."

"Double wow!" I can't see her face but her voice cracks.

Joe pulls a guard-style shirt over his head.

"This girl you've been talking about," he says. "She's a Brit?" He looks awfully confused.

And no wonder. He's a smart guy, but this morning I told him I was a time traveler and he thought I was talking about the best time of year to vacation.

"Colonel Fairfax, get those detonators ready," Sophie says.

He pulls more stuff out of the pack.

Despite the muffled sound of gunfire in the distance, hope is starting to filter back into me. Sophie seems to know what she's doing, and with this kind of firepower, maybe we can grab Yvaine and get out of here.

"Aunt Sophie, I got a message from Dad. Did he send you one too?"

She drops one of her lock-picks. "Damn! Not since the Tocks forced him to jump. With history so fubared, I was trying to distract myself from never seeing him again with helping out the ARA here, but now that I've found you—"

"I know where he is!" I've always loved being the bearer of good news.

She stops with the lock-picking and leaps toward me, reaching through the bars.

"Screw this place — drop us downtime and we'll get him right now."

God, I'd like to see him. But I can't just leave with Sophie.

"I'm on cooldown for at least ten more days."

She frowns. "What's cooldown?"

"What Yvaine and I call the time between traveling."

Joe holds up a stick of dynamite. "Stop yabbing about the temperature and get that door open." He lays the explosives in a row on his bed and fits each one with a clockwork mechanism.

"Let's just get out of here." Sophie grabs for my arm.

I leap out of reach. "I can't leave without Yvaine."

Sophie sighs. "I respect that." She goes back to work on the lock. "So you're normal — a couple of weeks between jumps? Hah! I'm the family freak."

"What do you mean? Aren't all travelers freaks?"

"My refractory period — what you call a cooldown — is only ten minutes."

"Wow!" I say. "That's great. You're ready to go already?"

"In about two minutes, but my range is only a couple days

and I never end up where I want. I'm not much of a time traveler, more a time tiptoer."

I didn't realize it varied so much.

"I'm almost ready with this door," she says. "Once I open it, Joe can escape and history will change. That'll bring the Tocks down on us fast."

"How will they know? Timequake?"

"Right," she says. "We won't feel it, being in the same present, but we'll feel whatever they do downtime to screw us over."

The whole thing is hard to get my head around. Opening the door is like letting the Tiny-Tock get away. The Tocks must have gone back in time to manufacture the treason charge and tip off the goon squad.

"Tick-Tocks don't have cooldowns?" I ask.

"Just those damn thirteen chimes and however long it takes them to dial in their destination." She squeals like a schoolgirl. "Lock's almost ready."

"Why didn't you tell me what I was?" I say.

She frowns. "Time got away from us? Let me make it up to you. Where's this Yvaine of yours?"

Joe has finished gathering up his dynamite. "She's probably in the women's maximum security wing."

Sophie nods. "I know where that is."

"You better get him there fast," Joe says. "The boy's so in love he might melt."

My face sure feels hot.

Sophie positions herself carefully with one hand on the lock-pick.

"Joe, when I open the door, blow the ward and lose yourself in the chaos. Just don't get shot by our side, the diversionary force is about thirty strong."

"What about me?" I rattle the bars of my cage.

She keeps one hand on Joe's door and reaches the other toward me.

"Grab my hand. After I open the door, I'll hop us out of here — only about five minutes, but brace yourself for a rough ride."

I reach through the bars to take her hand. She twists the lock one last time and kicks the door open. The building shakes.

Then we're yanked uptime.

The *in-between* flashes like a strobe light and we're somewhere else. My face hurtles at something white and I barely get my arms up in front of me before I hit.

Good thing. That some*thing* is a toilet some*body* forgot to flush.

"Oh God," Sophie says. "Why can't I land on my feet like a normal person?"

She's half under the stall partition of an industrial-looking restroom. Her torso is in with me, her legs clear through into the next stall.

"Charlie, be a dear and pull me out?"

Sophie clutches her remaining pistol, an old-style revolver Humphrey Bogart might've used. We slip out of the restroom and into what looks to be the prison guard equivalent of a teacher's lounge. Big Bertha's slightly thinner twin sits at a desk and talks into some kind of clockwork contraption with a mouthpiece shaped like a badminton birdie.

Sophie streaks over and puts her gun to the guard's head. "Don't move."

Bertha 2.0 looks sufficiently cowed.

"Charlie, get her weapons."

I slide around and unbuckle the woman's belt, claiming her billy club and a set of manacles.

"We're looking for the girl named Jane Doe," I say. "Tiny, pink hair, came in here three or four days ago for high treason."

CHAPTER TWENTY-TWO: UNEXPECTED

Bertha 2.0 talks very slowly. "That one was tried yesterday and sold at auction."

Pent up frustration bursts in my brain and I swing the billy club at Bertha's face, but the look of terror in her eyes stops me before I connect.

Sophie mashes the gun against her temple.

"Who bought the girl?"

"I have to look in the file."

"Slowly, then," Sophie says. "My nephew here's got a short fuse."

I'm starting to feel like a creep about that, but I glower at Bertha for effect. She rolls her chair over to a file cabinet and thumbs through a series of manila envelopes.

"Here," she says after a minute. "The Lord Proprietor's household."

"Who is he?" I shiver inside. He's the guy Mr. Fusée works for.

"William Penn IV," Sophie says. "His family owns Pennsylvania."

How do you own a state?

We leave Bertha handcuffed to her file cabinet.

"I thought we couldn't shoot anyone," I say.

Sophie grins. "They don't know that." I follow her down a corridor until we're stopped by a sliding door made from steel bars.

"What now? How do we rescue Yvaine from this Lord Proprietor?"

"We find a way." Sophie pulls out her picks and sets to work on the lock. "I might as well get this open, but if we can hold out another four or five minutes I can hop us out of the building entirely."

"Into a latrine?"

"One time your dad and I popped up smack in the middle of the Battle of Gettysburg."

"Been there, done that. Different war," I say.

"A rush, isn't it?"

Not really.

"Actually, Yvaine's pretty good at landing where she wants." I try not to picture the Lord Proprietor taking inventory of his new slave girl. "She hopped us from London eighty years to her old house in France, right under the kitchen table."

Sophie smiles. "Damned impressive. The further I go, the crazier the exit. It's better with your father, but alone I don't dare go more than a couple hundred yards."

"Why's that?"

"When you travel together, your skills blend. So with your dad I can go much further uptime without picking up so much angular velocity."

"Yvaine didn't know that."

"Not surprising. There's a lot we don't know. Like why the Tocks are trying to make history into a hell-hole—"

CHIME! A Tick-Tock drops out of a hole in the ceiling behind us. He lands quiet as a cat and draws his sword.

"Use the gun!" Aunt Sophie yells while she fiddles with the lock.

I snatch the pistol from her belt, point it at the Tick-Tock, and squeeze.

The trigger won't budge.

"The safety!" she yells.

I've never shot a gun, but the Tick-Tock is only about five feet away. I flick the switch on the side, aim, and squeeze again.

BAM! The unexpected kick knocks the weapon from my hands. But I must have hit him or at least grazed him — he stops, unbuttons his blue police coat, and examines the gauges and dials decorating his clockwork innards.

"Done!" With a rattling scrape Sophie slides the door open and drags me through.

The Tick-Tock lurches after us. My aunt pulls the door shut right in his face.

The bars bang against the jamb and rebound, sliding to a

stop a couple inches ajar. We back away as the Tock thrusts his sword between the bars but makes no move to open the door.

"Hurry!" Sophie says, dragging me by my arm.

The Tick-Tock just stands there, watching us. He's got the crack on his face, so this is Rapier, the same one that was after Ben Franklin. He glances around, then uses a single finger to spin one brass dial on his chest after another. The Roman numerals and double hands on one look exactly like a clock face.

"Why doesn't he open the door?" I say as we turn the corner.

CHIME. Countdown to time travel.

"Tocks are way out of phase," Sophie says. "More than us. They can't move anything."

CHIME.

"The hell they can't! This one grabbed me in London, dragged me down the street."

CHIME. The sound is fainter as we leave Rapier behind.

"You're lucky to be alive, but that's different. I said they can't move any*thing*. We're out of phase too, just not as far. They can move time travelers — or kill them."

CHIME.

I guess that explains why the Tick-Tock just stood there in Ben Franklin's churchyard when I closed the gate in his face.

"So closing a door stops them?"

CHIME. I can barely hear it now.

"For the whole minute it takes them to wind themselves up and travel into our future. The only thing I know that holds them up for long is a really high-voltage shock."

Sophie's got all sorts of valuable info.

We plunge into a big open gallery filled with prisoners clustered at the bars of their cells. They cheer and bang against them and reach their hands out when they see us running but we veer away. I glance down to see row after row of cell blocks stacked beneath us. We're on the top floor of what must be a ten or fifteen-story shaft. Jail all the way down!

We're almost cut off by a couple guards at a T-shaped junction but we put on the juice to get ahead of them. The officers swing into pursuit just ten feet behind us, legs pumping and clubs held high.

In front of us, a heavy ward door opens and a squad of rifle-armed guards hustles through.

With the Rapier Tick-Tock right on their heels.

"Hands above your heads!" shouts a guard with shiny things on his shoulders. "You're trapped!"

Four gun barrels are leveled in our direction. Sophie doesn't even pause, just hurtles right at them.

"Stay with me, Charlie!"

Holding my hand in hers, she hops up onto the rail of the balcony and gives me a tug.

She's crazy for sure and I must be too, because I plant my free hand on the rail and plunge over the side with her.

Chapter Twenty-Three:
Plans

Philadelphia, March, 2011

My stomach somersaults as we tumble down the gallery shaft. The ground floor rises toward us just as fast.

"Uptime!" Sophie cries.

My neck jerks as our descent reverses and we pop up into the swirling whirling *in-between* —

Then slide out sideways onto a long table.

I lose my grip on Aunt Sophie as we spill across a sea of silverware. Plates, glasses, and food break, tip over, and splatter in our wake. By the time I roll to a stop, I have to extract a fork lightly embedded in the meat of my palm.

"Major," a familiar voice says, "do you have something against shepherd's pie?"

"How long since I left you in that cell?" Aunt Sophie asks Joe Fairfax once we're off the table and I've pressed a napkin against the fork wound.

"Two days," he says. "I thought you must be dead or captured."

She runs her fingers through her hair, picking out bits of mashed potatoes and peas.

"You know me, always popping up unexpectedly."

His smile is bright against his dark face. "I'm not going to complain. And we've made progress here."

Sophie holds up ten fingers then points an extra one.

"You'd better have. The king gets here in eleven days."

"Why's he coming?" I say.

"2011 is King Charles's Silver Jubilee, the twenty-fifth anniversary of his reign, so he's touring the empire. And when he comes here, he'll be celebrating up at the Lord Proprietor's palace."

I have to stop myself from running out into the street and hailing whatever passes for a cab.

"You've got it bad," Aunt Sophie says when we we're alone.

"I have to find her," I say. "Back in France, time gave us the weirdest preview of Yvaine and me as a couple. Like seeing the future. We went downtime two weeks and kind of ran into ourselves."

"Your residuals?" She grins.

"Yvaine called them time-ghosts."

"Close enough." Sophie leads me to the kitchen and pours a glass of water. "How'd you feel about yourselves?"

I help myself to a cold beer from the icebox. The taste makes me think of Yvaine.

"Confused," I say.

"Residuals are just the universe's way of putting a normal-person gloss on our abnormal existence. Your dad's got a theory, says travelers have an extra dimension of motion, what he calls meta-time. Whatever the current history is, like this no-America Philadelphia, the entirety of it — past, present, and future — is our meta-present. The history you grew up with, that's in our meta-past. It doesn't exist for us anymore."

Big bummer, since that's where my mom is.

"We can't travel there?"

"Sorry, Charlie. We're stuck in our shared time traveler meta-present. You and I are standing here getting older. Eventually we'll die and meta-time will go on the way regular time goes on for normals. If you double back on yourself you'll just find time-ghosts." She snickers. "Phantoms the universe creates to explain us away."

"But if we change things back," I say, "doesn't the meta-past become the meta-present again?"

"Easier said than done."

"Didn't Dad have to change time to send his message?"

She nods. "Any forward communication does. But you have to be careful. Little alterations have a way of snowballing — and Tocks are good at spotting changes."

Yeah, I've seen that in action.

"Anyway, your Yvaine's in the present — *this* present — so first things first."

Sophie takes me to what, judging by the guards at the door, is the rebels' inner sanctum. When we find Joe I ask him why every inch of wall inside is plastered with photos.

"Since we plan on taking out the king at the Jubilee banquet," he says, "we've been infiltrating and documenting every aspect of the preparations."

"Can I look at them?" I explain the whole Yvaine-should-be-at-the-palace thing.

"Knock yourself out," he says.

The black and white — well, brown and white — photos are sharp enough, but I have to climb on a chair to see the ones tacked up by the moldings. Looking at them, I get a sense of an enormous ballroom with big columns and tables for hundreds of guests. But other photos show preparations, decorations, and entertainment, including giant metal birdcage-things in different shapes and sizes.

"What are all these cages?" I ask.

"The party's theme is the diversity of the commonwealth," Joe says, "so they've hauled in captive animals from all over the empire. Tigers and snakes and the like. Of course, the real snake sits on the throne."

There are a *lot* of photos. While I slog through them,

Sophie goes to shower and Joe joins some of his cronies at a table across the room.

With my courthouse mugshot experience and Bréguet's backward-facing son in mind, I'm betting we time travelers don't photograph well. I study every picture, every person, and every part of every person until I'm exhausted — hey, I broke out of jail and fought a Tick-Tock today. Running for your life really takes it out of you.

One cluster of photos shows a bunch of girls posed on long tables. Their attire is, well, minimal, barely more than bikinis, and their limbs contort about each other like a giant game of tabletop twister. I'm not in the mood for soft porn right now, I just—

Spot something. Just the one shot. A single image of a leg, twisted up with a bunch of other girls', but I'd know that little peanut-shaped birthmark anywhere. I call over to Joe.

"What's the deal with these girls?"

He drifts over to look.

"Yours mixed in with them? Makes sense if she's young and pretty. They're buffet decorations."

"I'm still confused," I say.

"That's because you're a human being and not a Royalist," he says. "Think of those slaves as human sculpture. Just a bunch of pretty flesh holding up platters of delicacies."

"And your team is sneaking into this party?"

"We are, but if I'm catching your drift, you'd better know our tickets are entrance only. Even if we succeed, the security forces will make sure there's no coming home."

"I don't care. I'm coming with."

The rebel base was once someone's house, but the windows are boarded over and the occupancy has at least octupled. It reminds me of our rank little cellar back in London, but with running water and toilets. Even if the toilets are powered by clockwork mechanisms, I'm still glad to have them.

After my first shower in a month, I find my aunt talking to a dark-skinned hard-muscled woman in bright-colored fatigues, with strong features and short black hair.

"I found Yvaine's photo," I say. "She's going to be at the king's party!"

"Do you two need privacy?" the dark woman asks. She has a lilting accent, maybe Indian.

"I'm sorry, Parvati," Sophie says.

The woman smiles. "Just find me when you're ready for bed." And with that she gives my aunt a full-on kiss on the lips.

"How come you never told me?" I say as soon as Parvati leaves.

"You never asked." Sophie smiles. "If you think it's hard being a time traveler with Yvaine, imagine what a crimp the whole boy/girl pair thing makes in my sex life."

Kinda sad. Me, I'm fine with the way the rules glue Yvaine and me together — more than fine. Now if I can just rescue her, get Sophie back to Dad, and fix the world, I'm eager to pick up where we left off on that whole pair thing.

"Where did you and Dad get your 411 on time travel?"

"Some from our parents," she says, "but mostly Fink concocts his crazy theories from studying the *Brief History*."

"Which is?"

"*A Brief History of Meta-Time* is our name for what old-school time travelers managed to write down. Way back in meta-time, before the war, somebody knew how to make metal sheets that are basically immune to time. But we've only collected a few, and the sheets are all scattered every which where and when."

"We found one in France!" I pull it out. "Can you read it?"

Aunt Sophie sighs. "Ciphers give me migraines, but your dad has it mostly worked out."

"This one has something to do with a clock inventor named Bréguet." I tell her what happened in France.

"I was wondering where all this gearhead bullshit came

from. Give the page to your dad if we find him. Fink deals with the Regulator mumbo-jumbo." She pats one of the two pistols strapped to her hips. "I keep us alive."

I remember Dad's pile of pages. "That word, *Regulator*? I found it on this page, in Latin."

"Not surprising," Sophie says. "He wrote most of the pages we have. But he's been dead for meta-forever, since the time-war. He was the first traveler — we're all descended from him."

"Shit! Then Yvaine and I are..." I'm too upset to finish the sentence. And my aunt looks *amused*.

"All travelers are related," she says. "But don't worry, I'm sure it's distant. Anyway, your grandparents were third cousins and you turned out fine. We sometimes marry normals to mix things up."

Like Mom.

"Not to mention," she says, "the Tocks don't leave many travelers to choose from."

I feel a little better. But I can almost hear Yvaine's voice in my ear saying *Dinna worry, Charlie*, and it makes me miss her so much I change the subject.

"What's the Tick-Tocks' deal?" I ask. "Why do they hate us?"

She grabs her head with both hands and twists savagely. I cringe, but she seems pleased with the resulting neck pop.

"Your dad has some new theory he's working on, but it boils down to the Tocks showing up because travelers messed with history. Karmic pest control, if you will. That's why the family motto is *Man is not God*. Our parents beat into our heads that we should only observe, never change."

"So why are you helping Joe's rebels?"

She grins ear to ear. "I was never big on rules. That's Fink's department. And motto or no motto, slavery is wrong."

"Will Dad be mad at you?"

"He'll get over it. Besides, not all travelers think that way.

There's a whole group that used to believe in changing the timeline."

"Used to?"

"Fink makes a big thing of it, calls them *manipulators* because they changed things and maybe worked with the Tocks. But like us, they're mostly dead."

"I don't think I get it."

"Me neither." Aunt Sophie rearranges herself on the couch. "Speaking of Fink, tell me exactly what his letter said."

"He's stuck in Shanghai, 1948." I give her the details.

"Even if we rescue your girl," she says, "hell if I know how all three of us are going to get back to 1948."

"There's no way I can take both of you downtime together?" I'm pretty sure I know the answer, but I want to be sure.

"If you bring me, you'll just leave Yvaine stranded here. Then in China, since I can only take either you *or* your father, it'll just be the same situation but with two guys instead of two girls."

"Who gets left behind if I open a time-hole while both of you are touching me?"

She shrugs. "It's kind of random."

"They can't jump in the hole afterward?" I ask.

"Suicide, Charlie."

"You sure?"

"Saw someone try it." She makes an ugly face. "They went into the void and never came out."

And that was one of my better ideas. I'm guessing that leaves Plan B, but I don't think she'll like it.

"That doesn't seem to be true of the Tick-Tock's hole," I say. "My first time, I followed one from the Philly I grew up in to London two hundred years back."

It's not easy to surprise my aunt, but the look on her face is incredulous.

"You jumped in a Tock's hole?"

I grin. "Yvaine thought it was crazy too."

Aunt Sophie kicks one leg up onto the back of the couch —
good thing she never wears skirts.

"The Tick-Tocks and us both open time-holes," she says,
"but Fink thinks the Tocks use a different mechanism. Their
holes last longer and they dial in their destination before
they start chiming."

Here goes.

"We're pretty much agreed," I say, "that Tick-Tocks are
literally time machines, right?"

"Sentient, mobile, *deadly* time machines."

"And you said electricity could knock one out?" She nods.
"So if we stunned a Tick-Tock, maybe we could just dial up
Shanghai, 1948, open a hole, and jump back."

Down come the legs and off the couch comes Sophie, who
starts pacing.

"Jesus, Charlie, there are so many things wrong with
that idea."

"Such as?"

She jabs a finger at me. "First, it's dangerous as hell —
the shock only puts them out for a few minutes. Second,
there *are* no electrical transformers in this present — the
Tocks have seen to that. Third, they only show up when
you *don't* want them."

I'm tempted to jab a finger right back at her, but I only
have two points.

"This Lord Proprietor guy seems to have a Tick-Tock
working for him. And I know a little something about
electricity."

I tell her how Leyden jars work.

"They're all about the high voltage," I say. "If we chain a
couple big ones together we can deliver tens of thousands of
volts — just once."

"Well, then," Sophie says, "if you're right about the Lord

Proprietor's Tock, we can be pretty sure where he'll be." Her fists are balled on her hips and the scar on her face stands out against her fair skin. She's pumped.

"Tocks know damn well we travel in pairs," she says. "There's nothing they like better than to grab one, then wait for the other to trot in like a lamb to the slaughter."

We get to working out the details.

Chapter Twenty-Four:
Empire

Philadelphia, April, 2011

The plan is, well, zany.

The three of us — Sophie, Parvati, and me — pose as pickle vendors. Parvati doesn't totally understand what we're up to, but the pickle thing was her idea. Salt water helps boost the capacity of batteries, and when I started testing my Leyden jars it reminded her of pickling back home. Thankfully, having our brine-filled capacitors packed with spicy Indian pickles doesn't seem to interfere with holding a charge.

The security team at the palace strip-searches us, studies our forged Identikeys, inspects every molecule of our stuff, and makes us all eat a pickle from each jar. Good thing these little gherkins are small. I'll burp salty vinegar for hours as it is.

The giant pickle jars are installed in the back of a street vendor cart with a clockwork pedal-powered unicycle up front and sideboards painted with colorful cartoons of a pickle-chomping monkey god. All three of us are wearing cheesy Indian costumes — when I saw myself in the mirror, I looked like a pale-faced Aladdin with orange hair. But wheeling our pickle cart into the circus atmosphere of the ballroom, we blend right in.

The hall is already chaotic, and the guests haven't even shown up yet. Lush fabrics and gold swag cover every surface, tables are piled with party favors, the staff includes costumed Chinese in silk robes, highlanders in kilts, Arab sheiks, African tribesmen, Indians of both the dot and tepee variety — you name it and it's here.

A full dozen Indian elephants, complete with gold-turbaned riders, wander the periphery, contributing an odor to the place that's not exactly celebratory. Live peacocks roam free while hundreds of exotic birds and miscellaneous creatures squawk, roar, or howl from silver cages placed around the room.

Being part of the Indian contingent, we establish our little pickle station not far from the tiger cages.

The big cats are, after all, part of the plan.

"There he is!" Sophie points across the room.

The Tick-Tock's easy to spot, all crisp and in focus in his blue outfit. He looks shorter and heavier than I remember.

"I don't think that's Rapier — the one from the prison."

Sophie chuckles. "Your dad and I never gave them names, but we've seen a couple different types."

"Are they individuals or models?"

Her eyebrows shoot up. "Individuals, I hope to God. We've never seen two of the same together."

"The other one in France, with the rifle, he's Longshot. This guy's more than a foot shorter."

"I've seen this tubby bucket-of-bolts before," she says. "He forced your father downtime while a huge one with a broadsword chased me. But I hopped an hour into the future and gave him the slip."

"A two-handed sword like the Kurgan? Let's call that one Claymore!"

Sophie chuckles. She's the only other action movie fan in the family.

"What's this Tubby packing?" I ask.

She shrugs. "I couldn't see. He was fast."

It bugs me that Rapier/Fusée might be lurking around somewhere. The last thing we need is a second Tick-Tock popping up.

"What if Tubby sees us?" I ask.

"Stay close, and be on the lookout for your girl. He'll be waiting for our move. This is a chess game. He knows the two of us can come and go as we please, but he also knows we want her."

I guess that's true. My cooldown came off yesterday, so I'm free to travel, and Sophie's is too short even to worry about.

"Parvati?" Sophie touches her on the shoulder left bare by her pink and yellow sari. "There's your target. The stocky guy in the official uniform by the ostrich cage."

"Who?"

"Concentrate," Sophie says. "Between the flightless bird and the koalas."

"The pudgy guy?" Parvati says. "I didn't notice him."

"Tubby. He's not very memorable. Focus on the blue and silver uniform. Point him out for me."

Her brow furrows. "Tubby's my target," she mutters.

"How come she can remember his nickname?" I ask Sophie.

"I'm not sure. But it's not a real name, it's a description if you think about it. You know, like when people can't remember a name they sometimes use a title, the way Joe calls me Major."

"There's a lot we seem unsure about."

She nods. "Keeps us on our toes."

Turns out Tubby is on Yvaine duty.

She enters the ballroom by a small door near the kangaroos, part of a line of ten other girls all roped together by silver cord, all dressed in skimpy silver camis and tiny silver shorts — silver being the theme for decorations, attire, everything celebrating the king's Silver Jubilee. The group is even wearing Yvaine's preferred footwear: none.

I can't believe I have the self-control just to watch. For the moment.

A handler leads them to a long table. Tubby follows and settles into a nearby seat to watch. His clockwork head swivels toward us, then returns to Yvaine.

The urge to go to her is so strong it's like a physical tug, like if I'm not careful, I'll be dragged across the room banging into tables all the way. But I know our only hope is sticking to the plan.

Yvaine's handler helps the girls up on the table. One by one, they crawl and twist into odd and suggestive positions, as if following a well-drilled procedure. Yvaine is soon all but lost in the tangle of limbs, but Tubby being not five feet away makes her easy to track. A line of more modestly silver-clad slaves comes in, bearing platters heaped with exotic fruits they arrange around and on top of Yvaine's pile of girls.

"I've always been partial to fruit," Sophie says, but the quip seems forced. "Parvati, see where Tubby is? That's the spot."

We have to keep reminding Parvati, who keeps tugging at her sari. Up until today, the only thing I ever saw her wear was fatigues.

Guests in elaborate neon-colored costumes are starting to filter into the room. Our plan — really our tack-on to Joe's plan — requires the king to be present and the party in full swing. I stare at the visible bit of Yvaine, just an arm, shoulder, and a touch of blond. If she sees me, she gives no indication. At least she's alive and, as best I can see — which isn't saying much — hasn't been treated too badly.

I tell myself she's a tough girl.

When the king shows up, there's a lot of trumpet blowing, cheering, and the like. But really it's just a loud yet brief interruption in the already underway festivities. I can't see the king himself but I can tell where he is by the way the crowd revolves around his position in the room.

Meanwhile, we scoop pickles into bowls and hand them to disinterested partygoers passing our cart.

"You better get into position." Sophie gives Parvati a quick hug. "Work the tables near Tubby and get on him fast as soon as Joe makes his move."

"How is a strip of fabric going to hold him long enough for you to get over there?" she asks — again.

"To him, silk isn't any different than steel." My aunt's looking more at me than her lover. "He can't move anything in phase, that's the key. Well, that and surprise."

Parvati sighs at what little of that she understood, straps little cymbals onto her fingers, and takes up her long silk scarf. She slides through the crowd until she's about halfway between us and Yvaine, then begins her routine.

I watched her practice all week, but I can't say it helped.

"Belly dancing just isn't her calling," Aunt Sophie says.

Parvati works the party, swaying back and forth, draping people with her thin pink scarf. What noise her finger instruments make is completely lost in the hubbub.

"Any moment now," Sophie says.

I look through the crowd, paying particular attention to the animal cages. Joe is nowhere in evidence, but scattered around I see faces from the rebel base.

Parvati wasn't the only Indian hiding out with us. There were more than a dozen, mostly guys in turbans, and now I spot several of them riding atop the elephants. They've been slowly touring the edges of the room all evening, offering rides to lords and ladies.

But now someone blows a whistle, and everything changes.

In a flash, the four exit doors swing shut and four enormous gray forms lie down to block them. The guests go crazy. The remaining elephants plunge through the crowd to block entrances to other parts of the building.

Let's just say that at a party, a stampeding pachyderm is cause for screaming.

Then Joe's people let loose the cats.

A nearby man screams as a lion brings him down. Animals and people scatter everywhere. We're talking total chaos.

Tubby holds his position, scanning the room, but Parvati approaches behind him. She loops her long pink scarf over him and cinches it tight across his arms, pinning them to his sides.

"Go!" Sophie says.

We sprint toward Yvaine and the Tick-Tock. The Tock thrashes about, but Parvati does as she was told and hangs on, tying a knot behind him. Unable to move her, he's trapped.

For now.

It's only a twenty-second run to Yvaine, but the scene is utter pandemonium. Nearby, a hissing ostrich has cornered a group of diners. A crazed chimpanzee on a table to my right shovels food into his mouth.

Sophie shoulders people aside like a pro football player, then makes a flying leap toward Parvati and the Tick-Tock. As soon as they touch, I see the briefest flash of starry white void. She and the Tock rise into the *in-between*.

"Where'd they go?" Parvati says.

I don't answer because I'm running towards Yvaine. This morning, Joe convinced me to carry a stopwatch. Fifteen minutes. That's all we've got.

Chapter Twenty-Five:
Rescue

Philadelphia, April, 2011

The buffet that includes Yvaine is already coming apart by the time I reach her. I hurl a platter of grapes to the floor and lift my girl up out of the mess.

Her eyes look huge in her face, which is a mask of smeared makeup.

"Charlie?"

I kiss her, very gently. She feels warm, feverish almost, her skin slicked with sweat.

"You comed for me," she says, but her voice sounds funny, slurred even.

I hold her by the shoulders and take a good look at her. She's lost some weight, and her neck's scabbed over.

"You're high!"

"They maked me." The dreamy tone of her voice is terrifying. "Held us down at first, but it feels so good."

Behind her, one of Joe's men skewers a red coat with a serving fork. I can't feel the slightest bit of pity for him, not after what they've done to her.

Yvaine strokes my face. "Other fools have tried t'do worse by me."

I check my watch. Thirteen minutes left. The silver cord around her waist has her tethered to the pile of fellow slaves.

"We have to hurry," I say.

"It be sewed into me smallclothes," she says.

I tug on the cord. It's not like a steel cable or anything, but I'm not going to be able to cut it without some kind of tool.

I grab her waistband and tug her shorts down and over her feet. Little did I imagine the second time I got her pants off would be in front of two-thousand people.

Fortunately, she's wearing a silver thong underneath. A couple of her buffet-mates take a card from our deck and start wriggling out of their shorts too. I figure the more distraction the better — not that there isn't already plenty.

Injured people lie everywhere. The mauled, the trampled, whatever. A group of guards tries to form up in the middle of the room, but Joe's men scatter them with elephants.

They won't allow any guns inside, he told me yesterday, *so when we turn their amusements against them, they'll be defenseless.*

I shudder. This isn't something I want to be a part of, even if it is *part of the pattern of history*, according to Aunt Sophie. If our plan works, it'll all change anyway. In this history, millions didn't die in the World Wars — but in mine, we abolished slavery. Who the hell knows which is really for the better?

Yvaine stumbles and I pull her up.

"We have to hurry," I say.

"The juice be wearin' off, makes me so tired."

As it happens, we're standing right next to a coffee and tea station. I snatch up a whole coffee pot — lukewarm by now — and hand it to her.

"Drink as much of this as you can."

She makes a decent go of chugging it. Coffee dribbles from her chin and beads off the shiny top to trickle across her belly.

I glance at my watch, then at the pickle cart nearby.

"Where be the Tick-Tock?" Yvaine says between gulps.

"They'll be back soon, and we have to be ready."

She flings the coffee pot away. But it's practically empty.

"Where is he? That prick-tock be the one killt me parents."

I put my hand on her arm, grateful for her anger or the coffee or time or whatever has sobered her up. Her skin still feels clammy, but my girl is back.

I glance at my watch. Eight minutes left.

"I found my aunt," I say, "and she took the Tock into the future."

"It be possible t'carry them uptime?"

"Apparently. See that cage?" I point behind me, my eyes on her face. "She's going to be inside it in seven minutes."

"With the burly cat?" Yvaine says.

I turn around. Holy crap. Joe's men opened all the cages, but the tiger's still in there, pacing back and forth at the far end.

"We're going to hit the Tock with..." I realize she doesn't even know what electricity is. "Man-made lightning. I need to get it ready." I look at her, standing there barefoot, her little ribs visible under the skimpy coffee-stained cami. "Do you think you can get the tiger out of there without getting hurt?"

"Unless he dinna like meat."

She's still got a shit-eating grin on her face. So while I don't like it, and the plan was dangerous as hell *before* the tiger got lazy, what choice do we have?

We decorated the pickle jars with silver foil in advance. The lids have the central conductors, and I already rigged them in parallel with wire disguised as ribbons. The contraption isn't charged yet, since electrocuting random pickle-loving guests would be uncool. Before I hop on the unicycle part of the cart, I check the big knife-switch to make sure it's open — as in disconnected — again, electrocution equals bad.

Leyden jars will hold a charge and release it when grounded, but you have to get the electricity in there somehow. A couple days ago I had one of Joe's engineers modify the cart's pedal-powered mechanism. Now, I pull the lever that drops the unicycle's drive chain onto a different wheel and start pedaling furiously. Instead of moving the cart I'm spinning a big disk of glass against a rabbit fur pad. The contraption looks innocuous, but I can hear the satisfying crackle of static as I pedal. I only hope there's time to build a big enough charge.

My test at the base took five minutes, but I've wasted some time with Yvaine and can only spare three, so I pedal like that guy from my history who's held the biking record at 81 mph since 2002. And I'm not suggesting he's a time traveler just because I can't remember his name.

I have a great show to watch while I'm pedaling. Yvaine heaves what looks like a haunch of mutton in front of the cage. She runs behind the door — thank God! — and tries to get the tiger's attention.

Gulp. Me, not the tiger.

Reminding myself to breathe becomes harder and harder. Yvaine is tossing bits of meat at the cat's head. I just got her back and here she is teasing a tiger.

But the big cat slinks toward the cage entrance, striped tail swishing behind it — screaming crowds must make it nervous. It snatches up the chunk of meat and bolts away.

Yvaine jogs back to me just as I finish with the bike. She's wearing that oh-so-pleased-with-herself smile.

"Stay away from the cart," I say. "Touch a jar, and you could die."

"Toff rescue, timid tigers an' killer pickles."

"This whole plan is crazy," I say. "In two minutes, my aunt is going to reappear in that cage with the Tick-Tock. His hands are tied, but she has to get out. You slam the door shut the second she does, then get away from the cage."

"Won't work," she says. "He'll chime his way t'freedom."

"I know, but if I can throw this switch, the power in these jars will stop him."

She shrugs. "I hopes you be right."

"I have to attach this cord first. The lightning moves along the wire, from the jars to the cage."

I scoop up the coiled cable and dodge across the twenty feet or so to the cage, then tie the end around one of the bars.

"Less than a minute!" I kiss Yvaine. "Get in position behind the cage door — and be careful."

The deadline comes and goes.

"Hold your place!" I yell to Yvaine from my position by the switch.

I'm nervous, but not too much. Sophie said she often overshoots. I just hope it's not too long.

The fighting has died down. Most of the people have been herded to the far side of the room. I can see Joe up on a podium with the king and lots of overdressed folk. They're setting up cameras. I really don't want to think about what Joe's going to do.

Where the hell is my aunt?

I don't know, but she's not the first returnee to the cage.

The tiger lopes back inside, sits down, and starts licking his paws.

"Yvaine! The cat—"

Now, two minutes and seven seconds late, Sophie makes her entrance. She and the Tock pop into the cage and slam into the side wall. It's like her arrival in Joe's cell, except for one detail. My aunt falls backwards onto the embiggened house cat.

He squirms out from underneath her, hissing and snarling. Sophie tries to regain her balance, gripping the bars, but the Tick-Tock is fast, even with his arms still tied to his sides. We watch in horror as he kicks her to the floor of the cage and stomps on one of her legs.

Even twenty feet away I hear the bone snap.

Yvaine's standing by the cage door on her toes. The tiger's at the far end, with Sophie and the Tick-Tock between. When the Tock raises a foot to kick Sophie again, the loose ends of silk flutter—

And the tiger starts to bat at the scarf like a kitten bats at yarn. In the process, his claws rip into the Tock's blue suit.

It's at this awkward juncture that Parvati returns.

"No!" She screams at the door of the cage, ready to rush in.

Yvaine shoves her sideways, toppling her to the floor.

The tiger has the Tick-Tock off balance but isn't doing us any favors because his claws have now shred the sash. In a heartbeat, the Tock's hands are at his waist and back up again, this time with two wicked brass daggers. Ignoring the cat, he pivots toward Sophie.

"Burn in hell!" Yvaine yells.

She flops into the cage, scrabbles across the floor, and grabs the Tock's ankles. A churning hole in the universe opens over her head—

They both disappear into the sea of stars.

The tiger hisses, arches his back, tail up, then bolts out of the cage and off into the crowd.

Shit, shit, shit! Where'd they go?

I leave my switch and start running. Electricity's useless with Sophie in the cage anyway — the shock would kill her.

"Frigging Tock!" Sophie says, dragging herself toward the mouth of the cage. Parvati, still on the floor where Yvaine knocked her, crawls over.

I hear the clanging of metal on metal.

"Charlie!"

Turning, I see Yvaine hanging beneath a gigantic birdcage

Caged with the beasts

filled with parrots and one pathetic and squishy-looking Tick-Tock. The cage is barely bigger than he is — his arms are smooshed up inside with his legs dangling below. Somehow, she managed to exit the *in-between* with him inside and herself outside.

She lets go of his ankles and drops to the ground.

"Bonny trick, if I does say so meself."

It is, but the Tock twists around in his cage — which, while not so great for the parrots, allows him to get his hands closer to his torso.

"The cable!" Sophie yells, her voice ragged with pain.

She's right. The Tick-Tock, his blue jacket open, is working the dials on his chest.

CHIME! Very bad. Twenty-six seconds until an angry Tock's loose in time. If we can't shock him before he leaves, we'll lose our chance to jump in his hole.

"Yvaine!" I yell. "Get that wire from the old cage to the new one."

Sophie starts untying the cable. Sweat beads her face, and I know that leg has to be excruciating — I give her serious points for grace under pain.

CHIME! Yvaine runs to the tie-off for the Tock's suspended cage. Whoever hung it threaded the chain through a big loop in the ceiling and clipped it to the base of a column.

CHIME! I take the cord from my aunt while Yvaine unhooks the chain.

CHIME! The Tock and his cage crash to the ground but Yvaine, way lighter, rides her end up into the air, clinging to it with her fingers and toes.

CHIME! She swings across the short space and leaps to the top of his cage.

CHIME! "Throw me that wire," she calls, "then fry up the bastard."

CHIME! I toss the half-coiled cable up to her and turn.

CHIME! I'm halfway back to the pickle cart.

CHIME! Reaching the switch, I see Yvaine tie the cable to the chain atop the cage.

CHIME! "Get away from the metal!" I scream, my hand poised on the big switch.

CHIME! She jumps into the air and hops sideways.

CHIME! The second her feet are clear I throw the switch.

CHIME! Just before the switch closes, the Tick-Tock's hand shoots through the bars and grabs her.

CRACK! Sparks fly from the switch, the jars, the cable, the cage.

Chapter Twenty-Six:
Clockwork

Philadelphia, April, 2011

When my eyes clear, Yvaine and the Tick-Tock are practically side-by-side, him slumped in his cage, her prone on the ballroom floor next to it, his mechanical fingers around her wrist.

I run to her, kick his hand away, and kneel.

"Yvaine!" I shake her gently, relieved that she's warm. But her open eyes are staring but not seeing. I put my ear to her mouth, then her chest.

Nothing.

No, no, no! We were so close —

CPR. I took it in gym this year but don't remember much. I clasp my fingers together, place my palms on her chest, and press a couple times.

Hard. They said hard. Count to ten. Ten hard jabs.

Nothing.

I pinch her nose, put my lips to hers, and blow. Ten times.

Was I only supposed to pump? — I can't think — I pump again. I blow again.

I'm barely aware when a shadow falls over me. It's Sophie, leaning on Parvati for support. She gasps in agony as her lover lowers her to the floor.

Parvati kneels across from me. She puts her brown hands on mine and pushes — not just hard, rib-breaking hard. Five times. Ten times. Fifteen —

"Owwwwww!" Yvaine's eyelids flutter and she sucks in a long, pained breath.

"Did an elephant stomp on me chest?" Yvaine whispers.

I hold her, stroke her hair. So close. So close. I feel like I've been shoved through a pasta machine.

Sophie opens the cage with the Tick-Tock. Her face reveals new depths of pain.

"Charlie, he won't be out long. Let Parvati take your girl."

I know she's right, but I take a folded handkerchief from my pocket and press the contents into Yvaine's hands.

"The police took the thistle," I say, "but I made this instead." It's just a flower from outside the rebel base, dried.

She kisses me and—

"Charlie!" Sophie yanks me away.

I turn to the Tock. With his porcelain eyelids shut, his face looks even blanker than usual. I'm close enough to see his horsehair-thick eyelashes and the white of his cheeks, painted with red. His legs are jammed under the heavy cage and when we try to shift him, we find that metal men are heavy. But I easily tear open his jacket to expose his guts.

Whenever I've seen the Tock's chest, the parts were all whirling and spinning. Now his innards are still.

I start with the easy dials. The clock with its twenty-four roman numerals is set to noon. Fine. The next one is brass, with the letters J, I, M, A, M, J, J, A, S, O, N, D.

It has to be the months, despite the weird February. I turn the brass dial to the second J, June.

The next dial has thirty-one roman numerals. Dad wanted to meet on the first of the month, so I roll it to thirty and give us a day to situate.

There's a brass cylinder with white and black enamel rotating numbers, like the counter on an ancient VCR. It has seven digits and reads 0002011 AD. Seven fricking digits?

I spin the adjacent wheel and it advances to 2012. Wrong way. I reverse. It's going to take me half a minute to get to 1948.

Yvaine leans over and pulls the two nasty brass daggers from the Tock's motionless waist.

"He killed me da and mum with these," she whispers. She takes the belt too and shoves the blades into the holsters.

Sophie points to two of the three remaining dials. "These are longitude and latitude."

Both of us memorized the coordinates for Shanghai, picking a spot a hundred yards out into the harbor so we won't pop up in the middle of a wall or a mountain. Sophie starts dialing.

"What about the last gauge?" I ask. It reads eighty, but eighty what?

She shrugs. "We'll have to risk it."

I finish with the year about the same time Sophie has the location dialed in.

"What do we do next?" I say. Not like there's a big button labeled GO!

"Is he wound?" Yvaine says. "I seen 'em wind theirselves."

There are two hexagonal brass sockets and a little T-shaped key dangling from his waist by a chain. It fits the sockets. I crank to the right.

I only last a minute before my wrist cramps up and Sophie has to take over. I can see a big spring inside tightening. We finish one, then wind the other.

Still nothing.

"What now?" I say.

"The swinger," Yvaine says. "Dinna you start a clock with the swinger?"

I stare at his guts.

She must mean a pendulum. He has a big brass one in the middle of his stomach.

"What if he wakes up?"

Sophie gives the pendulum a flick. Always a thrill-seeker, my aunt.

There's a metallic ticking as thousands of gears and whirling bits spin to life.

CHIME. His limbs don't move.

CHIME. Sophie gives Parvati a too-hot-for-TV smooch.

CHIME. "I'm going to miss you," she says.

CHIME. "Where're you headed?"

CHIME. "Long ago and far, far away."

CHIME. "I don't understand, but I know I'll see you again," Parvati says.

CHIME. Sophie tousles her hair then turns to me. "Get close, Charlie, but not too close!"

CHIME. I pull Yvaine to me. Her Tick-Tock blades look mighty peculiar belted over her silver thong.

CHIME. The gears and moving bits inside the Tock are speeding up, some of them just blurs of motion.

CHIME. The Tock's porcelain eyelids pop open. His brass irises expand. His arms jerk, then move to his spinning chest.

CHIME. "Bugger us!" Yvaine draws one of the Tock's daggers from her belt and holds it ready.

Sophie wrestles for control of the mechanical arms as the Tock's fingers grope at his dials.

CHIME. His innards are all a blur now. Where his heart should be, a lopsided red and gold thing whirls around, faster and faster. A shiver runs down my spine. It looks like a big cousin to Bréguet's whirlwind.

Within the non-space formed by its motion, the world opens to the *in-between*.

CHIME. The lights in the room dim. Yvaine thrusts her blade toward the Tock, but I grab her from behind with both arms, nearly lifting her from the ground.

The Tick-Tock drops into the hole that opens beneath him. The seething boiling hole. Sophie's almost dragged in with him, but kneeling on the solid floor, she braces herself as he drops away.

Chapter Twenty-Six: Clockwork

I feel Yvaine trembling. "If we goes in there," she says, "he'll be waitin'."

Sophie turns to us. "I'd go anywhere for your father." She pivots on her good knee and lets herself fall into the void.

"She'll be back," Parvati says. "Sooner or later she always comes back."

Yvaine watches Sophie's form shrink inside the hole.

"We might be jumpin' into hell."

I glance at her. "We could go separate, my cooldown's over."

"Save it. I trusts you." She holsters her knife.

We jump in together.

Chapter Twenty-Seven:
Sunk

Shanghai, downtime

Our passage through the *in-between* feels rushed, harsher. We tumble end over end. I grip Yvaine's hand so hard the skin turns white. But I don't dare let go.

And I'm dizzy. The feeling of vertigo doesn't end when we pop out into hazy daylight. I can see a low city below me, and as we plunge downward toward a sheet of water dotted with ships, I realize what the Tock's extra dial was for: height.

"Feet down!" I scream. A shred of good sense reminds me to bring my free hand up to pinch my nose.

Then we hit.

WHAM!

Our velocity drives us under. The water feels like ice and tastes like salty sewage.

Yvaine thrashes like a madwoman. Holding onto her is harder here than *in-between*.

I open my eyes to see Sophie struggling with the Tick-Tock. He's below me, one arm raised above his head, the other clutching her bad leg and dragging her down with him.

I want to go to her, but they're sinking too fast and I have my hands full. Bubbles pour out of Yvaine's mouth as she twists against me. I try to kick my way upward, but God, she's making it hard.

We break the surface and I gasp for air.

Time has changed Yvaine's hair — wet black strands stick to her blueish lips as she spits and chokes. A rough swell smacks her back under and she grabs at me, threatening to haul us both down.

I get my hands around her middle, under her arms, and kick like a madman. She pulls me under every other wave.

"Don't fight me!" I yell between breaths. "Scissor your legs and stay upright."

She coughs and coughs, but we manage to keep our heads above water.

The image of the sinking Tock is burned into my brain. Poor Sophie.

"Can't... swim," she hacks out between coughs.

"Tell me something I don't—"

A piercing scream erupts out of nowhere as someone falls out of the sky and plunges into the water. The huge splash settles to reveal my red-faced aunt. Time has given her hair a Chinese-style dye job like Yvaine's.

"Damn... son of a... wouldn't... let go!"

She starts an aggressive dog paddle. The harbor's jammed with boats, mostly Bruce-Lee-style junk ships but also a couple Titanic lookalikes.

Yvaine keeps struggling. I kick furiously but my thirty-something aunt with a broken leg makes better time.

By the time we reach the wharf, my numb limbs, powered by sheer willpower, are long past the point of exhaustion.

We cling to a crude wooden ladder bolted to the stone quay. None of us are in a hurry to climb up.

"You traveled t'get free?" Yvaine asks Sophie. My aunt winces. Her face is white.

"Had to tug off my pants first and kick him away. Didn't want him following me. Hurt like a bitch."

Yvaine looks so odd with her long, straight Asian hair. She climbs the ladder halfway, revealing that her silver cami has become a red silk pajama top and her thong white granny panties — both soaked, of course. She must be feeling better, since she slaps her own cheek on the way up — not the one on her face.

"You found a sassy one, Charlie," my aunt says.

Yvaine nods. "Been called that before."

"What'll happen to Tubby down under?" I ask.

"The fat Tock?" Yvaine says. "Call him Backstabber." She twists her hips to show off his knives, still belted around her waist.

Sophie says, "You didn't feel a timequake after I jumped away from him, did you?"

I shake my head.

"I hope he rusts at the bottom," Yvaine says.

"If they really can't swim," Sophie says, "we could try to drown them all."

"Leave me home if you do," I say.

Yvaine hangs off the ladder rail to let Sophie climb past. Without her pants, my aunt's leg is visible. It doesn't look good. The calf is swollen and purple, the foot twisted at an unnatural angle, and she moans with every rung. Not that she complains.

Yvaine follows, with me right behind her. Despite the cold water and my exhaustion, I can't object to the view.

On the dock above, a wide boulevard separates the wharf from an impressive row of western-style buildings. Rickshaws fill the street, but I also see the occasional unicycle. The crowds are mixed, mostly Chinese in robes and dark beanies or conical straw hats, with some Europeans in muted formal clothes thrown in — the men in really tall top hats and the women with their hair dyed black like Yvaine and Sophie. There's no sign of the neon colors and punk styles we saw in the future.

An occasional passerby gives us the odd glance. I really need to find my women some pants.

We spend a while plying the locals for information, a process made easy by our newfound mastery of the language.

The good news is we've arrived in Shanghai, June 30.

The bad news is it's 1955.

"The Tock must have turned the year dial during the struggle," Sophie says.

Yvaine puts her hands on her hips, newly clad in stolen silk pajama bottoms.

"There ain't no way Charlie can take us both back a few years?" she says.

My aunt shakes her head. "Too bad he didn't roll his dial the other way. We could all three go forward, but only two back."

"Dad said he'd keep coming every first of the month," I say. "Would he keep at it this long?"

"I would," Sophie says.

We discover there's still an emperor in Peking.

"It seems the Prince of Heaven now reports to Parliament," Sophie tells us after grilling a friendly passerby for political details.

"What about the communists?" I ask.

Yvaine squats on the side of the street and picks her toenails. Her expertise is more in acquisitions. Not only did she lift pants for her and Sophie — local laundry includes a ready supply of silk pajamas — she even liberated a handful of cash from a careless shopkeep.

"I asked," Sophie says. "Hunan province is in revolt, led by a socialist leader named Mao. Time preserves what it can, but I suspect he'll make little headway with the British fully in control. In our old history, the Japanese invasion really shook things up."

I only know the bold strokes of Chinese history — lots of dynasties and all that — but I'm happy to see less clockwork stuff here than there was in screwed-up Philly. The British all wear oversized pocket watches, but the locals don't seem as keen on them.

"Where we supposed t'meet your da again?" Yvaine asks.

"His letter just said 'the old place where my mother might find her favorite beverage.'"

"Knowing Fink," Sophie says, "he probably means the antique tea house by Yu Garden."

I grin. "Is that a restaurant?"

Sophie nods, and we both laugh.

"Why that be funny?" Yvaine asks.

"He *loves* restaurants," Sophie and I say at the same time.

"We need a doctor," I tell Sophie in the morning. Her leg is even more swollen.

"In mid-century China?" she mutters.

"Do you want gangrene?"

"Barber'll take it off," Yvaine says. "Folks often live."

If we don't get Sophie looked at soon, I'm worried it might come to that.

My go-go girl doesn't look so great herself. She didn't sleep much — who did? — and is all fidgets, tapping her feet, scratching her arms, picking at herself. Her skin looks clammy and her pupils are huge.

I put a hand on her knee, half to comfort her, half to still the incessant motion of her legs.

"Is everything all right?"

A pained look crosses her face. She grabs her belly, bolts into the corner, pulls down her pajama bottoms, and spends a long time looking really uncomfortable.

Sophie says, "Juice withdrawal looks like a bitch, but at least she gets to keep all her limbs."

"You're not going to lose your leg. Yvaine'll look after you while I go find my dad."

"I can take care of myself—"

Her attempt to move elicits a scream loud enough to wake the dead.

"That be settled," Yvaine says.

I squeeze Sophie's arm and kiss Yvaine. The teahouse is only a hundred yards away, floating over a grubby pond on stone pillars. It looks like some fairytale building out of Chinese Disney, all red painted wood and crazy peaked pagoda gray roofs, complete with hanging paper lanterns.

Dad better be there, and he better know a good doctor.

Chapter Twenty-Eight:
Age Gap

Shanghai, Summer, 1955

Inside, the teahouse is a cramped maze choked with foreigners and sweet smelling smoke. I work my way through room by room, table by table.

If not for his extra-sharp time traveler aura, I'd have trouble recognizing my dad.

He was always tall — but lanky, like me. Now his midnight silk robe tents across his big belly, and he has at least two and a half chins. His dark hair is shot through with gray and braided down his back. His eyes are the same: bright with intelligence and alight with curiosity.

His table is strewn with plates of food, and his chopsticks are poking at the remnants of a huge meal. Across from him is a silver-haired Chinese guy so fat he makes my dad look like Abbot to his Costello.

"The sea cucumber in abalone sauce is particularly fine today," he says.

"I prefer the frog's legs in bird's nest," his friend says, the motion of his jaw making his wispy white beard dance.

I walk up to the table. "Got your note, Dad."

My father drops the oyster skewered on his chopstick.

"Charlie?" He forces himself to his feet, nearly toppling the table, and wraps me in a bear hug.

**Eight years and
eight thousand meals**

For a minute, I imagine he's just come home from one of his trips, and while the warm bulk of his belly against me messes with the fantasy, it's amazing to see him. Things are going to be all right now, no more of this crazy by-the-seat-of-our-pants—

"I knew you'd come! I cajole Master Li into joining me every month."

"Pull my beard and buy me sixty-six dishes," the fat old man says.

I'd love to hang out and catch up, but Sophie can't wait.

"Dad—"

"Forgive my manners." My father steps back to introduce Master Li, who gives a little bow, really more of a nod. "Sit down, Charlie. You look starved—"

"Dad! I brought Sophie, but we need a doctor."

That gets his attention. He grabs my arm.

"Master Li, can you settle the bill and arrange for Doctor Wu to meet us at your house?"

Outside on the bridges, I jog toward Sophie and Yvaine, quickly leaving Dad behind.

"What happened to you giving me piggyback rides up and down the art museum steps?" I call back over my shoulder.

He puts on a burst of speed — for about five seconds — then returns to his walrus waddle.

"Seven years happened… and about seven thousand meals."

I have the grace to drop back so we arrive together. Yvaine looks really worried. My aunt looks even worse than she did when I left. Dad bends over her — no easy feat.

"Little sis," he says, "Just can't let you out of my sight, can I?"

Sophie grins — also no easy feat.

"I missed you too, Finkwinkle."

Dad knows how to get things done. He flags down a large rickshaw and pays some guys — coolies, he calls them — to help load Sophie inside. Soon we're dodging traffic.

"Is your name really Finkwinkle?" I always assumed Fink was one of Sophie's inside jokes.

"Your grandparents had a perverse streak," he says. "They thought a ridiculous name no one noticed was too funny to pass up."

"Methinks Finkwinkle be a leprechaun name," Yvaine whispers louder than she should.

Sophie winks at her. "Fink traded his forties for forty pounds."

My father scowls as he wedges a seat pillow under her leg.

"That be only the half of it." Yvaine's trying, none too hard, to keep from losing it.

Sophie elbows me. "I like this girl."

The thinner three of us laugh. The rickshaw is tilted to Dad's side, even with Sophie in the middle and Yvaine and me on the other side.

We approach a stone wall and a pair of servants open big wooden gates. Master Li waits in a courtyard sur-rounded by beautiful structures and gardens — what he modestly calls home.

"I set the bone and gave her something to make her sleep," Doctor Wu says when he returns from the garden bedroom where we carried Sophie. "She must drink nine cups of tea each day." He hands a servant a scrap of paper that must be the traditional Chinese equivalent of a prescription and tugs at the rat-tail of white hair snaking from under his black beanie. "Strength of an ox, that one, but she must not leave bed for a month."

"I'll make sure of it," my dad says. I don't envy him the task.

"If her fever rises, send word." Doctor Wu bows and glides out of the room.

"Master Li, thank you again for hosting," Dad says.

"My friend, after seven years, I think this is your home too." The big man smiles. "Fortune has blessed you. Family reunited, injuries on the mend."

"And a lot to talk about, Dad," I say. "Like how to fix this mess so Mom remembers who we are again."

He takes a seat on a bench and looks out across the ponds stuffed with oversized goldfish.

"So you met her?" he says. "In the new future?"

"You mean the future where she's married to our neighbor and has to wheel herself around the house?"

He doesn't answer.

"Dad, why didn't you tell me I was a..." I glance over at our host, not sure if I should finish the sentence.

"I have no secrets from Master Li, Charlie. And besides, brilliant as he is, time only allows him to understand so much."

Master Li checks his pocket watch — ominous and out of place in this zen setting — and smiles.

"I'll have the chefs prepare an eighty-eight course dinner for luck."

Didn't he eat like a thousand dishes of puppy tails in ginger sauce an hour ago? Just thinking about a long meal makes me want to collapse.

"Dad, don't you think we ought to rest up tonight? Maybe start the celebrating tomorrow?"

"You're probably right," he says.

But Master Li looks like somebody just consigned him to gruel and water for three days.

After he leaves, my dad wanders over to a niche and picks up a china bowl.

"I've learned a great deal here," he says. "Master Li is the greatest historian China has produced in centuries. Even the emperor thinks so. He personally inscribed this bowl with a poem praising Li's work."

Looking around at the lavish estate — it's like a private park in the middle of busy Shanghai — I'm thinking Master Li must also be the richest historian China has produced in centuries.

My father gets a dreamy look on his face.

"Of course, Master Li and I have our separate areas of expertise, his being the detailed course of history as currently represented on the timeline, mine the effect of fulcrum manipulation on the fifth dimension."

"Is he speaking English?" Yvaine asks.

"Shanghainese actually," I whisper. Then louder, "Dad, try to cater to the TV audience." Still, I take an odd satisfaction in being lectured — God knows that's mostly what he did when he was at home.

"Sorry." Dad puts the bowl down.

"Why didn't you tell me what I was?" I say.

"Sophie gave me an earful about that too. Charlie, I should have, but I didn't want to spoil your juvenescence."

Where does he get these words?

"Yeah, Dad, I had a great childhood being a friendless loser and not knowing why."

"We call that causal-dampening," he says. "I should begin with our history — what little I know — since we time travelers have no normal means of recording our culture. Even if we write down our experiences, time erases our efforts whenever we travel, except for—"

"*The Brief History*?" He's not the only one who knows stuff.

He raises an eyebrow. "You *have* been talking to Sophie. Much of what we know comes from pages written by the Regulator, the first and most brilliant of all time travelers."

Through my jacket, I pat the brass page I've carried since France. But in the ongoing spirit of petty payback, I decide to show-and-tell later, after I get some real answers.

"But first," my dad says, "tell me everything that happened since I last saw you."

I launch into the story but try to whitewash Yvaine's career choices, not to mention her love life. While the part about Ben Franklin is impossible to avoid, I downplay the whole Billy thing. The Rapier-in-the-church bit has Dad riveted, but when I start in on France — editing for a PG rating — his gaze wanders and he picks up the china bowl again.

Then I mention the buried brass page.

He drops the bowl back on the pedestal, where it rocks back and forth.

"Dad, it's here, but—"

He zooms across the room to snatch it out of my hand. Zooms. At his weight.

"Gee, would you like to borrow it?" I don't think he even hears me, he's so riveted by the text. "I could only make out a few words," I say.

His two and a half chins jiggle when he nods.

"This is the Regulator's work. His cipher is complex, but I broke the key some years ago. I'll take it to my study to translate."

Chapter Twenty-Nine:
Pages

Shanghai, Summer, 1955

After the servants bathe and dress me, I go looking for Yvaine. As her room is nowhere near mine, this involves crossing a stone bridge over an ornamental fish pond to traverse a courtyard filled with rocks and lanterns — all this before I figure out which building she's in.

The house is more a collection of Asian bungalows nestled in a giant garden. The windows are just reddish wood latticework, so I peer into a couple rooms.

And hear my father talking to Sophie about the page.

"It's been two years since I had anything new to work with," he says. "But I've made progress. Three years in, a historic oddity and several camels led me to a tomb in Xian, where I found seven more pages."

"Traveling without me is so old-fashioned," Sophie says.

"Better than popping up inside a dumpster."

She chuckles. "Now that's the Fink I love. Have your precious pages revealed the secrets of the eons?"

"That's how long since I held my wife. Eons."

"So you're my even older brother now," my aunt says. "Doesn't mean the end of the world."

"I'll probably never see her again — probably a good thing." A big sigh. "Look at me. What would Renni say?"

"Twice as much of you to love!"

"She'll never forgive me for stealing Charlie."

"That isn't your fault. Besides, he was never hers to begin with."

I slip away, not wanting to hear any more than I already have. I stumble over to a stone dragon crouched on a mossy garden wall.

We travelers belong only to each other.

When I finally find Yvaine's room, she's lying on the bed, a low wood thing, wearing a half-belted silk robe. Her legs are bent and her bare feet press a folding screen against the wall.

"Methinks I'll likely sleep for a month."

I flop down next to her. She smells all clean and soapy. It's not exactly what I'm used to, but it's nice.

"I'm sorry I couldn't get you out of the Lord Proprietor's palace faster."

She snuggles over to me. I can see a lot of thigh.

"You could've flown back here with Sophie. But you didna do it."

"After our night in France, I'd carve off my skin with a cake spatula to get you back." And I'm only half kidding.

She opens her robe. "It's just me body you want?"

I feel my face fall.

"Oh, Charlie. I likes t'tease you." She rolls over so our noses almost touch. "Like I did me da's terrier."

"So I'm your pet?"

"I loved that dog. He was loyal and not a mean bone in him."

She kisses me on the forehead, my nose, my lips. We make out for a few minutes until she scoots back against the headboard and runs her fingers through her damp hair.

"Was it miserable being a slave?" I ask.

"The worst of it be that demon juice. Me head feels like a tanner's hide, but if someone pressed an infernal juicer into me hand, I mightn't be able t'say no."

"I'd smash it for you."

Chapter Twenty-Nine: Pages

I feel her forehead, which isn't clammy like yesterday. Then I move my hand down to her neck. She puts her hand on mine.

"In the palace an' last night, the juice brought me the most unholy dreams. Donnie, Billy, Ben, me folks. They comed as corpses an' whipped the flesh from me bones."

Imaginary spiders crawl up my neck.

"You don't have to worry," I say, "juice hasn't been invented yet."

"I ain't so sure." She uses her toes to play with the hair on my legs. "In that hackney, the one pulled by men instead of horses, I smelled sweet smoke. It be the same."

Probably opium. "You promised to stay away from it."

She takes my hand and puts it on her belly, sliding it under the silk.

"Distract me."

The only thing she has on underneath is the belt with Backstabber's daggers.

"Unusual girdle," I say.

She chuckles. "Only thing I have t'remember 'em by." I guess she means her parents, not the Tocks.

I tickle the soft skin of her belly.

"Lower. Me tummy still hurts something fierce."

She doesn't have to ask twice. Under my new attentions she purrs.

"It'll be okay now," I say. "You saw how much Dad knows. We'll get all the answers, figure this out."

She makes a sad little sound. I stop.

"What's wrong?"

"Sorry." She captures my wandering hands and presses them against her stomach. "I be thinkin' of Billy again. How holdin' him seems a lifetime ago. A wisp in the London fog."

It does feel like that. Even the steam and clockwork Philadelphia is starting to fade, becoming a place of mist and mirrors I might never see again.

I wake with Yvaine still asleep beside me.

Napping wasn't my intention, but I guess it's just as well. I leave her to sleep and go to find my father. The sun has set and the gardens are lit by red paper lanterns.

Dad's study looks very Chinese. He's seated at a burgundy wood desk scribbling on a pile of paper, the shiny brass page in front of him.

"Any progress?" I ask.

He looks surprised to see me. "This may be a very important document. The cipher is computationally exhausting, utilizing a Lagged Fibonacci Generator, but manageable with the key."

"Can you teach it to me?"

He nods. I lean over his wide shoulder as he converts each symbol into a number, runs it through a big formula, then writes down a normal letter.

"Why is it in Latin?" I say after he works his way through the first sentence.

He shrugs. "Maybe the Regulator wanted to use a language prevalent in history. Or perhaps he was Roman, or a medieval priest."

"Or a snobby English teacher."

He ignores me, working letter by letter. I turn my attention to a refrigerator-sized iron safe. The door is ajar, so I peek inside.

There are stacks of silk-wrapped bundles. I peel back a bit of colored fabric to find the telltale too-sharp-for-this-world brass. More pages.

"How'd you get so many?"

"Your grandfather left me eight. The rest I found myself." He never looks up from his work. No surprise there, but he hasn't seen me in seven years — couldn't he muster up a little more enthusiasm?

"These are what passes for Grandpa's cufflinks in our family?"

"Except," he says, "deadly machines don't kill you over cufflinks."

"I saw Rapier with a page," I say.

That earns a glance. "Who's Rapier?"

"The Tick-Tock with the fencing blade in his walking stick."

"That one's bad news." He turns back to the cipher. "It's hard to tell, but he might be in charge of the others."

Figures I'd have the boss-Tock on my tail.

Dad taps the brass sheet. "Looks like your girl's father had the page about Abraham-Louis Bréguet."

Yvaine's grandfather, actually, which I might mention if he took a little interest.

"Her name is Y—"

"I call these pivot pages." He helps himself from a plate of stuffed buns.

"What's that mean?"

"The Regulator lived a long time ago — in traveler meta-time — but he recognized that the manipulation of history was fraught with danger. He espoused a pivot or fulcrum theory, and many of his pages detail historical junctures susceptible to large-scale time manipulation. Often smart people in important situations."

Like Ben Franklin, source of my whale-sized guilt.

Dad reads from the translated page in front of him, droning on about the importance of Bréguet to the development of mechanical technologies and the effect of volatile French politics on the sponsorship of his work. I'm glad he understands this stuff — that's why I came here — but...

"Aren't you the least bit interested in what happened to Mom?"

"Bréguet's a well known pivot," he says after a pause so brief I'm not sure it happened. "Following the big quake, I identified him as a major fulcrum for this timeline."

"Care to paraphrase?" I say.

"Even in the proper history — the one you grew up with — Bréguet was regarded as the greatest watchmaker of all time. But the Tick-Tocks altered something, furthering

his inventions. In this timeline, his Springtorb did for mechanical power what the dynamo did for electrical power
— particularly given the reduction in electrical research
created by Ben Franklin's absence." He pierces me with the
glare-of-all-encompassing-disappointment.

Since he won't ask, I fill him in on the rest of France — leaving
out the part where Yvaine discovers she's the granddaughter of
a major fulcrum — and Philadelphia-gone-bad.

"Clearly I miscalculated," he says. "Your approach for
bringing Sophie here was reckless and brilliant, but if you'd
studied the Regulator's work..." He scowls, further deepen-
ing the great mystery of whether he thinks I'm wunderkind
or dumbshit.

I thumb through the pile of rice paper scrolls inside the
safe. They seem to be translations of other pages. There aren't
many — just twenty-one — more a pamphlet than a book.

"So if we travel with these copies they'll be ruined?" I say.

"Turned into something harmless, like contemporary
poems. That's why the invention of phase-shifted brass was
so important."

"Let me guess. The Regulator cooked that up too."

My father nods. "There's even a page about it. Unfortunately,
the technique is rather unclear."

I find the one he's talking about. The Regulator dude
pontificates on the subject of causal-dampening and phase-
shifts. Apparently, he discovered some process to make
certain metals out of sync by an infinitesimal margin just like
us time travelers. He calls the result temporal-metallics. The
material is immune to time-assimilation, which I assume is
his term for whatever changes phones into notebooks.

When I look up, my father stretches his arms over his
head, then offers me the plate from his desk.

"Pork bun?" he says through a mouthful.

I take one to humor him. It's pretty good, like a BBQ pork
sandwich made from Chinese restaurant spareribs.

"Do any pages hide some secret for killing Tick-Tocks?" My turn with the full mouth.

"Unfortunately not. Mostly they're just lists of historically important people, philosophy, or technical discussions about time travel."

"Have you been to the far future?" I ask. "Maybe all the answers we need are just posted on the web — or whatever they have then."

"Only as far as 2030," he says, "but your computer-laden future is gone, replaced by a new one. And uptime travel offers its own challenges. Sophie's talents have their uses, believe me, but her range is limited and she's a poor navigator to places she hasn't been."

"Yvaine doesn't have a problem with it."

He shrugs. I doubt the name registered. At least Mom and other normals have an excuse for not paying attention to me.

"What *is* the deal with the Tick-Tocks?" I say.

His pudgy fingers move stiffly, laying out several sheets of paper on the desk. He looks so much older — and acts it.

"The vagaries of living in meta-time — my eight-year vacation being a case in point — make it difficult, to be sure, but the time-war seems to have started when a rogue group took the radical stance that the consequences of time manipulation on normals were irrelevant. These *manipulators*, as I call them, altered history, creating a future where mechanical technology was paramount. The Tick-Tock future. During the ensuing conflict the original timeline was restored, but some Tick-Tocks survived, remnants of a time that time itself forgot."

"Oh," I say. "Then they want to go home too?"

"In a manner of speaking."

I'd sympathize if they weren't inhuman killing machines. And while my dad might be a brilliant scholar and I'm just a talented upstart, it's obvious that the Tocks are big fans of the Regulator's work, just like Dad. That, plus knowing we travelers basically made the Tocks possible...

"These pivot pages seem pretty dangerous," I say. "Are you sure they're not a how-to guide for *changing* the timeline?"

"The Regulator wrote them as cautionary instructions," he says. "As in how to *avoid* letting America's founding fathers get killed."

"If you'd warned me, I'd have known better," I say. "You're supposed to be the parent here, right?"

He finally looks up. "We all have to take responsibility for our actions."

I toss the page I'm holding back in the safe. "Don't you think it's possible that this Regulator might not be what you think he is?"

"The pages make clear that the Tick-Tocks are nemesis to those with the hubris to alter time." He looks pissed, but at least he's paying attention. "Travelers observe, Charlie. They don't change!"

"Except when their daddies don't tell them they're travelers, and — forget it. So what's your brilliant plan to save Mom and Ben?"

"Haven't you been listening?" He stands up. "Man is not God. Research and understanding are the key, not impulsive, and quite possibly suicidal, action. When Sophie recovers, we all travel to Rendezvous D: Giza Egypt, under the Sphinx's nose, New Year's Eve, 1886. My investigations indicate a cache of pages buried nearby." He takes a deep breath. "I'm afraid the timeline must remain as you left it."

He can't be serious! But he is. I'm so mad there's no telling what I might say if I stick around.

I slam the door on the safe and walk out.

Chapter Thirty:
Dinner

Shanghai, Summer, 1955

Yvaine and I sleep so late we have to rush to get dressed for the mid-afternoon über-dinner I'm dreading. I'm not just mad at Dad, which I've been plenty of times, I'm really disappointed in him, a much less familiar feeling. He and I used to argue, but this is bullshit. And Sophie isn't allowed out of bed, so she won't be there to smooth out his butthead tendencies.

"If the pock-marked old lady's tofu is too spicy," my dad says after we're seated, "try the crab in garlic and ginger."

The table is big enough for twelve, round with a lazy susan in the middle, just like in an American Chinese restaurant. As big as it is, there's barely room for all the food. Yvaine sits beside me, holding a chopstick in each fist like a toddler holds crayons. She pokes at something with the consistency of Jell-O.

"Isn't the duck blood wonderful, child?" Master Li asks.

She thrusts both chopsticks upright into her rice bowl and uses her fingers to grab a drumstick from a tiny chicken apparently sliced by Freddy Krueger.

Dad frowns and Master Li watches Yvaine's hand like it's a roach in the kitchen.

"What's this?" She's tugging at the bird.

"Chicken without sexual life," Master Li whispers, his face about the same color as the rice.

Yvaine shrugs and chomps down on her drumstick.

"Chopsticks," my father says, "are left upright in bowls only at funerals."

I snag Yvaine's and lay them beside her bowl.

"Enough with the Chinese etiquette lessons," I say. "Let's talk about how we screwed up history. I can't believe you're just going to let Mom rot uptime. And what about Ben Franklin?"

"I'm not the one who left him to die in a burning church," Dad says.

"It's not like we had a choice!" Master Li frowns at me and I lower my voice. "We were trapped behind the altar with a collapsing roof and an angry Tick-Tock, no escape in sight."

"Charlie be spot on," Yvaine says. "If there'd been even a wee chance, I'd have stayed."

"You should have told me," Dad says.

"I did. Guess you weren't listening."

It goes right past him, far as I can tell.

"After the big quake I researched the new timeline," he says. "In this present, there is only marginal documentation from Benjamin Franklin's Boston childhood. As to the Philadelphia printer, the brilliant satirist, the great scientist, the master statesman, the editor of the Declaration and the Constitution, and perhaps most important, America's advocate in France? Nothing." A pause for effect. "Although no known Regulator page mentions him, clearly he's a major pivot."

His know-it-all tone coming on top of everything else heats my blood hotter than the tea the waiter's pouring.

"Can I get a real drink?" Yvaine asks him. "Ale or gin?"

My dad glares at her. "Alcohol encourages a loss of self-control and mistakes no time traveler can afford — like having a fulcrum's baby."

Yvaine scowls. "A ful*what?*"

Dad pulls an eyeball out of a whole fish and pops it in his mouth.

Yvaine pulls a knife out of her belt and spears a dumpling.

Master Li pulls himself together. "Child, cutlery may be used tableside in the West, but in the Middle Kingdom all food is sliced in the kitchen."

Yvaine freezes, but only for a moment. With the rapt attention of me, my dad, and Mr. Li, she pops the dumpling in her mouth — then jabs the blade into the tabletop.

Master Li shrieks. "That table belonged to a eunuch serving the Ching Kanxi Emperor!"

Yvaine grins. "This dirk belonged to Backstabber. An' now it be mine!"

My father gasps. "You took it from a Tick-Tock?"

This is my first good look at the knife. It's about ten inches long total, a third hilt. Both handle and blade look to be made of brass, and inside the handle is a sea of tiny Tick-Tock gears. The whole thing looks extra sharp — not just the blade, it has that in-focus look peculiar to time travelers, Tocks, and the pages.

"I think the daggers are made of temporal-metallics," I say, "like the Regulator's pages."

My father leans forward. "Can I see?"

Yvaine glares at him.

I put my hand on her leg. "He might be hen-hearted, but he's no prig," I say, hoping Dad isn't up on his Cockney slang.

Yvaine slides the blade over.

My father shows it to Master Li. "What's in my hand?"

The old man looks confused. "An English butter knife?"

"Almost a foot long?" Dad says.

"I'm not sure." Master Li's brows furrow. "Would you like another order of the husband and wife's sliced lung?"

"Take the blade from me," my father says.

"I'll request a new set of chopsticks if you need them," Master Li says.

Dad turns to me, spreads his hands, and smiles big.

"See! Far out of phase and showing a high level of casual-damping. All phase-shifted matter, including us and Tocks, does to some degree. I'm sure you observed that normals never even notice when Tick-Tocks brandish arms." He presses something on the knife handle.

CHING. The gears inside the hilt whirl and the blade collapses into the base. He presses the button again, and — CHING! — the blade is back. He looks at Yvaine and smiles, not the big smile but the sweet smile. You don't see that one very often.

"I don't suppose you'd let me keep this to examine?" he says.

She hasn't taken her eyes off the dagger for an instant.

"It's mine," she says between clenched teeth.

CHING. My father retracts the blade and hands it to her. She plays with the switch herself a few times, then draws the other blade and does the same.

I look at the weapons and sigh. There are two of them, and we could each take one. But I know better than to ask.

"The Regulator invented the special pages, right?" I say. "Don't the daggers seem awfully similar?"

My dad frowns. "As I said, all phase-shifted matter."

Yvaine flags down a servant and he brings her a small bottle of clear liquid on a tray. She takes a swig.

"Not bad but tastes like rice."

"Three-flower liquor is very strong," Master Li says.

Yvaine takes a gulp. "So how do we fight the Tick-Tocks?"

My father picks at a dish with his chopsticks. He's actually more interested in her question than his food.

"Temporal-metallics are virtually indestructible. I suspect the harbor water immobilized this Backstabber when he sank, but someday he'll be hauled up, probably not much worse for wear. Rumor has one entombed beneath the sphinx."

He's willing to face a Tock for a few metal pages but not to save Mom?

He glances at Yvaine, who looks to be making good progress on her three-flower liquor, and continues.

"The laws of nature, whether established by God or whatever, do not favor change. We're out of phase with the normal flow of time, which creates resistance to our efforts, our very presence. Causal-dampening."

"Like the way people don't notice our weird behavior," I say, "or the way we can't kill people?"

"Indeed," he says. "But time is not all-knowing — a strike against the God theory — and is unable to predict complex cascading consequences. It can be fooled by indirect manipulations."

"We can make a wee change," Yvaine says, "if it not kill anyone."

She pushes herself back in her chair and draws her bare feet up to her lap.

I roll my eyes. On our way to dinner, I tried to get her to wear the shoes the servants put out. Fail.

Master Li looks away.

"Yvaine, dear," says my father, who apparently does know her name, "you're embarrassing our host. Women's feet are a culturally charged issue in China."

Yvaine drops hers back to the floor.

Dad snorts. "The universe deals with minor time traveler alterations by allowing the change but reducing repercussions. Such causal-dampening prevents Master Li from understanding this conversation."

"There will be repercussions if we alter the seasoning in the shark-fin soup," our host says.

I get it. "No wonder it's hard for normals to photograph us."

"Enough blarney," Yvaine says. "The Tocks got Ben killt. Stands t'reason we can change it back."

"It never would have happened if you'd stayed out of the way." Dad sighs. "Because the Tick-Tocks are further out of phase than we are, they're able to affect time even less. But they're more clever, more aware of history. They draw travelers to pivots, weak points where small changes beget big. Once we're in position, they give us a shove and let the pins fall."

I think of how Rapier was waiting at the door to Independence Hall when I jogged past. How he dropped me on the same street as Yvaine. How she led me to Ben Franklin.

"I get it," I say, "but it's not fair to blame us. It's your fault or the Tocks', take your pick."

He shrugs. "Tick-Tocks are not all-seeing, just patient and good at working with what they have. Yvaine, how did you first meet Ben Franklin?"

Yvaine takes another swig of booze.

"Donnie sended me to him to brace up some swag."

"Stolen property?" my dad says. "Why would Donnie return it?"

"We was just the agent. Ben's place was burgled, so he went to the Thief-taker General t'get it back."

"Jonathan Wild?" Dad asks.

Yvaine takes another sip. "You know him?"

"Hasn't everyone read Fielding's novel?"

"Rapier goes by the name Mr. Fusée, Dad!" I don't even try to keep my voice down this time. "And he worked for the Thief-taker General!"

Yvaine's mouth forms into a pretty little O.

"Was him who brought Donnie the loot. I forgot on account o'never seein' him, but Donnie sayed Fusée asked for me in particular."

"There you go — indirection," Dad says. "The Tick-Tock lined up one of you, then the other, carefully orchestrating baby steps leading to Ben Franklin's death."

"But why does the Tocks hate us?" Yvaine asks.

Dad laughs. "I doubt emotion plays into it. We simply have to stay beneath their notice, or escape them if we can't."

"We make of it what we will," she says softly.

Dad looks like he's at the limits of his patience. "And what's that supposed to mean?"

"Sometimes it be best t'run, sometimes t'fight."

There's an awkward pause. I grab Yvaine's liquor bottle and take a sip. It's better than gin, sweeter, and it does taste like rice. Dad gives us both his you're-about-to-be-grounded look.

"Yvaine," he says. "Is it possible your father might have used the Bréguet pivot page to help the Tick-Tocks manipulate the timeline?"

"Lobycock indorser!" Yvaine says. "Tocks killt him in front of me."

"Your family seems to make a habit out of changing history! If you'd stayed away from the fulcrum—"

"Hey!" I say. "How would she even know who Ben Franklin was? She's from the past!"

"Ben still liked me for me," Yvaine says. "Billy's still me son. Mine."

"We can't change things," Dad says, "only observe. We have no right altering the lives of normals, for better or for worse!"

"If you can't mess with normals," I say, "why'd you marry one?"

I can't believe my dad is speechless.

Yvaine giggles. "Mayhap she was a good cook."

Dad points at the door. "Young lady, get yourself to bed. We'll talk when you sober up."

Yvaine knocks her empty bottle over on the table. "I was learned that if you breaks somethin', you makes it right."

She sets the bottle upright and struts out of the room.

I want to go after her but I don't — yet.

"Dad," I say, "we have to go back to save Ben Franklin. Think about it. Billy! Mom! *Slaves* in twenty-first-century Philadelphia—"

"You've done enough damage. Playing with the timeline brought the Tick-Tocks in the first place. This is what you get when you take up with a girl who can't control herself!"

"With dirty feet." Master Li shakes his head. "And no manners."

"Well, you didn't have to be such a jerk!" I say. "Who cares about what happened in a history no one remembers? Yvaine's right, *we make of it what we will.* And your precious Regulator can regulate my ass!"

On that brilliant note, I turn and go after my girl.

Chapter Thirty-One:
Date

Shanghai, Summer, 1955

What a cold asshole my Dad is. Or can be, anyway. He's always had that side to him, but the years alone haven't done him any favors. As I make my way to Yvaine's room, my neck and shoulders knot just thinking about it. Looking back, not only wasn't Dad around much the year before this little adventure, but he's never been one for social gatherings — or tact. And the food obsession is nothing new either, it's just out of control now.

I'm relieved to find my girl sitting on her bed with her knees drawn to her chest. She changed out of the robe-like dinner dress and is back in red silk pajamas.

I sit on the edge of the mattress.

"My dad doesn't mean to be mean, you know."

Yvaine elbows me in the ribs.

"Ouch! What did I do?"

"The Fink meant it," she says. "You was right t'call him hen-hearted. Look how Sophie fought for him, an' he be too lily-livered t'fight for his own wife."

She folds her arms around her knees again. A full moon shines through the latticework and makes the tears on her face glitter. I brush her hair away from her eyes. It's so weird how different she looks with a dark mop — not that I don't like both versions.

"I makes me own choices," she whispers. "Good or bad, they be mine. And Da didna help no Tocks."

"I know," I say. "I don't care about that. I've made more than my share of mistakes, but they're still our choices. If that makes us *manipulators*, who the hell cares? If my dad wants to blame anyone, he should blame himself. He could've warned me."

She takes my hand and rubs her fingers against mine. Which, for such a simple thing, is pretty darn cool.

"You're not like him," she says. "You never be mean to me. You and me da be the only men who weren't — well, besides the terrier."

I smile at her. "I'm not your dad — or the dog."

"Good thing, too, or I couldna do this." She kisses me. Thoroughly.

I kiss her back, all the while squeezing her hand. I want to squeeze as hard as I can — it's just this urge, this need. I'm pledging that I'd do anything, I mean *anything* for her, and hoping she would for me, too.

"Rank cull," she whispers. "Your da dinna deserve Sophie. Her I like."

"He's just scared." And stubborn.

"I be too, but we needs fix things for your mum and Ben and Billy. Even if I never see him again..."

She looks down and blinks. I stroke her arm.

"We'll make things right." Or die trying. That's part of *anything*.

She pulls away and puts both hands to her head.

"I thought the drink would help, but me head be packed with turds, an' ants be crawlin' all over me skin."

She lets her torso flop back onto the bed. I use my free hand to knead her calf where the silk has pulled up to the knee.

"This help?"

"Dinna stop," she says, her voice soft and an octave lower.

I work my way around her limbs, massaging. My own skin tightens, and my heart races, but I feel like the blood has been drawn away somewhere else. Ever since that night in France — hell, long before that — I've been dreaming about touching her. Really touching her.

She pulls her sleeves and pant legs as high as they'll go to give me more to work with.

I lean over and kiss her again.

"I be itching all over," she whispers into my mouth.

I go back to it, growing bolder, trailing my nails over her skin.

"Anyway," I say, "I'd make all the same choices again. Even knowing about the Tocks. You might think this is selfish, but the only part I'd change is Ben Franklin dying and that week and a half in Philly without you."

She puts her hand on the back of my neck and pulls me close.

"Charlie, I be some mighty hypocrite if I calls you selfish."

"What about stealing Billy and your dad's page?"

She unbuttons her top, pulls it off, and rolls over so I can rub her back — which I assume means I've been forgiven.

I lean down to kiss her neck. She tastes good, soft and a little like garlic lo mein.

"If we stay together," I say, "always stay together, always trust each other even if we argue, even if the other one does something stupid…"

"We can always move on and start anew," she says, "until one of us ends up dead."

She unbuttons my shirt. We go back to kissing. The rubbing becomes, well, a different kind of rubbing. It's less hurried and way more indoors than the first time.

Part of me knows I'll have to be damn careful. But I don't want to be. More clothes come off. I try to unbuckle Yvaine's belt, the one with the daggers.

"Not those," she whispers.

She pushes me down to the mattress and straddles my waist. The way she flips her hair back makes me think of the first time I touched her, grabbing her arm in Ben Franklin's church courtyard.

It's a whole lot better the second time.

Afterward we just lie there, all sticky and twisted together.

"We should stay here until we've learned all we can," I say, "and if Dad still won't help, just go fix things ourselves."

I feel her nod. "We needs a plan. For Billy, I can choke on me pride."

"What if we go back to that night when we all got drunk," I say. "Our time-ghosts and Donnie will be at *The Rose*. We can go to the hideout, take Billy, then force Ben to leave the city with us. If he isn't there a week later, he can't die."

"T'is not a bad idea. But we needs work out them details."

I hear yelling outside.

"What be that?" she says.

I wrap the sheet around myself, get up, and stumble over to the lattice window. I look back at my girl in the moonlight — stark naked on the bed except for those daggers — and take a mental photo I'll never forget, then slide the window open.

A man-sized blur tucked into a ball somersaults through and lands in the center of the room. No mistaking Backstabber's tubby figure. He's not wearing any clothes either, and his carapace is covered in barnacles. As soon as he sees Yvaine, he slaps his hands against the empty spots on his hips where his daggers used to rest.

She screams.

And I attack him with the only thing I've got.

I whip the sheet off me and over his half-crouched form. He twists and turns underneath, but the falling sheet forces him all the way to the floor.

"Turn-down service, sir," I say as I grab Yvaine's hand and we sprint from the pavilion.

We burst buck-naked into Sophie's bedroom. My aunt's already awake and struggling to get her splinted leg out of the bed.

"Tocks!" I'm so winded that's all I can get out.

She looks me up and down in my birthday suit.

"Where's your father?"

"He can feast in hell!" Yvaine says.

"We came here first," I say, "but after the way Dad was at dinner, I'm not sure I care where he is."

The sinking feeling in my gut doesn't agree.

"He told me what happened," Sophie says. "Fink can be an inflexible pig, but he means well."

"Sophie!" It's my dad's voice from the garden outside. Through the open sliding door, I see him lumbering our way.

BANG! Fragments of wood dust fly as a hole explodes in the doorframe.

Perched on a roof across the way, silhouetted by the moon, Longshot reloads his rifle.

"Dad!" I scream. "Sniper on the roof!"

Sophie grimaces as we help her up.

"Bloated ass or no, I'd do anything for Fink. He gave up his whole life to partner with his dyke kid sister."

I crawl to the window and peer through the lattice. BANG! The frame above me shatters, sending me back to the floor.

"I couldn't leave the pages!" Dad calls out. "If the Tick-Tocks get hold of them—"

"Fink, I'll hop to you," Sophie yells. "Be ready to grab me and head downtime." She turns to me. "Meet at Rendezvous D—"

I know, the sphinx. "We have a mess to clean up first," I say.

She nods. "Just be there." Then she vanishes in a flash of *in-between*.

BANG! Feathers kick up from the bed where she sat. I turn to see Longshot snaking across the roof for a better shot.

Pinned down in the buff

CHAPTER THIRTY-ONE: DATE

Before he can reload, I dive into the corner and grab Yvaine. Given our state of undress, skin-to-skin isn't a problem. Outside I hear the grunt and thump that signals Sophie joining my dad.

The Tick-Tock levels his gun at us.

I flip the switch inside myself and let us fall.

Chapter Thirty-Two:
Back Again

London, downtime

We tumble out of control through the *in-between*. The part of Yvaine I happened to grab was her ankle, and being joined hand-to-foot doesn't make for a comfortable fall.

I have to focus on where I'm going. I picture that night in *The Rose*, but not wanting to land in the back room, I think about the alley, imagining ourselves peering inside through the window.

Which makes me angry. Even though I won, I can't help but resent Donnie. Hell, there'd be something wrong with me if I didn't. I keep seeing his long face gloating over me as Stump has me by the throat. The details stick out in my mind. The way his tongue juts out, just a bit, when he rammed his sword through that journeyman in the church.

I don't even keep count as the years spin round and round us —

Until the cold night embraces us as we tumble into a hedge. Leaves and branches scrape my bare skin when we roll into the dirty space between some bushes and a ten-foot brick wall.

"I don't remember any bushes behind *The Rose*," I whisper.

But there's something familiar about the place, even if I

can't see much through the shrubbery. I doubt we're in the countryside, judging by the sounds and smells.

If Yvaine is any indicator, we look quite the pair — hair every which way, dirty and scratched, not a scrap of clothing between us other than her knife-belt. The air is colder than a witch's tit. My skin ripples with goosebumps.

Yvaine presses herself against my naked back. "Smells like London," she says.

Part of me leaps to agree. "Do you think Sophie and my dad got away?"

"That tub o'lard? He didna travel for years, so his cooldown be all sorts of ready."

"Stubborn or not, he's family—"

A creaking noise, metal on metal, sounds in front of us. I push aside some branches for a better look.

It's a girl, closing the gate in the wall behind her — the source of the creaking. She's wearing the wide-hipped dress and bonnet of the eighteenth century. Alerted by our rustling, she turns to face us.

It's fake Yvaine! Her eyes betray no recognition.

"You two catchin' a tumble in the green?" she says.

Real Yvaine, the in-focus and naked one, has squeezed herself under my arm.

"Jesus, Joseph, and Mary!" she whispers. "Charlie, you bringed us back to the bloody churchyard."

Now that I can see past the branches, I know she's right.

"Yvaine?" real Yvaine calls out.

The fake version of my lover looks puzzled. "What d'you want?"

"Dinna go inside," real Yvaine says. "Run away from this accursed night. Find Billy. Ben dies in there!"

Fake Yvaine makes the sign of the cross, then jogs to the door of the church and raps on it.

Damn! My own thoughts betrayed me, homing in on this godforsaken night instead of a week earlier. Any minute, Ben

Franklin will open the door for fake Yvaine, then Donnie, Stump, Carrot, and the fake me will storm in.

"We have to stop her — them — us," I say, extracting myself from the bushes, which is easier said than done when you're naked.

"She be a time-ghost," Yvaine says. "She'll do what I does the first time."

We stand for a second, shivering. Shanghai was hot and humid, but here the air is just raw. We need clothes. Now!

"What if we jump Donnie and the crew?" I whisper. Having been there the first time, I know they're focused on fake Yvaine at the door, not scanning the courtyard entrance for naked clones.

"I dinna think that'll work," she says, "but take this in case." She presses something hard and metallic into my hand.

One of her knives, with the blade collapsed.

I give her a quick kiss and tiptoe towards where I know Donnie and my fake self are hiding. Walking outside in the buff is really... drafty. And so cold it hurts.

But we're too late anyway. The church door opens. The invaders race across the fifteen feet and are inside before I'm halfway there. Yvaine and I race to the big door just in time to have it slam in our faces.

"Shit! Shit!" is all I can say.

"After you closed the door, what happened next?" Yvaine says. "I remembers Donnie hits Ben and I helps drag him out."

Think, Charlie.

"The boy. I let that little apprentice boy out and he comes back with the mob. If we can stop him, Donnie won't burn the building down."

"You be foxy clever," she says. "How we goin' t'do that?"

There isn't time to think about it, because the door cracks for a second and the apprentice slips out. He looks around, then sprints off.

He has shoes, but I'm faster. I tackle him just before he reaches the entrance to the street.

"But you just set me free!" he says when he catches a look at me. "And what 'appened to your clothes?"

I push the button that ejects Yvaine's knife and press it to his neck. I can't hurt him, but as Sophie said, he doesn't know that.

"Are you goin' t'cut me throat with a tobacco pipe?" he says, struggling.

Forgot normals don't see Tick-Tock weapons for what they are.

He freezes and his eyes go wide when naked Yvaine pads over and crouches right in front of his face.

"Mother of God," he says, given his view.

My hand over his mouth, we drag the boy into the bushes and I squat on his chest while Yvaine strips off his clothes. We use his own belt to hogtie him. One of his stockings goes in his mouth, the other around his head to make sure it stays there.

I end up with his pants and jacket — no shirt — and both too tight. Yvaine takes his knickers and blouse. His shoes are too small for me and Yvaine doesn't want them.

"I'm real sorry about this," I say as I cinch the buckle tight around his trussed, naked form.

"Someone needs find him top of the mornin'," Yvaine says. "If this be fatal, time would've stopped us."

I hope to hell she's right.

"The building might not burn now," I say, "but we still have to get Ben out."

In her baggy white shirt, knee-length underpants, and knife belt, Yvaine looks like a very sexy pirate.

"The roof?" She glances up. "Carrot be up there soon."

Another easier-said-than-done deal.

I find a spot where the courtyard wall is low and manage

to pull myself up. When Yvaine jumps I grab her hand, but she almost drags us both off and I have to let go.

"Try again," I say, letting more of my weight dangle over the far side to counterbalance.

Once we're up, we walk along the wall until it adjoins the building. There's construction scaffolding around one of the wing-like stone supports. We climb from deck to deck, but it's slow going and my feet hurt. Yvaine follows right below me.

"If you'd taked us where you were s'posed to, I be holdin' Billy by now."

"I thought I was," I say. "Guess time had something else on its mind."

"So did you."

We reach the small platform at the top of the scaffold. It's separated from the roof proper by about eight feet and decked with loose boards laid across a wooden frame. I tug a plank free and, with Yvaine's help, sling it across to the stone gutter to form a bridge to the church.

"I'll go first." I put a foot onto the four-inch-wide plank and glance down. The courtyard looks so far down a shiver of vertigo runs through me. "Fifty feet up, at least. Don't look."

"Better yet," she says, "dinna fall."

"This is more than a little crazy," I say. "We're both on cooldown too. You used yours in Philly, what, two or three days ago?"

I look straight ahead, hold my arms out to the side, and run across the board to the stone roof. Once there, I crouch down and turn to Yvaine.

She strides across likes it's nothing. We clamber up onto the slate tiles and slither to the crest of the roof. There we find an almost flat path and a set of steps, making it easy to walk around.

If you don't look down.

We make our way to the part of the church above the door. There's a bit of a commotion below, so I drop to my belly. Yvaine does the same and we crawl over to the edge.

The crowd with the torches is in the courtyard, just like I remember the first time around.

"Damn," I say, "did the apprentice get free?"

"I dinna see him."

I scan the crowd. Their leader waves at the mob, then the church.

Our Tick-Tock nemesis, Rapier. We creep back from the edge.

"Bugger!" Yvaine says.

"How the hell did he know we're here?" I say. "He's putting things back on track. His wrong track."

"I bets he an' his clockwork mates be throwin' a party later."

My mind races. Could Dad be right? Is what we're trying to do hopeless? I shake the thought out of my head. Dammit, the Tocks change stuff, so why can't we?

"Must've been us tying that apprentice," I say. "Rapier detected that little alteration."

Yvaine groans. Her face is a pale blob of white against the dark roof tiles.

"Rescuin' Ben be a mighty challenge if we can't never change anythin'."

I pat the knife handle shoved into my pants pocket.

"Temporal-metallics like Backstabber's daggers are supposed to be indestructible. Maybe we can push one into Rapier's guts and jam up his works."

Yvaine rolls her eyes. "That make the whole lightnin' an' tiger plan sound easy peasy."

Chapter Thirty-Three:
Rooftop

London, Spring, 1725

We hear a familiar voice from the chimney near the back of the church.

"Carrot," I whisper. "He'll be up any minute. We ought to hide somewhere — let him, Stump, and Donnie go, then slink down and try to pull Ben up."

"We can't," she says. "Dancer knows where Billy be."

Good Lord. "And he's going to tell us?"

"We needs make him," she says.

Crap. She's right, but the task seems impossible. Okay, okay, so's rushing down the chimney, killing a Tick-Tock, and getting Ben Franklin back up and off the roof to safety.

"We can ask Carrot," I say. "Maybe we'll get lucky."

"Carrot!" Yvaine says when his sooty red head appears below the chimney grate. "D'you ken where Dancer hid Billy an' Nancy?"

"How'd you birds get up 'ere?" he says.

"We snuck into the future, then traveled back in time," I say.

"Good. Then you can help me with this." He taps the copper mesh that forms a little tent over the stonework opening.

I don't know what Carrot thought I said, but the universe made sure he bought it.

I grab the metal grid and yank. It comes free easily, not being nailed down or anything, which makes sense — Carrot opened it himself in the original history. Yvaine offers her hand and we both pull him out.

"Much obliged," he says. "And Sassy, what 'appened t'your dress?"

"Billy and Nancy." Yvaine squeezes his hand. "Where they be?"

"Donnie didn't never say. Why don't you ask 'im when 'e come up?"

Carrot must have missed the whole mortal enemies memo.

"Never mind," I say. "You should get out of here." I point to the plank bridging the scaffold.

"Donnie wants you t'find us a safe place t'hide," Yvaine says.

"But I 'as to wait for Stump." Carrot pulls a thick coiled rope from his shirt and starts feeding it down the shaft. "I must needs pull 'im up. 'e can't never climb with one 'and."

Stump's welfare may not be my first concern, but I do like Carrot. I want to get him out of here before he gets hurt or causes some change the Tick-Tocks might notice.

"We takes care of Stump," Yvaine says. "Locate us a fine hidey-hole then meet us near that 'pothecary down the street."

We all but push him out onto the plank. He drops onto his belly and slithers across like a millipede.

When we get back to the chimney, we hear a loud pop below and the tinkle of breaking glass.

"Must be Dancer blowin' the crypt," Yvaine says.

My heart sinks. Right now, fifty feet beneath us, that poor boy is dying again. It's sad to think of all that suffering caught on auto-repeat.

Stump's annoying cockney voice hollers from the chimney.

"Carrot, pull me up, you ruttin' bastard!"

"Should we?" I whisper.

"We must needs surprise him. He likely ken where Billy be."

Together, we drag on the rope. Stump might be short but he's not light.

He complains from below, mostly about how he hates heights and cramped spaces, but we don't answer, just haul. As he starts to emerge, I grab his arms and pull him the rest of the way out.

"What the 'ell!" he says.

Yvaine takes hold of the rope, which he's tied under his arms, throws her weight against it, and runs down the tiles to the tiny lip at the edge of the roof.

Stump pops out of the chimney like a cork from a champagne bottle, spills onto the slippery slate, and — howling all the way — slides right down the roof and off the side.

"What'd you do?" I scream.

"Dinna worry about him," she says. "Time be on his side."

True enough. When I make my way down to join her, I find the rope snagged on a bit of stone and Stump dangling about three feet below the edge, his feet perched on a gargoyle head.

He's blubbering. "Pull me up! Pull me up!"

"The mighty Stump be cryin'?" Yvaine says.

"Pull me up!"

"First you tells me where Donnie planted Billy an' Nancy."

"I dunno," he says. "Dancer never told me."

"You can do better than that." Yvaine lies down and jerks his chain, forcing his feet off the gargoyle so he swings freely.

He screams. He shrieks. He cries like a baby.

"Yvaine!" I put a hand on the rope to hold it steady.

"He's not gonna die," she says, "but Billy might."

"Stump," I call out. "Where's Billy? I promise we'll pull you up if you tell us."

"I dunno!"

Yvaine goes to grab the rope again but I stop her, brace my feet on the lip, and strain to pull him up.

"What you be doing?" she says.

"He doesn't know."

She pouts but lets me haul Stump back onto the lip.

"That bitch be crazy," he says when he rolls to safety, "but I owes you one."

I pull two knives from his belt before he has a chance to recover.

"We don't want to see anyone hurt," I say. "Right, Yvaine?" She shrugs.

I cut the loop of rope around Stump's torso and help him up the sloping roof until we reach a stone protrusion he can cling to.

"Well, look-see what we has here," a new voice says from behind and above.

I turn to see a wigless, sooty Donnie perched on top of the chimney. Evidently, Carrot isn't the only skinny guy who can climb.

"You two vermin stick in me craw worse than a cloud of flies on shit."

"Dancer!" Yvaine screams. "Tell me where me baby is."

"Right. I'll do that very thing." But Donnie isn't even looking at her, he's scanning the layout of the roof. Behind him the flames leap higher and higher.

"Just tell the whore," Stump says. "Maybe then she lets us alone."

He said he owed me one, but that's just pathetic.

Donnie laughs.

Yvaine charges at him.

The whole building shakes. There's a deafening roar as the front half of the roof collapses, a column of flame and cinders rising from the gap.

Donnie holds tight to the chimney.

Yvaine slips, falls, slides toward the edge.

I dive, catch her arm just as she goes over, and jam my feet against the lip.

CHAPTER THIRTY-THREE: ROOFTOP

While I'm trying to pull Yvaine back up, Donnie pads over to the plank.

"Carry on your family reunion in hell," he says, kicking off his red shoes and putting a stockinged foot onto the wood.

"Dancer!" Stump calls out from his perch a few feet above. "What about me?"

Donnie sighs. "I'm always needing t'lend you a hand." He pivots on the board and offers his arm in Stump's direction. With the stolen bank notes protruding from his jacket like lace, he looks like a vaudeville dandy taking a bow.

"On me way!" Stump slides down the roof after him.

But he doesn't have a tenth of Dancer's grace. He flops onto the board and lashes it with his hand, but his weight tilts it to the side. As he flails with his stump, Donnie windmills his arms. The end of the plank slips off the roof, and both of them tumble toward the courtyard.

Yvaine gasps in my arms. "Billy!"

"We'll find him." I lean over, my head hammering. Bank notes flutter through the air. The mob below, which has been either watching the spectacle or beating at the flames, rushes towards a single still form lying on the stone pavers.

I can't tell which of them it is — and why is there just one body?

"Looking for little ole' me?" Donnie calls up. The agile prick is dangling underneath the very same gargoyle Stump half-perched on earlier. His feet scrabble at the wall and he tries to pull himself up, but the surface offers no purchase.

"Doesn't look like you'll be hanging around long," I say.

Yvaine grabs hold of the rope attached to the chimney and drags it out of his reach.

"Tell me where Billy is or you be kissin' dirt," she says.

He grins. "My dear nug, pull me up and I'll dock you extraordinary."

Yvaine hawks a loogie onto his face.

His grin only grows bigger. "Still the cockish wench me loves."

I'm not close enough to punch him in the face, so I snatch up a loose roof tile and hurl it. Yvaine gasps but a powerful gust of wind makes it miss by inches.

"I can still rile your new twang," he says.

"If there be any decency in you," Yvaine yells, "you'd send a babe back t'his mum."

"Parrish raised me," he says, "and look—"

The neck of the gargoyle shatters.

Donnie falls.

The roar of the fire drowns out the smack of his body against the hard ground.

Yvaine is sobbing.

"We'll find Billy," I say. "But we have to hurry. Ben needs us first."

She scrubs her eyes with her fists. We make our way back to the chimney.

I remember going with my mom to Arizona one summer — the temperature was 120 degrees, but the air blasting out of the church feels hotter. I haul up Stump's rope, drop it down the shaft, then swing my feet in and tell Yvaine to follow me.

"That way if you slip, maybe I'll break your fall."

But falling isn't the problem. In fact, the shaft is so narrow and rough that at times I find it hard to squeeze myself down. I have no idea how we're going to cram Ben up here.

I cough and gasp at the hot sooty air. It doesn't help that Yvaine's dirty feet keep kicking me in the head.

The journey seems endless but probably doesn't last more than three minutes. I'm pretty sure I leave a third of my skin behind as I crash down into the fireplace.

Donnie and Stump walk the plank

Roaring flames illuminate the church. Not ten feet away, I watch Yvaine's and my time-ghosts kiss behind the anvil and vanish.

"Make room." Real Yvaine kicks at my head and I scoot to the side.

The fake Tick-Tock stands for a moment on top of the anvil, just an ordinary-looking man in a blue suit.

"Tick-Tock time-ghost," I say. He vanishes too — about twenty-six seconds after we did.

Yvaine drops into my arms, then scrambles over to Ben and slaps him hard across the face.

"Ben! Wake up."

He shakes his head. He looks groggy.

We drag him back toward the chimney, which wakes him up some. But I'm not liking our odds. The ceiling above is a sea of rippling flame.

"Where am I?" Ben says.

About to burn to death, but I don't say that. Instead, I grab the rope and tug on it to draw more slack. The damned line breaks.

Could things get any worse?

CHIME! A hole flashes in the air. Rapier jumps down onto the anvil, sword in hand.

Chapter Thirty-Four:
Paperwork

London, Spring, 1725

The Tick-Tock saunters toward us, clacking his jaw and wagging his finger.

Yvaine and I struggle to hoist the woozy Ben to his feet. We stagger backward, but fire is everywhere and there's only so far we can go without char-broiling ourselves.

Rapier seems in no hurry. Ten feet away he fences with the air and clacks his jaw again.

Yvaine draws her remaining dagger, pushes the button to extend it, and holds it ready.

Rapier stops. His head tilts back and forth and he vibrates in place.

Something has finally pissed him off!

I draw my own dagger, holding it with my left hand — my right hand's busy holding up a Founding Father.

Rapier's head swivels back and forth between us. He moves again, sidestepping around the room. One of his booted feet toes into a burning pile of something: he stops to tug at his leg like he stepped on a giant wad of bubble gum. The flames tongue his calf, but he keeps tugging at his leg. Finally, he wrenches it free and resumes circling.

I retract my dagger and shove it back in my pocket.

"The fire!" I yell. "It sticks to him!"

I grab a heavy iron thing, so hot it burns my hand, and heave it across the room into some smoldering chairs. They shatter, throwing sparks and flames at the Tock. He dodges to the side, and is slowed as he passes through the fire, but he works past it and lunges straight at us, sword extended.

Yvaine shoves Ben in front of us.

Rapier streaks toward him, trips, and falls on his face. As he slides to the side he jingles like the broken Mickey Mouse alarm clock I had as a kid.

"He can't harm Ben," Yvaine says by way of explanation.

Founding Father as human shield. Can't say I'd think of that.

"Why do strangers all want to hurt me tonight?" Ben says.

"Over here." Yvaine pulls us back toward the anvil.

The Tock springs to his feet.

"I'll take Ben," I say. "Throw crap at the Tock! Anything on fire."

Yvaine paws through the clutter. Rapier eyes her as she grabs up some burning wood and hurls it his way.

"Over here, gearhead!" I scream, drawing the dagger again and waving it.

The Tick-Tock ducks to avoid Yvaine's projectile but swivels toward me.

A burning beam falls from the ceiling. Without looking up, he slides out of the way. Ben and I both cringe from the wall of heat — not that the room wasn't already an inferno.

"Bucket brigades..." Ben mutters. "Organized to fight fires and prevent loss of life and property."

The guy is strange.

I almost miss a new thrust Rapier aims in my direction. I use the dagger to knock his weapon wide. The brass blades throw blue sparks as they clang against each other.

"He be toyin' with us!" Yvaine cries. "Waitin' for us t'burn."

There has to be something else to stop him, but all I see are a couple little tools and piles and piles of papers. The heat and flames have even lifted some of them into the air —

Paper. Not exactly the ultimate weapon…

Unless your enemy can't move anything.

"Yvaine! Throw paper at him. As much of it as you can."

The Tock thrusts again, but I duck behind Ben. Rapier stops himself, then resumes our dance.

Yvaine grabs a stack of half-printed paper — more un-finished banknotes? — and hurls it at Rapier. The bundle comes apart, filling the air. Floating embers ignite some of the pages. Inside this mess, the Tock comes to a standstill. White papers stick to him, making him look like a mummy in a paper mill explosion. His sword seems to droop under their weight. He struggles to turn his head. Between sheets, I see his free hand twitching in a small space.

"More paper!" I yell. "Ben, you too. Keep it coming."

Yvaine and Ben hurl more bundles. The Tock pulls his free arm to his chest and gropes.

CHIME. He's trapped and he knows it, so now he's trying to bug out. Damned if I want him here, but I can't let him escape. He'll just show up again or pop back in time and do who-knows-what.

CHIME. I lunge into the paper storm, clutching Backstabber's dagger. Maybe I can get it in there and foul up his works.

CHIME. The papers part for me, but they might as well be steel plates when the Tock-made dagger slams against them, sending a jolt all the way back along my arm.

CHIME. Yvaine chucks something flaming into the swirl of paper. Now half the stuff starts to singe and burn, adding to the fun.

CHIME. Rapier and I both discover that by wiggling and worming through the wall of shifting burning paper it's possible to make some progress. For me this means I start to maneuver the dagger close to him. For him it means he drops his sword and snakes a hand in my direction.

Playing with fire

CHIME. He almost gets a grip on my arm, but I jam his brother's blade into the gears of his forearm and twist. Something metallic pops free and his hand goes limp. His mouth is locked open in a parody of rage. I notice his sword sliding down the swirling papers like a pachinko ball.

CHIME. I get the point of my blade near his chest, but the paper over the surface might as well be titanium armor.

CHIME. "Yvaine, help!" I yell as the Tock snags my wrist with his working hand. His grip is like steel, and I wince as he clamps down hard.

CHIME. The Tock and I struggle. Through the papers, I see Yvaine behind him, trying to work her own dagger into the jumble. I thrust my free hand through, scrape away at the banknotes on his chest, flip open his jacket, and uncover his dials.

CHIME. "Bastard!" Yvaine yells, working the tip of her weapon into his shoulder. The gears in his arm catch on the blade and go immobile.

CHIME. I work my hand and dagger free of the paralyzed mechanical arm. My face is close enough to his for me to get a detailed look at the fine crack in his porcelain cheek.

CHIME. "You are so out of time," I say, using my dagger to spin the dial with the months. Yvaine darts her hand into his jacket, groping beneath, and I barely avoid slicing her fingers as I work the dagger tip under a gauge and pop the whole face free from Rapier's mechanism.

CHIME. The spinning ruby-red whirlwind in his chest flares with the *in-between*, the bright firelight in the room dims, and Rapier drops into nothing.

We teeter back from the edge of his closing time-hole. Papers swirl into the space he vacated. There's a double metallic clatter as his sword finally makes its way to the floor and the month-dial joins it.

"Chicken-hearted knave!" Yvaine steps back, something shiny in her hand.

Maybe with a bum hand, no sword, and a broken chrono-whatever, he won't be a threat for a while. I retract the blade of my dagger, return it to Yvaine — and see what she's holding. A gleaming brass page.

"I saw this inside his jacket," she says. "Figured to make a habit of stealin' 'em back."

I smile. "I've got my own souvenir." I kick the fencing sword out from under the swirling papers and snag it.

"Charlie!" Yvaine shoves me to the side, just getting us clear of another collapsing beam. It's all very well to be free of the killer machine, but we *are* stuck in a burning building with no way out!

Glancing back, I see the chimney is filled with fire, so that's hopeless. I put my arm around Yvaine and we hurry over to Ben, who's retreated to the back wall.

The searing air cooks my lungs and threatens to boil my eyeballs. I pull Yvaine's face to mine.

"We're toast," I say.

She gives me a quick kiss, and for that sweet second the fury around us fades away.

Until the building shakes, just for a moment.

"Timequake!" Yvaine whispers.

"We have to open the back door," Ben says.

Door? I turn to find him tugging at a wall hanging of a fairytale Asian scene — which I hadn't noticed. The whole thing falls away to reveal a small wooden door.

The first time we were here, back when Yvaine warped me out, I scanned the whole wall. No wall hanging. No door.

Not that I'm complaining.

Ben gets the bolt and kicks the door open, letting in a blast of cool air.

Chapter Thirty-Four: Paperwork

The London mist outside is pure heaven on my skin. The three of us stagger into the courtyard, where lines of people pass water buckets to throw onto the fire. They look surprised to see us.

"Where'd that door come from?" I say.

"It's been there for decades," Ben says. "My boss, old Mr. Palmer, likes to tell the story about the fat man who showed up one day and paid him a fortune in gold just to install it — no reason given or asked."

Of course, until that timequake, no one told that story. Not only did adding the door, well, add the door, but the resulting timequake gave everyone memories to match.

I look back at the church entrance, filled now with a solid sheet of flame.

Thanks, Dad! I'll consider that a belated apology.

Chapter Thirty-Five:
Newgate

London, Spring, 1725

Of course, there's still the angry mob to contend with.

Ben tries to defend us, but his protestations fall on deaf ears. They're ripe for a game of beat-the-robbers. Despite a thorough job of groping and punching, they don't notice Rapier's sword tucked in my arms. Normals can't see travelers' weapons.

Come morning, Yvaine and I are hauled off, bruised and battered, in a manure cart. I manage to raise my head — before it's knocked back down — to take in a crowded square in front of a fortress of a building.

The mob is thickest as we pass the stocks. Back as a kid, visiting historical sites with my mom, it was fun to pretend to be locked between the wooden boards. But here it isn't just a bunch of laughing twelve-year-olds doing the jeering. Here the rabble pelts us with things I wouldn't touch if you paid me — like putrefying cats.

But we roll right past, through an imposing gate into a foul-smelling courtyard.

"Welcome t'Newgate Prison," Yvaine whispers as the guards come for us.

As a budding connoisseur of correctional institutions, I have to say the prison back in Philadelphia was paradise compared to what the inmates here refer to as *The King's Head Inn*.

On the bright side, the booking process is perfunctory and Yvaine and I aren't separated.

But we *are* chained. Thick black *Amistad*-style manacles on legs and wrists. It could be worse, though. They go through our possessions — again — without touching my new sword, our metallic page, or Yvaine's daggers.

After that, we're pretty much tossed through the door into hell.

The Newgate felony ward, as I learn it's called, is a warren of crowded corridors and doorless cells. It all smells like shit, and a whole lot of it since there are no bathrooms. Our bare feet are a sticky brown — best not to touch the scrapes and cuts on my face. Plus several fellow prisoners look like they should be home with the flu.

"Just say no to typhus," I whisper.

Yvaine leans against me. "If we get some chink, we must needs bribe the guards t'remove the irons."

"Money? In here?"

"For food and gin."

"They don't give us food?" Not that I was looking forward to the local fare, but since I've half starved a couple times of late, I'll take my chances with weevils and gruel.

"If we gets word to Carrot, maybe he'll sneak us some," she says. "If not, we be right skinny by the time we can travel."

"I think we have ten days to go."

She nods. "Trial be before then but not hangin' day."

"Maybe we can get some kind of message to Sophie and my dad."

Yvaine scowls.

"Hey, he broke his precious rules to add that door back at the church!"

"I appreciates that, Charlie. But dinna go askin' me to stitch him a quilt just yet."

The next morning I wake to find Yvaine cursing and kicking at a scrawny, scabrous guy who's groping at her underwear-clad legs.

A good whack across the head with my manacles sends him scurrying. And pathetic as he is, he must be richer than us, because he isn't in chains.

"I had it under control," Yvaine says.

"Can't a fellow protect his girl?"

She sighs and settles next to me. It would be a pleasant moment if not for the ambience.

We try to stand, but it isn't easy. We brace against each other and worm ourselves up the wall.

"See?" I say. "Teamwork."

"If I get too used t'it, I'll go soft," she says.

I kiss her, which hurts given my split lip.

Some of our fellow prisoners wander around like zombies. Others huddle in groups, shooting craps, and quite a few drink from skanky mugs. It's kind of like the most sordid rave imaginable. In one room, we find a disgusting man and a suitably disgusting girl rutting away, right on the floor. She doesn't look happy but she isn't complaining.

"Should we help her?" I ask Yvaine.

"She probably be tryin' t'plead the belly."

"What's that mean?"

"They dinna hang women that be with child."

"And you worry about going soft?"

We settle in the visiting gallery, which is hot and loud but has fresher air and more light than below. The scene is chaotic. A long row of prison bars divides the room. It reminds me of that place at the airport where people wait to greet family coming off the plane, only here nobody gets picked up and taken home.

I use the delay to translate the page we stole from Rapier. Working the formula without pen and paper isn't easy, and

I have to scratch the Latin in the grime on the prison floor. There are just enough words I recognize to tell it's a treatise on Benjamin Franklin, including a detailed timeline of his whereabouts and his impact on the future. The Regulator says, *presentia est necessarius secundum 1765 Anno Domini*: presence necessary after 1765 AD.

Tell me something I don't know.

"Rapier's to-do list in a nutshell."

"Whose side this Regulator be on?"

I shrug. "Dad sure has a man-crush on him."

"What's that mean?" she asks.

"It's when—"

Her face lights up. "There be Carrot!" She tucks away the page and gets to her feet.

Lost in cipher-land, I forgot we were in the visiting galley.

"I heared they catched some folk the other night," Carrot says from the 'free' side after we shoulder our way over to him.

Yvaine gives him an awkward hug through the bars.

"Thanks for coming," I say.

"Brought you this." He passes us a loaf of bread.

I try not to think about what's on my hands as we tear into it.

"It be stuffed with a bit of wedge," Carrot says.

Yvaine digs through the bread until she finds several small coins.

"We owes you again," she says.

"Just returnin' the favor, but I wishes I 'ad Donnie's salt t'buy off your trial. What 'appened to 'im and Stump?"

"They climbed up the chimney after you left," Yvaine says.

Carrot nods. "I not 'eared from them, but with that much rum cole I bets they split town."

I watch one of the guards let another pair of officers out through the gate, which gives me an idea.

"Think you could bring me a guard's uniform?" I ask Carrot.

"Mebbe. But ain't you be on the short side for a warden?"

I'm not so sure. Yvaine said a long time ago, *people see what they expect in us,* and the Tick-Tocks sure work that angle.

"See if you can, Carrot," Yvaine says. "You heared any word on Nancy?"

He nods, his face all smile. "She done turned up this mornin' lookin' for coin. She 'ad the little chit with 'er."

"Blessed virgin!" Yvaine stands on her tiptoes and tries to hug Carrot again. "He be all right?"

"Billy's right as rain. I'd of brought 'im but I didn't know you be 'ere for sure."

"Bring 'im, please." A tear streaks her dirt-caked face.

The first thing we do after Carrot leaves is find the right guard to buy off our chains.

"I feel light as a butterfly," I say, massaging my sore wrists.

"We have a wee bit o'money left for ale," she says.

"What about food?"

"We'll die of thirst first," she says, grinning. "But that was a clever bit about the uniform."

She leads me to one of the grubby tavern areas.

"We make of it what we will," I say.

"Exactly," she says, handing me a mug of beer. "Dinna worry, Billy be found and Ben be alive. And it takes 'em more than a week t'hang folk."

We toast the slow judicial process.

People here mostly leave us alone because of our time traveler vibe — ahem, because of causal-dampening — but I chase some scumbags out of a rank cell for a little privacy.

We're too wired to sleep just yet, although we probably should. Instead, I check for lookie-loos and we make a go at pleading the belly.

The Justice Hall is packed for our trial, our case having drawn no small amount of notoriety.

The white-wigged advocates give speeches, witnesses are interviewed, including the apprentice boy and Ben Franklin, and the jury deliberates.

All in about an hour.

"Do you find the prisoners guilty or not guilty?" asks a man the judge calls the recorder.

"Guilty," the foreman says with token weightiness.

It's hard to remain unemotional when you're given a capital verdict.

Guards — Yvaine calls them turnkeys — hustle us from the room. Ben Franklin is in the hall outside. He uses a shilling to buy a few minutes from our keepers.

"They'll send us up at Tyburn," Yvaine says. "Will you take Billy?"

"I tried to plead your case," Ben says.

He really did. His testimony spun the truth about as far in our favor as was possible, sticking more or less to the facts.

But the facts didn't sound so good.

"You must needs take him if we're to hang," Yvaine says. "You be his father, you has to."

Ben nods. He looks as nervous as I feel.

Chapter Thirty-Six:
Condemned

London, Spring, 1725

The sentencing is even shorter than the trial, but just as crowded.

We're "condemned to hang until dead" on a Monday over a month from now.

I try to shrug it off. The prison is bad, but in eight days its walls won't matter. We'll be gone.

Then two men enter the room.

One of them is Rapier. His blue suit is ratty, dirt clings to his mask, and one arm hangs limp and useless at the shoulder, the other at the elbow.

"Who's that with him?" I whisper to Yvaine.

"Jonathan Wild, the Thief-taker General."

The other man is short and ugly, but his coat and wig are fine and primped.

Rapier leans close to him, and Wild approaches the judge. They speak for a minute.

"On further consideration of the particulars," the judge announces, "this execution shall take place one week hence."

The slam of his gavel feels as final as it sounds. The noise is still ringing in my ears when I look up to find Rapier standing toe-to-toe with me. I stumble backward, but he edges after me until I'm trapped by a wooden wall and the turnkey's grip.

"No fraternizin' with prisoners," one of our guards says.

Rapier doesn't care. His hands might not be working but he uses his functional upper arm to open my jacket, then dips his face to my chest.

He's going to gum me to death? The guards have me good and pinned. I wait for the burning pain — but he steps back, the Regulator's page in his jaws.

"Sir," a bailiff says, "I must ask you to remove yourself."

The Rapier doesn't move, just stares at the sword shoved through my belt.

The bailiff grasps his limp arm and leads him away.

I'm still recovering, catching my breath as the turnkeys force us, along with several other condemned, to hold out our hands while a guard binds our thumbs together with a thin metal cord.

He winds it so tight it cuts deep into the skin.

They don't take us back to the regular ward but instead throw us into the Condemned Hold, a single room of stone with a slit of a window too high up for any prisoner to see through. Wooden bench-like shelves serve as beds and seats, with most of the half-dozen or so inmates perched or reclining on them.

The Deputy Keeper, who introduces himself as Mr. Rouse, cuts the cords around our thumbs as he shoves us inside. In the hour or so since our sentence, the pain's retreated to a dull ache, and the color of the affected digits has faded to white. Their release reveals thin red slices where the cords cut in, so deep I half expect to see bone.

And the real kicker is when the blood returns.

"Do you think Ben will come?" Yvaine asks after the pain becomes manageable.

I'm slouched at the end of one of the bench-beds. Yvaine's stretched out along the full length, her head in my lap.

"He'd better," I say. "I saw him before the Tick-Tock showed up, so I know he heard our sentence. At least he's alive, and if he takes Billy their futures should be more or less on track."

It's our own lives that are royally screwed.

"I hopes your mum remembers you again." Her eyes gleam. "And likes me better than your da."

"We'll just have to escape and find out," I say.

But I seem to have lost my natural optimism. Maybe it's this hellhole we're in, maybe it's the pain in my battered body, maybe it's Rapier's worming his way back here so easily. My English teacher, Mrs. Pinkle, had a word for what I'm feeling. She taught it to us when we read *Hamlet* last fall: melancholy.

Just because we're on death row doesn't mean we're isolated. If anything, the whole setup is more convenient but less private than the felony ward. Our cell is separated from a public room called the Lodge, which serves as a kind of prison guard social club where food and drink are for sale. Which, if we had any money, would be great.

As it is, I'm lightheaded with hunger and so thirsty the chamberpot might start to look appealing.

"Can I borrow some coin?" I ask one of the turnkeys as he passes.

"Let me guess." He grins. "You'll pay me back in two weeks."

"You don't want us to starve before you can kill us, do you?"

"Tell you what," he says, "Give you two shillings for your jacket."

One of the other prisoners told me the turnkeys sell souvenirs off the condemned.

"Ten," I say, "but you loan me yours until I don't need it anymore."

"I'll lose me job, but I can offer you a guinea for the girl's knickers," he says. "Today."

"And your uniform?"

He shakes his head. Not that I'd sell Yvaine's clothes, but it was worth seeing if I could talk the jacket off him.

"Set us free," I say, "and you can have everything we own."

That earns a laugh. "I likes you. A silver crown, and I'll rent you back your jacket till your final mornin'."

I accept. At least we have money to eat and drink.

The ringing sound of a turnkey's club on the bars wakes us from a fitful nap.

"Printhouse pillagers!" he shouts, using the nickname the papers gave us. "You got visitors."

The Lodge is open to the public for a couple pennies a head. This time it's Carrot, and he's brought Nancy and the baby.

"Billy!" Yvaine shrieks, reaching.

Nancy lets her hold him, although it's awkward at arm's length through bars. Billy doesn't look any older than I remember, but it's only been a couple days — for him.

"Carrot," Yvaine says, "can you run and get Mr. Franklin? He can often be found at *The Horns* tavern, near the priory."

"Me?" He leans close to whisper. "What if the other printers recognize me?"

"Send Nancy," I say.

While we wait for her, Yvaine sings softly to Billy. I catch myself wondering what our kids might be like. But first we have to survive Monday!

If we do, and if our kids are travelers, I'm going to tell them all about it. As soon as they're old enough to understand.

"Any luck with that uniform?" I ask Carrot.

"Couldn't find none." He presses a loaf of bread into my hands. "But take this."

I fish inside to find coins and a heavy-duty steel file.

"Bless you." But if there is a God, he sure as hell isn't watching out for us.

"Jack Sheppard used one of those t'saw through right 'ere." Carrot taps the bars. "But methinks they might've replaced 'em thicker now."

There are no guards around, so I set to work in the corner filing away at the base of a bar. Trust me, 'slow going' doesn't begin to cover it.

Nancy returns with Ben Franklin, who looks troubled.

"I spoke to the judge again. He told me flat out that Jonathan Wild would never allow a stay of execution."

"Magistrate's just some man with a purse heavy enough for his post," Yvaine says.

Ben shakes his head. "Treating government positions as prerogatives is inherently corrupt."

Yvaine says, "The real question be, are *you* going to do right by Billy and me?"

"I think I have it in me to be a better printer than a father, but I'm no shirk."

"Thank you." She pats his shoulder through the bars.

"If it's all right with you," he says, "I'll take him back to Philadelphia. I lost my position here. There's a postal frigate leaving tomorrow at dawn."

"Family be more important than place," Yvaine says.

Uh oh. In my original history, he was here for another year.

"You didn't do anything wrong," I say.

His turn to shrug. "Mr. Palmer was fair enough. Someone has to take responsibility, other than the insurer."

"You should start your own print shop in Philadelphia," I say, hoping to help keep him on track.

"I plan to. Plenty of things to keep me busy." His face lights up. "In fact, I couldn't help noticing the discharge of sparks you caused that terrible night. There was something about it that made me think lightning might be electrical in nature."

He isn't supposed to begin his electrical researches for

another twenty years. Looking at him, I imagine the gears spinning — not Tick-Tock gears but Ben Franklin super genius gears.

Yvaine pulls Billy's head close enough to whisper in his ear, then holds him out.

"Your son, Mr. Franklin."

Ben eyes the baby like he might bite, but he takes him.

"William, then," he says.

Tears are trickling down Yvaine's face.

"One more favor," I say. "When you write your memoirs, put in a sentence about William's mother. Say she was a good girl from Scotland, hanged at Tyburn. Give the date, too. The date's real important." *Indirect manipulations,* Dad said.

Now tears are squeezing out the corners of Ben's eyes.

"I'll also say she fought for her son to the end, showing her bold and generous character."

Yvaine says goodbye to Billy

Chapter Thirty-Seven:
Tyburn

London, Spring, 1725

In the morning, the turnkey who rented me my jacket claims his property and we're taken to the yard. The weather outside is cool and gray. I feel the damp against my bare chest. A blacksmith strikes off what shackles remain on the four of us who stand condemned.

I feel a quiver deep inside my groin. In Philly, that started a day or so before I could travel.

"My cooldown is almost up," I whisper to Yvaine.

Her eyes brighten. "Mine too. I'd say it be a close race, but Rapier always be one step ahead."

"How could he—"

A turnkey cuffs me hard with his stick.

"Quiet. Under Sheriff Watson is here."

An officious man demands a receipt for each of our bodies from the turnkeys. Damn creepy.

Next, we're muscled through the gate and onto the street. Several constables on horseback lead four carts. All in all, it's a pretty sorry parade.

Our perfectly rational escape plans fizzled — no uniforms to walk out in, not enough time before they hang me to file through the bars. But I've still got two crazy schemes. First, with Ben Franklin alive and on his way back to America, I'm hoping that when the timequake hits, Dad will reread the *Autobiography*. If he notices that date, Sophie should be all over the rescue plan. Failing that, we delay and hope our cooldowns reset. Yvaine's right next to me — I'll just step on her foot and off we go.

Turnkeys grab our arms and force us toward separate carts.

"Yvaine!" I scream.

"Watch out, Charlie!"

A sharp pain across my temple gets me about a thousand stars. These guards are really pissing me off.

They lift me onto the cart and loop the noose over my woozy head. But instead of cinching it about my neck, they pull it tight around my elbows and torso. A priest hops up next to me, so I'm squeezed between him and a turnkey.

"Call me Mr. Wagstaff." His white pilgrim-style clerical collar flaps in the breeze.

I tell him my name. He nods as he forgets it.

When our procession rolls out the prison gate, I'm surprised to find the street packed like Philadelphia at Thanksgiving. The cheering crowd would make a rock star happy. Kids line the rooftops, bare legs dangling. Every window is jammed with faces, and the constables have to use whips to clear the path.

Two new wagons join our procession, each loaded with a pair of coffins. Perched on one of these is a heavyset man dressed in black, a black hood over his face.

"Normally I sit with Mr. Ketch," Mr. Wagstaff says, nodding at the black blob. "But my stomach's unsettled this morning. Can't take his stench."

"He's the…" My mouth's so dry it's hard to talk.

"Mr. Jack Ketch, Esquire, King of Tyburn, the hangman," Wagstaff says. "Not that his mum gave him that name, but it's tradition to call them after a notorious predecessor who botched his duties."

I don't want to know how you botch an execution.

"Why're you here, sir?" I ask.

Our cheery little column halts before a stone church.

"As pastor of St. Sepulchre," Wagstaff says, "I offer solace to the damned. Take mass if you like."

I've never been much for church — nothing against it or anything, but the only time I went it was, well, boring. I glance back at Yvaine on her own cart, her arms held tight by her noose, her teeth nibbling at her lips.

Today, a nice long service might be just what we need.

Yvaine is maybe twenty feet ahead as we step out of the church into bright sunshine. She twists around to look at me.

"Me cooldown be back—" The turnkey boxes her in the ear.

I lunge forward. My own power is still a couple hours off, but if I can just touch her, we're out of here, leaving Mr. Jack Ketch, Esquire, at the altar.

I only get two steps before a blow to my shoulder knocks me to one knee. Two of the guards grab me by the arms.

"Turnkeys take such pleasure in their work," Wagstaff says once I'm shoved back into my cart. "Let me buy you a drink instead."

Sure enough, we pull up before a tavern and a screaming crowd. Pints of ale are passed around to guards, priest, and prisoners alike.

I'm required to clink mugs with my admirers. I look back at Yvaine and watch for any opening. We only need an instant's proximity.

The first prisoner stands in his cart and raises a pair of tankards above his head.

"I'll buy you all a round on me way back!" he yells.

The crowd on the street goes wild with cheers and toasts. Jack Ketch sits on his coffin throne. People press beers into his hands. He rolls his hood up over his mouth and chugs away.

Maybe if they get the hangman drunk enough he'll pass out. Maybe —

Out of the corner of my eye, I catch the too-sharp impression of someone near Ketch and the coffins. Someone out of phase with time. The surging crowd hides the traveler from view, but hope rises in me.

Only to be dashed when I spot Rapier's crisp blue-coated form. He must've checked out the hangman, then stepped back to get a view. Noticing my gaze, he waves with his 'good' arm. His bicep lifts but his forearm and hand dangle.

Doesn't matter. His being here makes my already slim chances of touching Yvaine even slimmer.

I've been afraid countless times since this whole adventure began, but I always thought that things would work out. I already lost my optimism, and now I feel like I've lost all hope. Without it, the fear I'm feeling is different, a growing certainty that man is not God, and that the course of history will drag us both to the gallows and hang us by the neck until dead.

Tyburn Fair is outfitted like an all-day summer concert. Where the stage should be, the gallows looms, three thick horizontal beams set atop heavy vertical posts like a grotesque wooden Stonehenge. On one side is a rock wall topped with shoulder-to-shoulder spectators. On the other side are enormous wooden bleachers filled to precarious capacity. The field between is packed with everyone from picnicking gentlemen wearing clean wigs and pressed jackets to gutter whores clutching dirty babies to their breasts.

The chance to touch Yvaine never comes. I'm wedged between turnkey and pastor, and two extra guards cling to the cart. Not to mention the press of people worming, jeering, and reaching between us.

Rapier seems content to let justice take its course. He remains at a distance as our parade halts near the gallows. One prisoner is in the cart in front of me, Yvaine is behind mine, the last behind hers. The first cart is wheeled under the beams and the loose end of the condemned man's rope tossed over. So drunk he can barely stand, the hangman takes several minutes to get the knot tied around the poor man's neck. He jumps from the cart, stumbles to his knees, but the crowd lifts him to his feet. He ties the rope tight to a gallows post.

Mr. Wagstaff stands near the cart, Jack Ketch staggers toward the horses. We wait as the roar of the crowd settles and the sea of humanity falls silent.

The prisoner reaches up to tug the handkerchief down, half covering his face. Jack Ketch slaps the lead horse on its rump, and the cart rolls out from underneath the doomed man.

The roaring cheers return a hundredfold. I watch in horror, expecting a Hollywood Western drop and snap. But the prisoner doesn't really fall. He kicks and thrashes within a small ring of constables that hold back the crowd, his hands clawing at his neck, his feet reaching for a foothold that isn't there.

The volume of shouting dies down, but he keeps on kicking and squirming. His efforts work the handkerchief free to reveal a purple face contorted with terror.

This macabre dance continues for what seems like hours. I glance back at Yvaine. Her eyes are wide open and her face drained of color. The afternoon can't be warmer than sixty, but her hair is plastered against shiny skin.

Back on the scaffold, the kicks grow feebler until, with a last spasm, they stop. Jack Ketch steps forward and whacks the body with a long stick, inducing a further series of convulsions. When these stop, he strikes again. The corpse doesn't twitch this time, just spins around like a gruesome piñata.

The hangman cuts the rope and the body drops. The crowd cheers and breaks through the constables to hoist the dead man aloft. His lifeless form is lifted on their hands, passed from person to person like a singer crowd-surfing the mosh pit.

My cart pulls up beneath the gallows. I've never been so scared in my life. I can't even count the number of times I nearly died lately, but this is the first one where I've seen a live action demo of my fate.

Wagstaff helps me to my feet and I scan the crowd, every pair of eyes reflected back on me. Are Carrot and Yvaine's old gang out there somewhere? Rapier has seated himself in the front row of the bleachers, about fifty feet away.

Jack Ketch joins us, staggers sideways, and almost falls back off the cart. Wagstaff was right: he does stink. Like piss and beer.

"Mr. Wagstaff," the hangman says, his slur thickening the words, "me needs fill Oliver's skull before droppin' this one."

The priest sighs. Jack Ketch slides back off the cart and into the crowd.

"You've a brief reprieve while our erstwhile publican relieves himself," Wagstaff says.

Which gives me an idea.

"Could me and my girl go out at the same time?" I say.

He scrunches his face, which makes him look like a hamster.

"That would be irregular."

I raise my free hand as if to speak, quieting the crowd.

"Seeing as me and my girl did rob the print house together," I scream, "shouldn't we hang together?"

The crowd cheers and someone starts up a chant:

"Printhouse pillagers, together! Together!"

Taking credit for a crime I didn't do bothers me, but it's all for a good cause.

"TOGETHER!"

"Let him have it his way," the officer in charge tells the others, "lest the mob make short work of us."

Yvaine's cart is drawn next to mine.

Chapter Thirty-Seven: Tyburn

Parked side-by-side under the gallows, we're only eight feet apart. I step to the edge and reach for her while she does the same.

But the party pooper of a turnkey yanks me back. Wagstaff pulls the noose up from my chest, drawing the scratchy rope across my neck.

"If we can't touch, go without me," I call.

"I won't leave you!" She bites at her captor and we make another lunge at each other. Fail. All we get is whacked. Hard. And Wagstaff tugs my noose tight.

"That swill-tub of a hangman be taking too long."

He can take all day as far as I'm concerned. But a cheer erupts as Jack Ketch returns from whatever corner he found to piss in.

I feel like joining in when I get a look at him. He's still wearing the black hood and pants, but the leather vest is stretched ridiculously tight over a torso even bigger than it was five minutes ago. After it ends his belly goes on, covered in thick hair. Every gray strand glints, sharp in the sunlight. Time traveler sharp.

The crowd cheers again as he lumbers up on the cart and checks my noose.

"I'll get your girl," Dad's voice says from behind the mask. "Your aunt is around here somewhere."

I'm so relieved my knees feel weak, but now's a bad time to drop.

"Rapier!" I whisper. "Your three o'clock."

We turn to see the Tick-Tock climb over the lip of the bleachers and jump down into the crowd.

He's seen Dad.

"Mind if I borrow this?" My hangman-father yanks Rapier's sword from my belt and leaps — none too gracefully — across to Yvaine's cart.

He bends close to her, fitting the noose about her neck.

He says something that makes her eyes snap and her mouth turn up at the corners, then scans the crowd. Behind him, the Tick-Tock fights through the mob that's drawn in all around us.

"Crown the boy, the bitch ain't worth it," says the guard Yvaine bit.

I'm alone on my cart, but my dad stands next to Yvaine, a hand on her noosed neck, the other holding the Tock's sword. Suddenly, he throws it high. Sophie leaps from the crowd, not far from me, and snatches it out of the air. I guess it's been more than a week for her because that leg sure looks better!

The throng cheers and settles to an expectant hush as Wagstaff tries to prep me. Rapier is much closer now, just a few feet from Sophie, slowly working his way through tight-packed bodies he can't move. Just like with the paper in the church, he has to wait for each little opening.

BRRIIIING! BRRIIIING! I hear the angry noise over the cheers and jeers: Rapier is ringing like a huge alarm clock. The crowd pays him no notice, but the horses tied to my cart rear and buck. They lurch forward, drawing the cart out from under me.

I drop — just a couple inches, but the rope around my neck is like a vise. My body feels like a thousand pounds dragging me down. I look for Yvaine, but my eyeballs seem to explode from my skull and my vision blurs.

I struggle to breathe. No air gets to my lungs. My chest burns and I swoon. My legs flail. I think of the man in the first cart and shudder: there's nothing for my feet to find. The burning tightness around my neck gets worse and worse. The crowd spins as I twist at the end of the rope. Sophie's nearly clear, but so is Rapier, and he steps between us.

Yvaine swims into view, still on her cart, mouth open like a fish. So little time, we had so little time together.... I'd have

Charlie dances at the sheriff's ball

thought everything would go dark, but instead it's growing white. Luminous and bright.

Spinning in place, I see Rapier and Sophie fighting, not eight feet away, just beyond the ring of constables. She feints, then bashes him in the face with the hilt of the sword. He spins, spilling two metallic pages into the dirt between the carts.

Sophie shoves past the guards to step around him. Rapier regains his balance and follows.

My dad surges toward the edge of Yvaine's cart, his eyes locked on the pages not five feet from him. But he steps back and hurls something into the air. A cascade of golden discs rains down around the Tick-Tock.

Coins. The constables lose control of the crowd. Everyone surges toward Rapier and the money, burying him in a wall of flesh.

My father grabs Yvaine again, the sun dims, a hole opens beneath them, and they fall out of sight.

Sophie steps forward and grasps my bare ankle.

"Done hanging out?" she yells.

And we surge upward toward the bright, bright future.

Chapter Thirty-Eight:
History 3.0

London, June, 1759

We land somewhere in the near future along the muddy shallows of the River Thames.

When we start wading, Sophie limps. I give her a soggy hug on shore.

"How's the leg?"

She's trying to wring out her skirts. I'm not sure I've ever seen her in a dress.

"Getting there, Charlie. Personally, it's been about six months since China."

"This is the third time you've rescued me, you know," I say, trying to ignore the maggoty dead dog bobbing to my right. Good thinking, installing that door in the church."

"We were in Giza, looking for those extra pages, and we felt some small quakes. It wasn't hard to guess where you'd gone, and your dad, brainiac that he is, remembered which building Ben Franklin had his workshop in. The problem was, we didn't know the exact *when*, so we took a shotgun approach and added something permanent years earlier."

I'd forgotten Giza. "The Regulator have anything new to say?"

"Your dad is still translating. We had to rush back to arrange that door, which put us on the downtime side of the big quake that got Franklin back on the map, but we crawled up to 1791 and got the scoop from his *Autobiography.* That's when we found out you jumped from the frying pan into the fire, so we had to turn around."

Good thing, too. Swallowing hurts, and I touch the raw ring of skin on my neck.

"Do I have a *Godfather* voice now?"

Sophie chuckles.

"We checked out the prison the day before your execution and found your time-ghosts. After that, *get the hangman drunk* was the best plan we could come up with. Did you arrange for that change to Franklin's book the night before?"

"I had about six desperate plans going myself."

"If you try that again," she says, "remember other travelers can never find the real you *before* the moment when you roll a timequake forward to signal them."

For us, *before* is a pretty subjective term.

"Do we have a plan to meet up with Dad and Yvaine?"

"Safe house in London, 1759."

Traveling with Sophie is really different than with Yvaine. We only have thirty-four years to go, but it takes us about a month to get there. Despite my aunt's short cooldown, jumping takes a lot out of us. She can only manage five or six hops a day, covering about two months each.

Part of the wear and tear is the landings — ditches, sewers, brick walls, basements, sweatshops, brothels, and such. When we finally make it to June of our intended year — on the roof of some barn outside the city — I insist we walk the rest of the way.

"We arranged this place on our way downtime," Sophie says as we turn onto a tree-lined street of beautiful Georgian homes and let ourselves in through a little iron gate.

"Mom would call this a Palladian facade," I say. "Do you think she's back to normal?"

Chapter Thirty-Eight: History 3.0

"We'll find out soon enough." She knocks on the door.

We look pathetic enough in our filthy rags that it takes a bit of work to convince the servants to fetch the owners.

"Charlie!" Yvaine comes streaking through the grand entrance hall in a silk dress four feet wide. Her hair is powdered, clean, and tied up with ribbons. Plus she's wearing shoes.

But she walks right into my arms all the same.

Dad insists on having the servants bathe and dress us before debriefing me. He looks good, even in a baby blue silk waistcoat and a powder white wig. He's lost some weight.

Yvaine's put on some, just enough that she looks less waify and a little filled out. She sits on my lap in the drawing room and laughs when I tease her about it.

"Your da's been havin' 'em cook for me," she says.

"How long has it been for you two? I'm surprised you haven't been at each other's throats."

"Just a month. An' he ain't so bad once I figured out what t'do with him."

I chuckle. "And what's that?"

"Regale him with me past and smile when I dinna do what I's told." She motions at a servant. "George, be a dear."

Despite the white wig, he can't be more than twelve. He fetches a tray and two glasses of wine.

Yvaine hands me one and takes the other. "Claret be even better than ale."

"Dad lets you?"

"He dinna like it, so I smile when I takes it."

Sophie and my father return. She cleaned up well too, although she's done a half-ass job of going period — men's knickers and unpowdered hair in its usual braid.

"Thanks, Dad," I say. "Again. I know trying to save Ben was against your principles, but it's good to be alive."

He laughs and offers me a meat pie from his pocket.

"Messing with history is still dangerous business, Charlie."

"Your Giza raid shed light on anything?"

He slumps into a chair with feet like eagle talons. "A cache of fifteen pages, including some of the Regulator's oldest known writings."

"And?"

He looks down. "I always assumed the history we grew up with was — more or less — the original. But now I'm not so sure. It's clear from the pages that the Regulator may have been involved in early manipulations."

I swallow the urge to say 'I told you so.' He did save my ass in a pretty big way.

"Everything I believed has been thrown into question." He walks over to me. "And letting my only son die over a debatable doctrine hardly seemed right...."

"We make of it what we will," Yvaine says.

"Your foundling might have a point," he says, "but we have more research to do. Careful research."

Yvaine sneers at him, but it seems a good-natured sneer.

"Did Ben Franklin's life get back on track?" I ask. "Is Mom going to remember us?"

Dad rises to go. "As to your second question, I hope so, and Yvaine can answer the first."

Yvaine hauls me halfway across town, but it's an easy trip — we just take the coach. Four men in Dad's powder blue colors bring it around.

"It be so peculiar t'have money and servants," she says.

The coach is pretty sweet inside, too, all silk and gold trim, but the ride is still bumpy.

It stops at a handsome brick house. The sun is setting and candlelight spills out from inside. We walk past the front windows, peering in.

"This room," she says.

Chapter Thirty-Eight: History 3.0

I step up to the sill and look. Two men and two women are eating dinner. The younger man is in his thirties. He's wearing a white wig and has a rather pronounced forehead, just like his father.

At fifty, Benjamin Franklin looks exactly like his portraits. His peppered gray hair runs down long from the sides of his head and not at all from the top. His round spectacles are on the table by his plate, and not far away is a copper and glass contraption that looks all old-school scientific.

"Me Billy's a William now," Yvaine says.

Wow!

"Have you talked to him?"

She sighs. "Fink dinna think it be a good idea. His life is as it should be. He's a barrister an' works for his da. Ben's a famous philosopher who represents the colonials in parliament. A real important man now, just like you said."

She leans in and kisses me.

"I told you so," I say.

She swats at me. "Dinna make fun of me talk."

But she kisses me again.

Returning to the house, we decide to head uptime in the morning. Sophie and Dad will follow — in their own slow-ass barn-and-ditch way. I'm eager to get going but in dire need of sleep.

Not to mention the fact that Yvaine and I haven't seen each other in a month.

"What about Bréguet?" I ask Dad after dinner. "Would the timequake from fixing Ben's life have cleaned up his inventions?"

"I think so," my father says. "Large-scale time changes are complicated, but the Regulator's Bréguet page indicates that in timelines with the French Revolution, he flees to Geneva, not his country home. When history is recomputed, any interactions with the Tick-Tocks should be nullified since their residuals will be in the wrong place."

Franklin family dinner

Chapter Thirty-Eight: History 3.0

"In English, Fink." I grin at him. He scowls.

"Basically, I hope it'll work out. And Charlie, if you don't mind, please call me Dad."

"Sure, Dad."

"You two are sleeping in separate rooms," he says.

But that doesn't stop Yvaine from leaving those new shoes of hers and tiptoeing over to my bed after the candles are out.

After breakfast, we gather our things. Rapier's sword I leave with Sophie. After all, she earned it. But Yvaine gives me one of her daggers, making sure the other is strapped to her hip.

We hug Dad and Sophie goodbye and go.

My aunt's cooldown might be handy in a fight, but traveling with Yvaine is way more comfortable. Not only does she make it back to 2011 in one jump, but we land right in the middle of the entryway to my house — on our feet!

I'm relieved to see the two names on the mailboxes: Montag *and* Horologe.

"Ready?" Yvaine says. She's wearing tapered jeans, Keds, and a cute little red hoodie.

I knock on the door.

And Mom answers! She's standing on her own two feet and looks just like I remember, but the minute she sees me, a puzzled expression crosses her face.

My heart drops into my groin.

"Did you lose your key?" she says.

I rush forward and practically crush her in a bear hug.

"I missed you, Mom!"

"Was the field trip that bad?" she asks.

The orange afternoon light streams in behind us. Yvaine must've nailed the date — while it's been months for me, for Mom it's only been hours.

Which is fine by me.

"Introduce us," she says.

"This is Yvaine, my girlfriend."

Mom looks at Yvaine, gives her a smile that would make a serial killer feel right at home, and winks at me.

"Hi, girlfriend. Did you two meet at school?"

"In history," I say.

I glance at Yvaine, who lets out a delightful giggle.

"Dad called my mobile," I tell Mom. "He and Sophie are coming home soon."

I hate lying to her, but she literally won't understand the truth.

"That's a relief," she says, "I was really worried after that strange incident with the police. I'm surprised he didn't call me, too."

She pulls her phone from her pocket. It looks weird — round and flat, about the size of a donut. She taps it, and the circular LCD on the front comes to life. Pixelated clock hands give the impression of an old-fashioned dial.

"No messages," she says.

"What kind of phone is that?" My voice squeaks.

"My iWatch?"

I rush into the room and over to the window, drawing back the curtains.

Down the street is the Philadelphia skyline. Skyscrapers and all. But where the Comcast Center should be is a hundred-story tower. Up its side in scrolling glowing LEDs runs the text:

Franklin-Bréguet Electro Data Corporation!

TO BE CONTINUED...

Find *Untimed*
online at:
untimed-novel.com

If you enjoyed *Untimed*, please consider taking a few moments to leave a review at the retailer where you purchased it. It need not be long. A few sentences and a rating are all that's required. These reviews really do matter.

ACKNOWLEDGEMENTS

First and foremost, I'd like to thank my wife Sharon, my mother, and my "story consultant" Bryan Visintin for reading each chapter hot off the presses as I finished it. Then reading again. And again. Then discussing each and every possible alteration. Big thanks to my agent, Eddie Schneider at JABberwocky Literary, and my publicist, Kimberly Kinrade.

I owe a great debt to the thousands of Fantasy, Science Fiction, Paranormal, and Horror novels, movies, games, and television shows I've consumed over the years. The details in this book wouldn't have been possible without several hundred writers of histories and whatnot that I gobbled up over the course of my writing. Not to mention the ever handy Google and Wikipedia.

I'd like to thank my professional editors: the incomparable Renni Browne, Shannon Roberts, and R.J. Cavender. 12,855 "changes" in line editing alone!

Proof reading was by Dave Lane, typesetting and book design by Chris Fisher, e-book layout by myself, and jacket copy editing by Beth Jusino. Thanks also to The Editorial Department champs Karinya Funsett-Topping, Ross Browne, and last but not least, Jane Ryder.

The awesome cover illustration is by Cliff Nielsen. The cover and logo design are by me (who says programmers can't Photoshop). The amazing interior illustrations are by Dave Phillips. The print edition is formatted in Book Antiqua, a font designed by Monotype. Thanks also to my long time business partner Jason Rubin for help with my working cover, logo, and for many lessons in Photoshop blending layers. I used CreateSpace.com to print private draft editions, Advance Review Copies, and the final trade paperback. LightningSource.com printed the hardcover edition. Further thanks to Stephen Rubin for pro bono intellectual property advice.

This novel was written entirely on Apple products (thanks Steve!) and in Scrivener, a specialized word processor for writers. If you write long form prose and are still using a dinosaur like Word, look into it. The paper version was typeset in Adobe InDesign and the e-book converted with Scrivener and Calibre. I did the conversion myself in a fairly automated fashion using some scripts I hacked up.

I also very much appreciate my loyal beta readers, especially those who read many drafts or offered up comments: Scott Shumaker, Jane Mullaney, Keren Perlmutter, Ben Stragnell, Lara Shanis (my third grade teacher!), Owen Rescher, Brent Askari, Andrew Reiner, Abbe Flitter, Brian Roe, Danny Pickford, Kimberly Kinrade, Catherine Young, Don Gavin, Zachary Perlmutter, Andrew Notaras, Eric Wunderlich, Bill Guschwan, Emily Perlmutter, Lauren Lewis, David Cotrell, Jason Kay, Mirella Abounayan, Greg Cooper, Valerie Flitter, Mike Gollum, Barbara Feldman, and Mitch Gavin. If I missed any of you who finished the book, I apologize, or you forgot to tell me!

Lastly, I'd like to thank you, the reader, whose eyes on this page hopefully mean you made it to the end.

All sorts of additional info can be found at my website: http://andy-gavin-author.com

Andy Gavin,
California, November 2012

Andy Gavin is an unstoppable storyteller who studied for his Ph.D. at M.I.T. and founded video game developer Naughty Dog, Inc. at the age of fifteen, serving as co-president for two decades. There he created, produced, and directed over a dozen video games, including the award winning and best selling *Crash Bandicoot* and *Jak & Daxter* franchises, selling over 40 million units worldwide. He sleeps little, reads novels and histories, watches media obsessively, travels, and of course, writes.

For more information, check him out at
http://all-things-andy-gavin/bio.

CPSIA information can be obtained at www.ICGtesting.com
Printed in the USA
BVOW040751250113

311585BV00001B/2/P